Downstairs something crashed. He stiffened at the muffled scream followed by a thick gurgling noise. Like poisonous gas, the smell rolled beneath the door. Black shields dropped over his eyes.

"They're coming, we must leave this instant," Ian hissed, already gathering the book and wrapping it in the skins.

"What's going on? Who's coming?" Gabriella's eyes grew wide.

"Can we talk about this later when someone's not trying to kill us?" He buckled on his sword sheath and shoved his arms through his coat sleeves before opening his window.

Church of the Damned, she had said. But who the hell were they and how did they track him to this place?

"But I need my purse...my passport."

He frowned, then grabbed her hand and tugged her into the hall and to her room. The passage reeked of them. They'd come looking up here as soon as they killed the Innkeeper and his wife. Damn savages. "Just grab your purse and coat. We must go now!"

"Why? Who are they?" Her eyes asked her question— what is downstairs that's terrible enough to frighten *you*?

"Vampires, lass, lots of them." He shoved the window up, pulled her into his arms and plunged into the snowy night.

Praise for [reviews]

Reviews for To Kill a Vampire:

From The Romance Reviews ~~ *The book not only surprised me, but it also put me on emotional roller coaster — fear that someone will die, anger over the behavior of some characters, even Angelica and Erik, to the tears at the end. The book left me breathless. Truly a refreshing story with new ideas of the mysterious world of vampires.*

From ParanormalRomance.org ~~ *Before starting this book I was expecting a typical woman meets Vamp, falls in love and off they go into the sunset, not literally that could lead to some crispy Vampires, but I was wrong. This is a gut wrenching story of how much would you give for the person you love.*

Reviews for Fate of the Fallen:

From The Romance Studio ~~ *Fate of the Fallen offered a unique look into a world that encompassed almost every paranormal element known, and I for one will be sorely disappointed if we don't see more from Eva, Rahab, and their fellow Demonators.*

From Night Owl Reviews ~~ *An excellent effort especially for a first book. Looking forward to what she does in the future.*

Requiem for the Undead

by

Sharron Riddle

Requiem for the Undead: Vampire Wars, Book One

Contact Information: info@riddlemeastory.com

Edited by Maureen Sevilla
Cover Art by Travis Miles

Riddle Me A Story Publishing, LLC
10519 Sky Flower Ct
Land O Lakes FL 34638
Visit us at www.riddlemeastorypublishing.com

Publishing History
First Edition, 2012
Print ISBN 9780615612478
Digital ISBN 0615612474

Published in the United States of America

Dedication

This book is dedicated to my wonderful editor, Maureen Sevilla; my great beta-reader, Renee Fenwick; and to my conscientious copy editor, Donna Confer, all who I consider my excellent friends. Thanks for everything, ladies.

CHAPTER ONE ✝

December 8ᵗʰ Carpathian Mountains, Romania

Ian followed the scent of her blood through the forest. Not the smartest way for a vampire to track, not if he wanted her alive. But tangling hot and thick through the bitter wind, her blood smelled too damn good.

The demon stirred in his brain, stretching, testing Ian's control.

The bones of his hands cracked and lengthened. *Damn.*

He paused in a shallow ravine along the mountainside, ripping a blood packet free from his nylon rucksack. Sharp points rippled over his teeth, tearing into the plastic. He sucked the bag dry in seconds, draining another before his claws receded. After the third he trusted himself to follow again.

Trees flashed by in a blur, the icy flakes glancing off his cheeks. Howling winds fought to rip away his leather duster. His sword slapped against his thigh as he ran. More than once he caught his hand slipping around the grip, a habit from years of hunting the rogues. Vicious bastards. Too bad there weren't any around. He wouldn't mind whacking off a few heads, get rid of some of this tension.

He slid down the steep slope, exploding from the woods into the unplowed road. Of course there wasn't a car in sight along the Transfăgărăşan Road. The route was too dangerous for sane people.

The woman, Gabriella, had abandoned her rented Range Rover in the center of unplowed blacktop. On the cliff high above him, the castle's jagged outline loomed against a winter sky. Low gray clouds curled around the crumbling turrets, clearly visible to him in the darkness. One of the few useful perks of vampirism.

He leapt the steep stairs to Poenari Castle—Dracula's castle. Well, the ruined remains of one once inhabited by Vlad the Impaler. Gabriella's scent lingered here, blocked from the wind.

1

His demon rattled the bars of its prison. The beast craved her flesh with such pained longing, thick black nails erupted through Ian's fingertips. He paused, battling for control until his own ragged nails returned.

He'd trailed Gabriella on foot from the town of Curtea de Arges, knowing the storm would hinder her drive through the Carpathian Mountains. The road was closed for the winter, and she'd been forced to wait for nightfall before sneaking around the barricades. He realized now how much he'd taken for granted—first, that curiosity would bring her here, to Romania, secondly that she would continue her quest despite this godforsaken weather, and finally that she was insane enough to chance the unplowed highway alone...in the dark.

He shook his head, wondering if he were equally crazy for following her.

A passage of decaying walls led to the rear of the castle. He jumped the rusted metal railing where her boots had scuffed away the snow. Here the mountain plunged straight down, nearly as steep as it was on the front side by the steps. He half slid, half ran through the deep snow, feeling a strange compulsion to laugh when he saw the path where she'd fallen and skated several yards on her ass. Then he chastised himself, realizing a fall on this mountain could have cracked open her fragile human skull. He needed the woman alive if the book truly existed.

If.

So much weighed on such a small word. Did an end to his torment truly lay hidden in the mountainside? No more pain.

After so many centuries, it seemed too great a thing to hope for. He sighed with bone-deep weariness and chanced a small sip of her scent. In through his nose, her fragrance hit him hard, the scent more like a flavor spreading deliciously over his tongue. Lord, how he missed the smell of a woman.

Lantern light bobbed up the steep far bank, a lace of yellow through pine boughs and gusting snow. So intent on watching her, ice cracked underfoot before he realized he'd reached a frozen stream.

"Ah, bugger," he muttered, shaking his foot.

The lantern flared with the fierce brightness of a lightning strike, blinding him a moment. Ian blinked and raised his arm just as the light flashed out, plunging the world into blackness.

"What the hell?" His eyes adjusted quickly to the change, and he dashed through the forest, up the far slope. He saw it then, what he had not noticed before. The outline of more ruins jutting out of the snow.

Her strange scent grew stronger as he neared the piles of collapsed stone. The demon inside him squirmed like a hungry weasel in his brain, but Ian fought him back. No matter how much he drank, the beast always demanded more. He'd thought the twelve pints he'd stolen from a hospital in Bucharest was overkill. Now he wondered if it would be enough.

Leaves crackled under the drifting snow. Pine and must from a cave mingled and swirled around him. Animals rustled in their warm winter burrows near his feet. He raised his chin, sniffed the air.

Wolves. He smelled them an instant before the first one bayed. Dozens of heavy paws pounded down the steep slope above him. They'd caught the woman's scent, and they were hungry.

He drew his sword.

* * * *

"Why am I here again?" Gabriella asked, her voice muffled behind the flap of her parka. "This is idiotic." She stared over the railing at the rear of Poenari Castle, shaking her head.

Grandfather had insisted she make this trek now, in the dead of winter. *Others are seeking the book*, he'd said. *So what*, she'd argued. One more ancient book of exorcisms. He had a library full of them. *But no, this book is different*, he'd pressed. *You always say that*, she'd countered.

They'd argued back and forth for a while until exasperated, he'd shown her a note, one cryptic line written on thick cream paper in an elegant scrolling script.

—The Church of the Damned seeks your most sacred treasure—

"Where did that come from?" she'd asked.

"Someone left it wedged inside the door of the archive building."

This had startled her. The archives were no secret, but no one but her people knew of its sacred contents. "What does that mean?"

"It means we dangle over a precipice of great change.

3

We must guard the scrolls. And you must obtain that text. If things go badly for us, it may be our only hope." Then he'd confessed the secret hidden in the book.

She had no choice. This was her family's charge, to keep such things out of wicked hands. Plus, he'd promised her a paid vacation in Tahiti once she returned the tome into his care.

And she'd need a vacation after this trip.

All she had to do was climb the mountain just past Dracula's castle. In the dark. During a blizzard. Brilliant.

She'd slipped in the snow as soon as she crossed the railing, spraining her ankle when she slammed into a tree near the bottom. A bottle of water shattered in her pocket, soaking her side and her leg. She hobbled down the slope, her feet shuffling dangerously when she hit the icy mantle of a narrow stream hidden beneath the deeper snow in the valley. She lifted the lantern, shining the light around until she found jutting rocks to use for crossing.

Halfway across the racing water, she froze. Hairs prickled along her neck. A strange force rolled out from the trees behind her. Something she'd never encountered before.

Had members of that strange cult followed her? Once she reached the far bank, she raised the lantern, casting light over the woods. She listened for the crack of a stick or the crunch of footsteps on snow. Nothing.

Stupid, scary vampire legends. This place had her spooked. Danger rode the same horse as adventure. She'd learned that truth years ago hunting relics in tight mountain caves, battling giant octopi that guarded scribed stone tablets deep in the Aegean Sea, and hacking through snake infested Amazonian jungles to find lost spells for raising the dead. This should be as easy as making instant coffee by comparison.

Still, something felt...off.

She huffed, glancing up the mountain to the towering ruins, getting her bearings. The ancient map had shown straight north from Peonari Castle. She tugged the GPS from her pocket and checked her direction before setting off. In a couple hours, she'd be back at the hotel, soaking in a hot tub. Maybe she'd have a glass or two of wine. Yes, focus on that, she thought.

Gabriella struggled up the next slope, wet and shivering, her ankle throbbing. She blinked her eyes against the prickling snow. Following the directions, she zigzagged

4

back and forth across the mountain's face, scanning the snow for any strange protrusions.

After several minutes of futile searching, a nagging worry burrowed in her brain. The entrance should be right here.

Had she missed it?

Dread skittered down her spine. Maybe it wasn't here at all. The map could be wrong. Perhaps she read it wrong. Her heart thumped against her ribs. She'd never made this kind of mistake. Her skill for translating maps was world renowned. How could she be so wrong?

Self doubt crushed her beneath its pitiless heel. Panic welled, confusion clouding her brain. She wanted to run, but she stubbornly set her feet.

Something outside her mind worked with incredible force to scare her off, to send her in another direction.

A spell. She smiled. A skilled practitioner had placed a protection spell here. Impressively strong magic, she thought grudgingly. Anyone who wandered too close would be steered away, terrified and feeling lost.

Dragging in a deep breath, she closed her eyes, feeling the air with shaking fingers. A subtle humming pressed against her palms, pulsing with nervous energy. Thrills of terror shuddered through her. She lowered her hands, shaking them out to cast off the effects of the magic.

She concentrated, using her own power to pull the complex weave out of the air. Like an invisible rope, she reeled in the energy of the offensive spell, spooling it around her body. She fought the rising panic as the spell bound her legs, tightening over her ribs. Energy coiled around her throat, choking her breath. A scream tore from her lungs, but she held her lips tight. Not a moment too soon, the last of the magical threads encased her mouth, pressing on her nose, covering her eyes like a blindfold. She gathered her own power and pushed against the binding spell, testing, clearing a space to speak.

"With ancient birthright called to be, of binding magic set me free!" She shouted with her last stale breath, raising her arms as if breaking out of brittle ropes.

A white light blasted from her hands, her skin, and right through her heavy clothes. Exploding power dispersed the aggressive spell, the bindings fleeing with a crackling, angry hiss.

She opened her eyes and squealed. In front of her, a

shadowy rock formation reared up through the night-grayed snow.

Adrenaline charged her spirits. She instantly forgot about her freezing wet clothes and the pain in her ankle. She'd done it! She'd found Biserica de la Lepros—Church of the Lepers.

She knew from her research an order of monks had built this cathedral in the seventeenth century as a sanctuary to protect the lepers from the outside world. The outer building had served as shared living quarters, though she was disappointed to find it had crumbled into rubble. No doubt, the building had fallen from the same tremors that had shaken apart Peonari Castle.

She scrabbled over the broken stones and mortar, praying the inner sanctuary hadn't collapsed, too. A deep crevice gaped in the granite mountain face, nearly hidden by tangles of ropy vines. She ripped aside the mesh and stepped through the threshold into another time.

"Wow," she murmured, crunching over broken tiles as small rodents rustled in the rotted remains of wooden pews.

She swung the lantern around, amazed at the size of the chapel. The cave ceiling soared above the room where a hundred people, maybe more, could have gathered. Water trickled through cracks, glistening on the granite columns that supported the walls and created a promenade leading to the dais. Much of the tile floor had buckled and cracked. Miraculously, the stone altar at the cavern's head remained completely intact.

Gabriella lowered her hood, slipping out of her pack as she hobbled to the chancel. Two steps led to the apse, where she collapsed onto the raised floor. Needing to tend to her ankle, she dug a small first aid kit from her pack. Since she had crushed her only bottle of water, she had to dry swallow two aspirin. After she looked for the book, she'd wrap her ankle, but a stiff bandage would only hamper her mobility. She tugged the map from the pocket, smoothing the yellowed paper over her knees.

Outside, a wolf howled. Several more answered. They sounded hungry.

"Seriously? Wolves? The blizzard and the ankle weren't enough?" She shouted at the ceiling. A clump of dirt fell from a crevice and cracked like an egg on her forehead. She spit out crumbs and shook out her hair. "Fine. So that's how things are gonna' be," she muttered.

She fished out a 9mm pistol from her backpack. She'd arranged in advance for the innkeeper to have the weapon ready for her when she arrived. Wolves were common in the Carpathian Mountains, and they tended to grow a little bold during the winter when food was scarce. If they ventured too close, a warning shot should be sufficient to send them running. At least, that was her plan.

She listened several minutes, hearing only the wailing wind. Satisfied no immediate danger prowled outside the cavern, she followed the map's instructions to the rear of the vestry. Like the tile floors, much of the laid stone had buckled from earthquakes. But, she was only interested in the fifteen squares between the wall and the altar.

"Now comes the fun part," she muttered, removing her gloves. One after another, she knocked on rock tiles until her hand throbbed from cold and her knuckles bled.

Soon she reached the rear wall. Only three tiles remained unchecked. A moment of panic gripped her. What if the book was gone? What if someone else had found it first? This wouldn't be the first time she'd followed an ancient map to its end, only to be disappointed.

She shuddered, trying not to think about those spells in the hands of some crazy cultists. Church of the Damned. That was a new one. There were plenty of fanatics out there, but Grandfather seemed seriously concerned about this one.

Her knees ached as she scooted to the next section, tapping the closest tile. A hollow cord sounded beneath the plate.

She froze in place a moment. Had she heard right? With throbbing fingers, she fumbled open a pocketknife, wedging the blade into the crack between the stones. The steel bent, and for a sickening moment she thought the shank might snap. Finally, with a grating lurch, the tile raised enough for her to cram her fingers underneath. Within seconds, she wrestled the square aside.

A metal box lay wedged in the tight space.

"Gabriella saves the world again," she sing-sang, wriggling the box from its hidey-hole. "Tahiti, here I come."

She dug a kerchief from her jeans pocket, working her numb fingers to rub away the years of grime. Lustrous gold gleamed in the lantern light. Her heart pounded as she pried it open. The lid squeaked on tired hinges. A chemical smell like sulfur swirled up from the bundle of animal skins. Preservatives, she knew, to keep the velum safe. She unwrapped the volume, reverently running her fingers over the carved letters in the cracked leather cover.

"*Votum pro Phasma Malum,*" she whispered in Latin. Requiem of the Undead.

Rustling and scraping at the entrance brought her chin up. She fumbled with the gun from her pocket, expecting wolves. Her frozen hands could barely hold the grip as she pointed the barrel at the dark gap in the wall.

She nearly screamed when the giant man stepped into the muted light. A black leather duster hung mid-shin over matching jeans, shirt, and hiking boots. Anomalous dark eyes stared with glaring intensity. The only color in that darkness was the red-gold tendrils that fell wildly around his wide shoulders.

Her muscles clenched, braced for terror that never arrived. In fact, a flutter of desire shivered through her belly. The face, so strong and striking, the sharp cheeked angles belonged on a marble sculpture chiseled by one of the great masters.

She would have liked to linger on that face a minute or two longer, but her eyes could only manage to focus on one thing—the sword he clenched in his hand—the blade dripping thick, dark drops onto the floor.

Blood. Its coppery sweetness broke her trance.

Shaking from fear as much as cold, she raised the gun.

"Are you one of them?" She demanded.

"One of who?" The man's thick brows pulled together, looking truly baffled. But why else would he follow her on a godforsaken night like this?

"Your friends from the Church of the Damned."

"I swear to you, lass, I've no clue what you're talkin' about..." He stepped further into the cave and she swung the gun higher, pointing the barrel at his chest.

"Don't move. I don't want to shoot you." Her hands trembled, her eyes blurred by frustrated tears. She'd clearly felt his energy moving through the woods. His psycho cult had sent him after the book and she'd led him right to it.

Why hadn't she trusted her gift? But she knew why. He'd felt different. Off. Human. But something else, too— something she'd never encountered in all of her travels— making her wonder if her senses were mistaken.

Apparently not, because there he stood, magnificent and terrifying all at once.

What is he?

"Take it easy," the man said, raising the sword.

Her finger slid over the trigger. She tried aiming over his shoulder without making it obvious. She didn't want to shoot the guy, just scare him away, like the wolves.

"Put the sword down, now!" she said with impressive authority, despite the fear quaking in her bones.

He slid his boot over the rubble, his arms opening. A gesture. Of what? She blinked and steadied herself. Sweat slicked her palms, making it harder to hold on to the gun. She'd never imagined pointing a firearm at anyone, and the gravity of it sickened her.

She shifted her grip, wishing her hands would quit shaking. The barrel kicked up, nearly wrenching the gun from her grip. The sound of a gunshot exploded, its blast deafening.

She screamed, watching in horror as his hands fell slack. The sword clanked onto the stone, though she barely heard the noise above the ringing in her ears.

He grunted and gripped his chest, scarlet rivulets streaming through his fingers.

"Shit!" She dropped the gun and ran to her backpack, digging out the first aid kit. "Oh my God, oh my God," she muttered. All the gauze in the box wouldn't help him, but she had to try. For God's sake, she'd just shot the man.

She rushed back to him, the kit clutched to her chest.

"Stop," he shouted, a crimson mist spraying through his lips.

She lurched to a halt near the center of the nave.

Something shifted on his face.

She blinked.

Her brain tried to reconcile the cracking cheekbones, jutting and stretching his skin with sharp points. His brow thickened, hooding his blackened eyes—no whites showing at all.

"W-what...?" Her heart pounded in response to his sneer, sharp points rippling down over his blood-smeared teeth.

She clapped her hand to her mouth, catching the scream as she stumbled backward.

He coughed, staggering a few steps.

Her boot hit the base of the chancel, and she fell hard on the step, her twisted ankle throbbing.

What was happening to him?

Every instinct screamed at her to run, get the hell out of

there. Unfortunately, running wasn't an option. The importance of the book eclipsed any other texts in her grandfather's collection. She wouldn't—couldn't let this man have it.

He erupted in a coughing fit, his chest convulsing.

Nervously glancing over her shoulder, she crawled to where the book lay, folding the cloth around it and closing the box's golden lid.

What had she done? Any idiot knew not to point a gun at someone unless one planned to shoot said person.

Bile burned up her throat. She pressed her fist to her lips, watching the beast-man choke, red-black droplets spattering the floor. Leaving him standing there bleeding to death without trying to help went against everything she believed in, monster or not. It took all of her will not to run to his side. Yet he had warned her away. Helping him could get her killed. And if she died, the book might fall into enemy hands.

She shoved the box into her backpack, sacrificing the first aid kit and a GPS to make it fit. Still watchful, she hobbled along the rough wall, the lantern shaking in her hand, flashing spectral shadows over the walls.

Gurgling liquid boiled up the monster's throat. He barked a final, choking cough, murmuring something she couldn't make out, and fell deathly silent.

"Please don't be dead," she whispered, turning back to him, sure she would find him lying dead on the floor.

He stood where she'd shot him, holding out a hand to her, his lips moving. She tried listening, but fear muddled the words in her brain. Something lay in his palm. The bullet? Impossible.

The ragged entrance beckoned just yards away. She wanted to flee into the night, get the hell away from this nightmare, but guilt held her frozen with indecision. Her gaze wavered from the monster to the cavern opening, where snow drifted over the floor.

A low growl rolled in from the night. Eyes glowed through the narrow crack, gleaming yellow in the lantern light. A second pair of eyes appeared from the darkness, and then a third, a fourth. Blocking her escape. The gun, she realized, lay in the shadows in front of the apse.

She had only two choices, both of them deadly. Risk the monster and try for the gun, or take her chances with the wolves. She took a step back along the wall.

* * * *

The pain faded quickly, but Ian still hacked and gagged, finally driving the bullet out of his chest and up the trachea. Muscles nimbly meshed together. Veins and vessels buffered their shattered walls, but blood had already flooded his lungs. Each cough spewed crimson spray over the floor. Damn embarrassing, not exactly the first impression he'd hoped for. What the hell had she been thinking, shooting him like that? With one last barking hack, something hard and metallic clicked against his teeth. He spit the bullet into his palm.

"What do you think of that, lass?" He held out the copper slug.

When he finally opened his eyes, he smelled the wolves and saw the girl looked like she was about to scream or faint, so he wiped the bullet on his jeans and shoved it in his pants pocket.

He swung around to face the wolves. The strike from his sword to their leader's ear should have scared them off, but hunger made them bold. The large black wolf stood just ahead of his pack, his tattered ear flat against the blood-slick fur. He snarled menacingly as seven smaller wolves pushed through the vines at the cathedral entrance, flanking him, lips curled back over glistening teeth.

Ian muttered a curse. He had no choice, but his only chance of protecting the girl could mean her death. Praying for control, he released the demon he'd battled since the gunshot.

His fingers stretched, knuckles growing thick. Black nails curled around his fingertips. Bones cracked and twisted as the beast erupted in its entire, grotesque splendor. He swept up the blade and raised the sword. His demon's triumphant roar shook the ancient walls. A loud crack echoed through the cavern. Splintering supports buckled and bulged. Dirt rained down from fissures cracking along the ceiling.

The girl screamed at the sight of him, pressing herself against the crumbling wall. She raised her arm defensively, as if such a weak gesture could save her. The beast growled a laugh at her before swinging around to meet the wolves.

The smaller animals paced nervously near the entrance, mewling and eyeing their leader. With an angry huff, the black wolf turned and bounded into the night. The others whined, racing out behind him.

He turned to the woman, sniffing her scent from the air. Ian felt the demon's feral craving, languishing in its sanguine seduction. She edged along the wall to the front of the chapel. Her boot struck some debris, sprawling her on the floor. He reached her in a blur, hauling her up by the hair and hugging her to his chest.

"Please, please don't," she begged. Tears streaked her filthy face, her fear exciting the beast.

A thin sharp tongue darted through his teeth, licking the glistening trails from her cheeks. Salty, like blood. His nose traced along her neck, deeply inhaling her exquisite bouquet.

His scent quickly lulled her. She slumped in his arms, smiling at him as her thin fingers tugged her clothing away to expose her throat. His body shuddered beneath the delicate hand that tugged his shirt from his jeans, creeping over his belly in search of his suddenly gorged erection.

He pressed his mouth to her neck, feeling the pulsing scarlet river. His lips curled back, lusting for the thrill of sliding sharp teeth into her velvet skin while pounding his hammer hard cock into the blazing heat of her feminine folds.

"Stop!" A voice—his voice—snarled from some dark place in his mind. Ian battled the beast, a terrible struggle with the blood feast so close. So hot. So very sweet.

He clenched his teeth and laid her out on the floor. Took several steps back, until her scent dulled in his nose, until he could no longer feel that fire smoldering between her thighs. Still salivating, he ripped his pack from his shoulder. Instead of flesh, his teeth tore into plastic, opening a pint bag of blood. He sucked it dry in seconds and went for another. Finally, the third pint barely quenched the thirst that burned like hot knives stabbing his throat, so he drank a fourth and a fifth.

At last, the demon reluctantly retreated to where it hovered eternally at the fringes of his brain.

Ian heaved a sigh and sheathed his sword beneath his coat.

The girl limped away a few steps before falling to her knees and Ian realized she must have injured herself when she fell down the mountain.

She crawled up the steps to the apse and reached for the gun.

"There should be a law against shootin' a man twice in

12

the same night." He knelt beside her in a flash, shaking the gun from her hand. "And it wasn't very ladylike shootin' him the first time. I'll hold on to this," he said, slipping the weapon into his coat pocket.

"What are you?" Her voice trembled.

He looked away, hating the fear in her eyes.

"I'm a monster." He watched as widening fractures veined across the main support columns. "A demon squats like a toad in my belly, sloshing in his bloody pond."

"What?"

He sighed and met her stare, seeing her face up close for the first time. A petite thing she was, with long dark waves framing a lovely, elfin face. Dark copper eyes, large and sensuous, slanted beneath thin brows. Lips like soft pink pillows. Even puckered in fear, he knew they'd be luscious to kiss. Pale freckles smattered her tear streaked cheeks.

He cocked his head, narrowed his eyes. This woman shimmered. He blinked to be sure. Yes, he saw it clearly now. The faintest glow haloed her like a pale winter moon.

Half consciously, he raised a hand to touch her hair, frowning when she cringed away.

"Don't touch me!" The dark eyes widened with fear.

"I didn't mean anythin'..." He started, but then he huffed. "Listen, I'll not apologize to you. You're the one went off half cocked and tore a hole in my favorite coat." He poked a finger through the bullet hole.

She cringed, but defiance wiped away the flicker of guilt. "It was your own fault, charging in here with your damn bloody sword."

"My fault? I was trying to scare off the wolves."

"Oh really? How did that work out for you?" She raised her chin.

A laugh exploded up his throat, echoing through the chamber.

"What's so funny?" She demanded.

"You are. You shoot a man, you nearly bump heads with a hungry wolf pack, you swoon for a vampire, and still you're full of hellfire, lass."

"Swooned for a what?" Her lips quivered a moment before she stiffened them in an angry line.

"A vampire."

"You were talking about demons and toads..."

"The demons are what drives a vampire. The toad analogy was figurative, muzzy, I've got no lily pads in my

13

gut." He tried not to smile, watching her face twist with disbelief.

"A demon? What do demons have to do with vampires?"

"That's what vampirism is. We've rented out the spare room in our psyches in exchange for immortality."

She stared at him. "But I thought...everything I've read says vampires are just...dead."

"That'd be un-dead." He shook his head. "And I'm sure you read all about us in the reference section of your fancy library."

Her lips tightened and her eyes sparked. "Of course not. They were works of fiction, just like you. I must have hit my head when I fell and I'm out cold. And since I'm in Transylvania, it only makes sense I'd hallucinate vampires. When I come-to, you'll be gone."

"You might as well believe in vampires, if you believe that fairy tale."

"Sure, because believing in a demon possessed stalker makes much more sense than being unconscious."

Ian ran a hand over the prickly stubble on his cheek. "A stalker I am now, eh? Perhaps I'm here for the same thing you are, lass."

"I knew it! You are one of them." Her hand flew to the strap of her pack. "I found the book. It's mine."

"Why do you keep saying I'm 'one of them'? Who do you think I am?" Curiosity overcame his flaring annoyance.

Doubt flickered in her eyes before she steeled herself. "Don't act ignorant. Why else would you be here if you weren't working for the Church of the Damned?"

Church of the Damned? What nonsense was this? "I swear, I have no idea who they are. My reasons for wanting that book are personal."

She sighed, her shoulders slumping. "I'm not stupid. I know you could take the book from me if you really wanted it, but I'm begging you to let me take this with me. I only want to keep it safe...and I really want to go to Tahiti. I seriously need a vacation."

Irritation roused the sated demon. "You're talkin' nonsense. I don't want to keep the damn book, but if you want to argue ownership, perhaps you should discuss it with the Romanian government. That book belongs in a museum in Bucharest."

She hugged the pack to her chest. "I'd hardly consider it stealing a national treasure when they never would have found the book in the first place. The map was a rare find. As far as I know, only three people in the world could have deciphered the codes. Besides, the box and book are not Romanian in origin, so Romania technically has no better claim to them than I do."

"'Tis easy to rationalize when we want something, eh?" He considered sharing how she really came across that map, but decided to save that discussion for later.

"My grandfather collects ancient religious texts. I'd dare anyone to claim they could care better for this book than he can."

"And we can't forget his granddaughter, the famous historian and restoration expert for the Chicago library."

"How...?"

"I've been searching for this book for a very long time." She'd taken the whole vampire topic much better than he'd expected. Perhaps he should tell her everything. He started to speak but she interrupted.

"Why?" she breathed. "If you're not working for Church of the Damned, what could you possibly want with it?"

He pulled a slow breath. "I told you, my reasons are personal. 'Tis a spell I seek, and a little help."

"What?"

"I need someone to perform the exorcism. Someone who can read and speak Latin."

"What exorcism?"

"You're a smart one. Think about it. I have a demon inside me and I want him out."

Her mouth fell slack. "And you want me to do it? Are you nuts? I'm not a priest. I...I'd probably just piss him off and we'd both be spewing pea soup."

Ian grinned. "You don't have to be a priest. That's no religious text, 'tis a spell book written by the Roman, Apuleius of Madaurus. He practiced magic, even after he was almost executed for it. He risked his life penning those spells. According to a diary I found, his family gave the book to an order of monks for safekeeping. The monks believed in preserving history, and they hid it away."

"You're telling me this text is nearly nine centuries old?"

Ian grinned, pleased she knew of Apuleius. She'd need brains and nerves of iron to rid him of this curse.

"Aye, so take care with the pages."

"How do you know so much about it? How did you know I'd be here, looking for this particular book?"

15

"I'd discovered the map was hidden inside a Gutenburg bible, but before I could get to it, your grandfather found it. I knew of your reputation enough to know you'd be out here searchin' for it." He hated lying, but the truth was complicated. How would she feel, knowing he'd arranged this entire hunt? He couldn't chance her turning her back on him. Not now, with the end so close.

She studied him thoughtfully. Finally, she sucked a breath through her teeth, her fingers drumming her knees. "If I help you, I get to keep the book."

Ian shrugged, smiling. "Of course. I hold no claim to it, and you've worked hard deciphering the map and trekking out here. Alone." He shook his head, glancing where snow still whispered through the crevice. "In a blizzard. At night."

"My grandfather said I couldn't wait any longer, not with those church people looking for it."

"Right, I get it." Though in reality, he didn't understand at all. He'd never heard of this group. How did they know of the Requiem? He patted the stiffening blood on his shirt, wishing he'd thought to bring a spare. Just in case someone shot or stabbed him. Not a rare occurrence in his profession.

She cringed and he felt a little guilty, but not enough to apologize. Not with a bloody bullet poking his thigh through his jeans.

She rubbed her hands together, blowing warmth into them. Her breath billowed beneath his nose like sweet spring grass on his Scottish Highlands, sending his head into a spin for a moment. He turned his face away, blinking his eyes to stop the room from tilting. What the hell? It was he who made heads spin, not some cheeky, mortal lass who glowed like she'd bathed in radium. Perhaps not so mortal. But then what?

"Grandfather's very smart, but he's eccentric. He says things sometimes." She looked up from beneath a lace of ebony lashes, scorching the faded embers in his chest.

"What did he say about that cult? Are they dangerous?" Ian frantically retraced his own moves. Had someone followed him? So keen is the focus of the predator, he rarely notices when he's become the prey. A truth Ian knew very well.

She waved her small hand. "He said the book contains powerful magic. Apparently there's a group of fanatics out there who agrees with him."

Ian raised a brow. "Aye, and one fanatic in particular."

16

She laughed a little nervously. "I'm not making fun. I'm just not as zealous in my beliefs of the occult. Personally, I think Grandfather spends too much time with his dusty old books."

Ian resisted an argument. No sense poking the demon. Already, he felt the beast peeking through his eyes, watching the moist pink tongue tracing her lips with the same desirous passion as a cat hunting a bird. Fighting the painful swell pressing against his jeans, he shook his head, but there was no breaking the connection. The demon saw everything he saw, tasted, and smelled, even felt all that he did. The only thing that belonged to Ian alone was his will, and most times, he battled over that.

"So what do we do now?" Gabriella asked.

In answer, two central columns rumbled, the granite shifting and grating. Chunks of earth dropped from the ceiling. Other pillars groaned in protest of bearing more weight. Solid rock exploded across the left wall, and with a deafening roar, tons of earth rained down in a cloud of choking dust.

"What we do now is get the hell out of here," Ian shouted above the thundering chain reaction. Hundreds of cracks stretched over the center columns. They had seconds.

"We'll never make it!"

"Like hell." Ian swept her into his arms. Holding her tight against his chest, he raced for the entrance. Supports sagged beneath the crushing weight. With a grinding surrender, the mountain crumbled around them.

CHAPTER TWO ✝

December 8th Carpathian Mountains

The cave-in roared through the mountains, shaking snow from branches. Ian raced through the night, the woman clenching his neck, her face buried against his chest. He let his nose drift into her hair, breathing the scent of berries winding a comfort through the human part of him. He swallowed back the painful longing, raising the shield to his emotions sharply into place, and he lunged up the mountain beneath Peonari's shadow.

Ian avoided humans in general, and women in particular. He'd stayed away from his own kind, too for more than a decade. Except for the ones he hunted. For those he kept the satellite cell phone in his pocket to take his assignments.

He skirted the broken brick walls of the castle as he crested the peak. Ignoring the stairs, he slid recklessly down the snowy slope to the highway, his hair whipping across his eyes.

His body offered little warmth for the woman. With the wicked winds and her soaked clothing, Gabriella was shivering violently by the time he settled her into the passenger seat of the rented car. He found the key in her pocket and twisted it in the ignition. Her eyes followed him warily as he buckled her in, her teeth chattering behind blue-tinged lips.

Ian smelled coffee, felt the warmth of it radiating from the back seat and quickly located the thermos. In her parka pockets he found a protein bar, a bag of peanuts and a smashed water bottle, which explained the wet clothing. He considered removing the wet things, but instead he slipped out of his coat and laid it over her parka. Cold air blew through the vents, so he slid them closed. She watched his movements as he held the coffee cup to her lips, taking a sip. Her face scrunched in pain and she turned her head away.

"Too hot?"

"Y-yes." She chattered.

He blew on the coffee with his wintry breath before trying again. She drank, slowly at first and then greedily.

Finally the engine heated enough to provide some warmth. He aimed the blowing air at her. After several minutes her shaking subsided to intermittent shivers.

"Better?"

"Yes," she said quietly, still staring at him in the weak instrument lighting.

"You should eat this, your body needs energy," he said, pressing the energy bar into her hand.

Unaffected by darkness, he watched her take small bites, wanting more than anything to touch her, to make contact.

How long had it been since he'd reacted so strongly to a woman?

That thought was too painful. He buried it deep. Not that it mattered. She saw him as a monster, and the stars only knew what she'd think once she witnessed what he demanded of her.

He pulled onto what he hoped was the road, heading down the mountain. Forcing himself to concentrate on the sounds of the whining motor, the rumbling chain-wrapped tires and the thump of the wipers scraping ice from the windshield—anything to distract his thoughts from her beckoning heat, her dizzying smell.

"I still can't believe it," she said. "It's like a dream. Like I'm imagining you now. And I'm not sure what to think. What really happened in the cave? It was so dark."

"'Tis no dream. 'Tis a nightmare at times, but no dream."

A face flashed in his memory. Angelica.

"I make no apologies for what I am, Gabriella. 'Twas a bargain made with a kind-hearted man who had the devil's gift to share with a dying soldier on the Scottish Highlands. He did what he did out of compassion, he was no fiend."

He thought of Erik, his best friend, who'd left them for reasons through no fault of his own. Demanding Ian's oath to watch over his beloved Angelica. Returning decades later to claim her. His intentions had never been cruel. He'd never expected to return. But Angelica had never lost faith in Erik, and Ian had kept his word, though his love for her had grown like sharp thorned briars. Bloodying his heart, but well hidden. No matter how deeply he'd yearned for it, he

19

knew her love had never rooted deeper than that of a good friend.

Ach, he must be free of this curse! Death was far more welcoming than an eternity of pain. His teeth clenched, and he fought back the demon, always lurking and waiting for any outburst of emotion or desire. And so long denied carnal pleasures, the demon desired the woman beside him badly. Every molecule in his body screamed in agony for wanting to bury himself in her soft, warm cleft. And ultimately to drink from her throbbing red fountain.

He cracked his window, raising his nose like a dog to the fresh air. He would never allow the beast to harm this girl. Soon enough, if the spell he sought were hidden between the brittle pages, he would be free of this blight. And if the gods were kind, he'd crumble to dust.

"I've been thinking this over, and I've decided you're not really a monster. If you were, I'd be dead, right? And as pleasant as your company has been so far..." She gave him a look that made him grin. "I'm fairly sure this isn't heaven, and it's too damn cold for Hell. So odds are good I'm still alive."

Ian snorted a mirthless laugh. "For now, but 'tis a battle to keep the beast from going after you. We'll finish our business quick as the wind, and I'll not be bothering you again. 'Tis a promise, lass." A promise he might have been eager to keep before he met her, but she'd struck a nerve in him, one much deeper than the maddening thirst. Deeper than the place he wanted to bury this blasted aching erection.

"So the spell you think is in this magic book is supposed to chase out the demon?"

"Aye," he said, relieved for a distraction.

"Why would he let you do that?"

"He wouldn't, not if he had any say. He's strong and he's fighting me, but I'm stronger. As long as I keep him fed, my will always defeats his." He remembered then, his own pack on the floor of the cave with the remaining pints of stolen blood.

"Just great," he muttered. If she had any idea how badly his demon craved her, how badly *he* craved her, she'd take her chances out there with the wolves.

Gabriella lowered her hood and pulled off her gloves. "So where will we do this...ceremony?"

"I'm not sure yet. Wherever we go, though, I'm thinking

you might want to keep a bucket of holy water at hand, just in case."

Ian slammed the brakes as a herd of deer leapt into the road. They spun around twice, the headlights glancing off trees, deer, rock and guardrails, but he managed to stop without crashing.

Gabriella's heart raced, a loud staccato in his ears, and her fingers clawed the seat. She took a deep breath, and he pressed the gas, taking it slow.

"A *bucket* of holy water?" she said after a minute. "Just in case of what?"

"If we can chase him out, I don't imagine he'll be too happy about it."

"No, I suppose not. But a bucket?"

"He's an evil creature, he cannot touch anything holy. I'm not sure what'll happen once he's out. You might want to douse yourself, so he can't get inside of you."

"Oh. Where can we find so much holy water?"

"My employer has connections at the Vatican."

She turned to him, her face bent in disbelief. "The Catholic Vatican?"

"Do you know any other?"

"Who are your employers?"

He smiled wryly. "My employers are the monsters who kill the worse monsters."

Her brow furrowed. "So, the Vatican knows about vampires?"

"Aye. Does that surprise you?"

The scent of fear curled out like fog from her skin. Her eyes shone in the dark as she lapsed into silence. Ian let her alone with her thoughts, knowing much harder things lie ahead.

They came through the last steep twist in the road, and the lights of small villages glowed in the foothills. As they continued their cautious decent, Curtea de Arges appeared in the valley like an old fashioned Christmas postcard with brick and stone houses and its gothic church steeples piercing the darkness.

"Where are you staying?" she asked.

"At the Inn, same as you. 'Tis the only one in the city."

"There's the Posada Hotel. It's much nicer."

"I stay away from the bigger hotels. Too many people." Too many tempting smells, he thought. "And you should talk. Why give up the luxury of a suite to a small room and a

21

shared bath?"

"People are nosy. When I'm hunting for something, I always travel as discreetly as possible."

He already knew this from studying her, but he nodded.

"The Inn is nearly empty. How did I miss you?" she asked.

"I came in late last night, and I had no choice but to spend the daylight hours in the room."

"But what about—?"

Ian sighed. "I know, I know. Sleeping in coffins and all that superstitious rot. 'Tis nothing but silly legends. I spent the day under the bed, away from the sunlight."

"Until about an hour ago, I thought you were the silly legend, so cut me some slack."

Ian felt his mouth twist up in a smile, stretching rarely used muscles. Yet Gabriella had elicited several tonight amid the swirling chaos of their meeting. He glanced to find her smiling, too.

"What?"

"Nothing. Just appreciating the profile." She smiled wider and he groaned. The vampire scent seduced her. "I don't even know your name."

Ian's cheeks heated, not an easy feat for one as cold as he. "Ian. Ian McShane."

"That's a beautiful name," she said a little dreamily.

Ian focused on the road, wishing she truly desired *him*, not this damned beast.

* * * *

In this part of Romania, horse drawn carts nearly equaled autos. But tonight the knee-deep snow discouraged both beast and machine, leaving the streets nearly deserted. Ian parked in the small lot behind the Inn. Gabriella protested when he offered his hand, finally ceding when she nearly fell on the lame ankle.

The Innkeeper laid down a book, his eyes growing wide behind round glasses as the pair of them struggled through the door. Gabriella hopped on one foot and both of them were filthy. Ian could only imagine what the old man was thinking.

"Elena!" The man shouted, hurrying from behind the counter. A small round woman rushed from a back room, wiping her hands on a flour dusted apron.

They spoke quickly in Romanian, both flashing looks at the couple now hovering near the fireplace in the small parlor. Soft firelight glowed warmly over dark hewn paneling, the only light in the room.

"What happened?" The old man asked in strongly accented English.

"A tumble down the mountain. Just a sprain, she'll be fine."

"Take her upstairs, Elena will run hot bath. You clean up when she finish and we have dinner for you then. A good hot meal fix her right up." He grinned beneath a thick gray moustache, patting a rounded belly.

Ian nodded and against her expletive filled protests he carried her upstairs where Elena already bustled between Gabriella's room and the Inn's only guest bathroom. Ian settled her on a chair and Elena shooed him out the door, eyeing his sword a little nervously. Gabriella lifted his coat from her shoulders and handed it up to him.

"Thanks," she managed before Elena slammed the door in his face.

He headed down the hall, Gabriella's pack hanging from his shoulder. He knew he should wait for her, but his patience had long expired.

Inside his room, he tossed his coat and sword onto the armchair and emptied the pack on his bed. The room was small with worn wooden floors and threadbare rugs. A narrow dresser stood beneath a wavy glass mirror. The bed squeaked and something hard poked his ass when he sat, but it was neat and clean, and they kept a fire going in the woodstove in the corner. Not that cold bothered him, but it would be nice for Angelica.

"Not Angelica. Gabriella, damn it!" he snarled. Why did that name continue to haunt him? After so many years, the pain of unrequited love still shredded his heart. He tore the lid off the golden box and ripped aside the skins.

Carefully, almost reverently, he laid the book on the bedspread. A long sought blessing and a curse. Deliverance and imprisonment. He sucked in a breath and opened the cover.

The pages he turned beneath his fingers were yellowed with age, fragile, yet powerful, revealing spells for binding spirits and calling up the dead. Every word was handwritten in Latin with expertly inked illustrations accompanying each incantation. Near the back of the book, he was surprised to find even a rare death curse. But where was the exorcism?

A light knock on the door interrupted his search.

"Who is it?" Ian closed the book and covered everything with his coat.

"Is Dimitrie," the owner said.

Ian swung open the door, and Dimitrie's eyes widened. "Is so dark. You no want a light?"

"What may I do for you?" Ian said, blocking entrance with his massive body.

"My gun. I would like it back now, please."

"Oh, of course. Please wait here." Ian left the door open and rummaged through his coat pocket, digging out the gun from where he'd stashed it back at the cathedral.

"Here you go." He smiled as he handed it back.

Dimitrie clicked the cylinder open and raised a bushy brow. "One bullet is missing."

"We had a run in with a wolf pack. She fired a shot to scare them away."

Dimitrie eyed the hole in his shirt, the dark stain.

"Snagged myself on a branch. No big deal, just a scratch."

The innkeeper remained dubious.

"Okay, the truth is she shot me. Thank God I'm a vampire so the bullet didn't kill me. Just pissed me off a bit, and I think I had every right, don't you agree? I mean, I hadn't even introduced myself and 'pop'."

The old man stared a moment and then burst into laughter, showing off several missing teeth. "Oh, you Scotsmen and your crazy humor."

Ian grinned and shook his head. "That's me, crazy Scotsman."

"So, how you end up with Miss de Chartres? She leave in car and you go by foot, after her."

"I found her stuck in the snow when she tried to pass the barriers to the mountain road. I pushed her free and went along...to keep her safe." Immortal life had conditioned him to lie. So much of his existence depended on it.

"Hmm. So long as she no bring wolf back." The old man winked.

Ian laughed and Dimitrie joined him a moment before growing serious.

"Still, I am missing bullet. They are no cheap." He clicked the gun shut and held out his palm.

Ian nodded and drew out his wallet, pressing two fifty Romanian Leu notes into Demitrie's palm. The man looked from the money up to Ian, who stood a head taller.

"Is too much, sir." He tried to hand one back but Ian raised his hands in the air, one still clutching his wallet.

"The rest is for your hospitality, and for taking care of Miss de Chartres."

The old man beamed and headed down the steps, humming an old Romanian folksong Ian had heard playing earlier on a scratchy vinyl album in the sitting room.

CHAPTER THREE ✝

December 8th Curtea de Arges, Romania

"Where is my book?" Gabriella hissed as she passed him in the hall, smelling of soap and wrapped in a thick robe.

"Safe in my room," he said, carrying a towel and clean clothes tossed over his shoulder. "They expect us to join them for dinner as soon as I've showered. We'll take a look at the spells later. I glanced through it, but I didn't find the one I was looking for."

Her face softened. "Oh. Don't worry, I'm sure it's there."

The hall was narrow, and Ian turned sideways to let her pass, swallowing a moan as she rubbed against his groin. He went hard as an iron rod and quickly turned away, unwilling to let her see the affect she had on his libido.

"Thanks for, um, saving me tonight," she murmured from her door.

He nodded and closed himself in the bathroom that was still filled with her scent. He sat on the toilet and rested his head in his hands, seeing her in the hall, all beauty and hellfire. Freckles over her cheeks, her long lustrous hair dripping down her back, just a curve of soft breast at the fold of her robe. He'd wanted to grab her right then and kiss her. No, not kiss her. He'd wanted to take her, make love to her; pound himself inside of her, over and over. Not the demon. Him. Ian McShane.

"No, I will not lay my heart out to be ripped to shreds. Never again." He stripped from his clothes, quite aware that his swollen cock did not share his sentiments of celibacy. With a snarl, he stepped into the shower and twisted the spigot, spraying himself with frigid water.

* * * *

"I thought you couldn't eat food," Gabriella whispered as they climbed the stairs after a meal of spicy sausage and mushroom fritters.

Ian huffed a sigh, weariness creeping into his bones. "More rumors, lass. I can and do enjoy food, but it metabolizes very fast. I drink a bottle of scotch and I'm sober in an hour."

Gabriella made a face. "I'd be sick."

They went to Ian's room where he moved his coat and sword back to the chair making room. But Gabriella sat on the bed next to the book and carefully began turning pages.

After a few minutes, she tilted up the book, pointing at a page for him to see. "I think this is it."

Even without words, the illustration on the facing page told him everything. A cantor dressed in robes bent over the supine body. The human's face distorted in pain and terror while the fingers of one hand twisted through his hair as if wrenching out a handful by the roots. The other hand raked the earth so severely, skeletal bones ripped through his fingertips.

Thrust up through the belly of his host, the demon howled at the sky, fighting to cling to the body. One arm punched through the chest, the other through the thigh, as if the beast could secure itself to the bones and the heart. The beast appeared as tortured as the human.

An intricate cross adorned the lower corner of the illustration, drawn inside a circle with words written in Latin beneath it.

"As the demon wrestles to remain inside the vessel, the human soul becomes his anchor. If the human's will is not strong enough, his soul may be ripped from his body and dragged down to hell with that of his parasite's," Gabriella read and sat up, her face ashen.

"Oh my God. Ian, are you sure you want to try this? It sounds terribly dangerous."

He swallowed, and nodded. "I will not change my mind."

Even as he said the words his eyes followed the lines of her long legs, one tucked under her as she sat on the edge of his bed. Her womanly scent wafted from that warm, moist place where the fabric pressed into her folds, and he found himself breathing deeply, his body reacting—

Downstairs something crashed. He stiffened at the muffled scream followed by a thick gurgling noise. Like poisonous gas, the smell rolled beneath the door. Black shields dropped over his eyes.

"They're coming, we must leave this instant," Ian hissed, already gathering the book and wrapping it in the skins.

"What's going on? Who's coming?" Gabriella's eyes grew wide.

"Can we talk about this later when someone's not trying to kill us?" He buckled on his sword sheath and shoved his arms through his coat sleeves before opening his window.

Church of the Damned, she had said. But who the hell were they and how did they track him to this place?

"But I need my purse...my passport."

He frowned, then grabbed her hand and tugged her into the hall and to her room. The passage reeked of them. They'd come looking up here as soon as they killed the Innkeeper and his wife. Damn savages. "Just grab your purse and coat. We must go now!"

"Why? Who are they?" Her eyes asked her question—what is downstairs that's terrible enough to frighten *you*?

"Vampires, lass, lots of them." He shoved the window up, pulled her into his arms and plunged into the snowy night.

CHAPTER FOUR ✝

December 8th Curtea de Arges, Romania

Gabriella buried her face against Ian's chest as he landed silently on the roof of the neighboring home.

"Hold on," he whispered before swinging her around onto his back.

She wrapped her legs around his waist, her arms clinging to his neck as he raced across the rooftops. Her stomach dropped every time he sailed across the gap between buildings. Her backpack bounced painfully against her shoulder—she'd had no time to secure it.

"What's going on?" She struggled to keep the fear from her voice.

"I think we found that Church of the Damned."

"More like they found us. How did they get here so fast? We just found the book a few hours ago."

"They must've been following one of us."

"What are we going to do?"

"Right now? Run like hell. There're too many of them to fight."

She glanced behind them and bit back a scream. Black shadows flooded through the open window, leaping from roof to roof like monkeys on steroids.

"Can you outrun them?"

"Not for long. They'll be using their demon's strength. I don't dare let mine out. It'd be like a lamb ridin' wolf."

"And I'm the lamb?"

"Aye. So I'm trying to come up with a plan B."

"What's plan A?"

"Being ripped apart before we get out of the city."

"That's a crappy plan."

"Don't I know it, lass. Hence the plan B."

The end of the street loomed ahead. She braced herself as he sailed to the ground, but she barely felt the impact. Using the slick road to propel them, he skated nearly a block before running again. He dashed into an alley, sweeping

29

between fenced backyards.

Ian slid to a sudden halt behind a tiny bungalow, nearly throwing her over his head with the lurch.

What are you doing?" she snapped, before she realized why he'd stopped. A snowmobile rested inside a wooden gate. Ian leapt the fence with the grace of a stag, despite carrying her. He slipped her to the ground before quickly dusting off the machine,

"Excellent." He grinned, his face sharp planes and dark shadows in the half-light.

How powerfully handsome he was, and he seemed to neither know nor care. Yet her breaths quickened, as amber waves tumbled over the golden stubble of his cheek. She'd known since the mountain that something about his scent seduced her.

He swung his leg over the seat and she climbed on behind him. Instead of frightening, she found his power fascinating. A useful tool to heighten arousal, she thought, then immediately admonished herself.

The snowmobile roared to life, shaking her from her musing. Seconds later, the back door burst open, pouring light over the yard as a man in red long johns raised a rifle at them.

Ian hit the gas and they crashed through the fence in an explosion of wood, speeding off down the alley. The crack of the rifle echoed around them. She ducked her head, expecting a bullet in the back. To her immense relief nothing struck her as they slid around the corner into the street.

Her relief disappeared in an instant. Nearly a dozen hideous creatures huddled across the road, looking equally surprised at their sudden good fortune.

"Damn! Hold on tight!" Ian swung around in a wild u-turn. The machine tipped sharply to one side, nearly dumping them onto the snow-covered cobbles.

She gasped, seeing the monsters in the gas lamplight. Sharp-boned and waxy pale, mouths brimmed with rows of fangs. Like the monster she'd seen in the cave, the one living inside of Ian.

Demons, she thought with a shudder.

The beasts raced after them, incredibly fast. She screamed when a hand grabbed her hair, jerking her backward.

"My sword!" Ian shouted.

Too terrified to protest, she plunged her hand beneath his coat and found the cold metal handle. In one sweeping movement she unsheathed the weapon and spun around, swinging the blade in a violent down stroke. The beast shrieked in fury, snarling as he tumbled away, his one remaining hand gripping his empty wrist spurting black blood in the dim light.

Something brushed her scalp. She yelped, her hand flying to her head.

"Shit! Shit!" The creature's fingers remained twined through her hair, still moving. She re-sheathed the sword and she tugged the hand away, tearing several hairs out with it. Grimacing, she flung the hand behind her, shouting to the beast just leaping up from the road. "Hey, I think you lost something."

Ian's laughter roared above the raging howls echoing through the village.

The others raced behind them. She gasped when one jumped at her, just missing her by inches. The engine buzzed and he accelerated further from their pursuers.

Once they reached open farmland, Ian left the highway, opting to travel over the fields in case the police came searching for the stolen machine.

"Get the phone in my coat pocket. Hit speed dial one," he shouted above the wind.

In their haste at the Inn, she hadn't thought about grabbing her gloves. Already her hands grew painfully cold and stiff, but she searched his pockets until she came out with the small phone.

She tried to see the screen as they bounced and jostled over the rough terrain. Finally figuring how to work the damn thing, she pressed the buttons.

A silky smooth, female voice answered, "Rogue Hunters, how may I direct your call?"

"What should I tell her?" she shouted, not sure if he could even hear her. Between the motor and the wind.

"Tell them Slayer number three needs the plane fueled and the pilot ready for takeoff as soon as we reach Budapest."

"I heard," the female voice said in her ear. Sounding more urgent now, she added, "Tell him the plane will be ready, hangar number six."

"I heard her," Ian called over his shoulder, and Gabriella rolled her eyes.

"And tell him to call in, as soon as he's in the air." The woman clicked off.

"I'm sure you got that, too," she said, slipping the phone away.

"Keep your hands in my pockets or you'll get frostbite."

She eagerly obeyed his suggestion. Her hands throbbed from the cold, but it didn't prevent her from noticing how the cords of muscles rippled beneath the leather, stretching and flexing like those of a giant cat beneath her grip.

Her stomach clenched in response to the sensation of the strength of his iron muscles beneath the coat, and she shivered as the warmth spread to lower, more sensitive places.

She'd never known a man in a physical way. It was forbidden, and her destiny pre-ordained. Until tonight, that hadn't been a problem. And with the demons chasing them, she didn't know whether to be relieved or angry.

"Are they coming after us?"

"If they're after this book, then I imagine so."

"Do you have to be so damned sarcastic?" Her words trailed off, and she suddenly felt overwhelmed. Monsters were chasing them, and here she sat with her arms wrapped around one, trusting her life to a monster just like them. What made him different from them—any better, safer?

Yet what choice did she have? She stood no chance against the others alone.

"What's a rogue hunter?"

His body stiffened. "We hunt others of our kind. Those who seek to kill humans, or to turn them."

"You have a...a company?"

"Yes."

Damn him and his simple answers.

"So who else knows about you guys? I mean, you have planes. You're obviously free to fly internationally."

For a moment her head spun, trying to comprehend the implications.

"We're an international company backed by several governments."

"Who?"

"Like the Vatican. They'd just as quickly deny any knowledge of us. But they understand and accept us as necessary. None are too happy about our existence."

"How? Where—?"

"There are many countries where we work under the

guise of our cover, Rockford-Houghton Pharmaceuticals."

"Seriously? That's you?"

"Erik Kestler, the founder, is one of us. He's a gifted scientist and a close friend."

She rested her cheek against his back. Her mind whirled with more questions, although she decided to wait until he didn't have to shout for her to hear his response. But ask she would. Whoever or whatever this man was, he completely fascinated her.

CHAPTER FIVE ✝

December 8ᵗʰ The Romanian Countryside

Ian relaxed a little when the lights of Pitesti appeared on the horizon. He'd worried they'd run out of gas before he put as much distance as possible between them and their pursuers.

He skirted the edge of the city until he saw the tower of Hotel Muntenia. City streets twisted through downtown clusters of tall buildings separated by parks and open spaces built along the Arges River.

He parked a block away from the hotel, helping Gabriella climb from the machine. The way she moved, slowly and stiffly, he knew she must be half frozen after the cross-country trip.

"Here, let me help."

She offered no protest as he slid an arm around her waist to assist, half carrying her to the front of the hotel. His eyes transitioned instantly from the empty black of the vampire to his own green as they stepped inside, allowing him to see more clearly in the bright interior.

Gabriella blinked taking in the lobby's brilliance. Still limping and shivering, she huddled against him as he scanned the lobby. No one sat at the car rental booth so he headed to the front desk. A young man in a starched shirt and jacket eyed them warily from behind the check-in counter.

Gabriella tried smoothing her hair, and he was dismayed to see her cheeks were wind-burned to bright crimson.

He asked the clerk if he spoke English, the only words he knew in Romanian without aid of his pocket translator. The thin blond man nodded, his lips pressed in an arrogant pucker.

"The car rental, it is closed?" Ian asked and the clerk nodded again.

"Could you please call us a taxi? We need to reach

34

Budapest tonight."

The man glanced at the clock behind him. "There is a train leaving in forty minutes."

"No, we can't wait. We need to catch a flight." Ian dug out his wallet and tossed the man two one-hundred Leu.

"Very well, sir. You may wait in the restaurant. I'll call for you when the car arrives."

"How long?" Ian nearly snarled.

The man's haughtiness vanished.

"Five, maybe ten minutes. I'll tell them to hurry, but with this snow..." He shrugged.

"Thank you."

"I don't think I'll ever thaw out," Gabriella said as Ian helped her into a chair inside the nearly empty restaurant.

Ian stood over her a moment, parting through her hair. He'd nearly lost Angelica this way, he would not risk Gabriella.

"What are you doing?" She tried to duck away, but he gripped her head in his hands, ignoring the angry spears hurling from her eyes until he was satisfied.

"Looking for bugs?" She shrugged away as soon as he released her.

"No. Scratches. Did the vampire's nails scrape your scalp?"

"No, why?" She smoothed her hair down, looking around but there were only a few busboys and a waiter lingering around, none paying any attention.

"A vampire scratch is poisonous to a human. It's deadly, the bacteria under the nails will eat you alive."

A festering stench rose like bile from his memories. Flesh rotting and sloughing in sheets off Angelica's body. The organs blackening and curling up like dead leaves. Angelica, smelling like rotted death. He swallowed, the face of his memory fading to the dark haired pixie with her moon dust skin, staring at him from across the small round table.

Gabriella shook her head. "No, I'm sure. He never got close to my skin."

Staff buzzed about the dim dining room, stripping away white tablecloths and placing chairs on top of tables. As Ian took his seat, a waiter approached, his face pinched.

He rattled something at them in Romanian. Ian let him finish his tirade and simply shook his head. "English?"

The man huffed. "Yes, of course. You are supposed to wait to be seated."

"We're waiting for a car. I need two cups of coffee and a pastry."

The man nodded and smiled less than genially. "We have a delicious apple strudel..." he prattled as if he'd recited the same line a thousand times tonight.

"Fine, one piece, please." Ian waved him off, irritated. He could feel the beast's excitement, scratching away at the edges of his brain like a monster clawing at a closet door. He forced himself to calm down. He'd never been good at containing his temper—another good reason to stay away from humans.

"I hope that's not for me," Gabriella whispered as the waiter headed to the kitchen.

"You need the sugar, it'll turn to energy and heat you up."

"I'm still full from dinner."

"Don't argue with me," he said a bit more harshly than he meant.

Her eyes narrowed.

"Please, I am just thinking of your health."

"My health is better than you think."

What a strange thing to say, sitting there lame and half frozen, he thought. He studied her obliquely until the waiter returned with two steaming cups in saucers and the dessert.

"We are closing soon, if you could pay now..." He held out his palm, which Ian filled with enough to cover their order plus a generous tip.

"*Multumesc.*" The man thanked him. He busied himself around the room with the other staff, removing salt and pepper shakers from tables ahead of the busboys who were doing the heavy work.

The clerk appeared at the door just as Gabriella finished the last bit of strudel. She set her fork on the plate and wiped her mouth with a napkin.

"Your car is here," the young man said and returned to the desk.

"Feel better?" Ian asked, shielding her behind him as they stepped outside into the swirling snow. He scanned the shadows, the streets and the nearby park for any sign of their pursuers.

"Yes, I do. Thank you," she said in a grudging tone.

He sniffed the air as he helped Gabriella into her seat, smelling nothing but trees and buildings and the icy wind. As the city faded behind them, he still kept a sharp eye on every car approaching from their rear.

Her scent glutted the small space, tearing at his defenses with a desire so fierce his teeth gnashed against the physical need, plunging through his groin, lusty thoughts of flesh and blood flooding his brain.

Why did she tempt him so badly? Blood was blood. There were subtle differences between one type and another, but always a sharp metallic smell. But hers was rich and sweet, unlike any human he had ever encountered. The thought gave him pause, and he glanced at her. Beating heart, pulsing veins, that distinct womanly warmth between her lovely thighs.

Saliva welled in his mouth, and he drew a deep breath, filling his lungs with her, craving just a taste.

The demon stirred uneasily.

She moved closer, leaning her head on his shoulder. He stiffened, fighting warring urges to shove her away or sink his fangs into her delicate neck.

Why her? The one he had chosen to help him end his torment? Why did she, of all humans have to smell so damn delicious? Was this his punishment? His price for the lives he had taken, for playing God and judging evil while his own soul reeked with the blood of innocents?

Her arm curled through his, and he turned his head away, ignoring the warmth of her body pressed against his. They would find a place to perform the exorcism, and if he survived, he would send her away. She could never see him as anything other than a monster, and for her own safety, it was just as well.

But she had touched him, and he wished things were different. Perhaps he could be someone she could care for. "Fool," he muttered to himself. He was not someone else. He was a vampire, a killer. He had loved once before, given so much, and had his heart shattered. Never again. He would never allow another to hold his heart, just to crush it. A life of solitude was his fate. And even the fires of hell offered more appeal than living so alone.

CHAPTER SIX ✝

December 8th Bucharest Airport, Romania

Ian shook her awake as they approached the airport. She blinked, surprised she had dozed off. The car drove straight to a hangar where a sleek black jet collected snow on the tarmac. On the tail, circled in gold were the letters R-H in fancy script. She recognized the pharmaceutical company's logo, laughing now at the double entendre. Rockford Houghton Pharmaceuticals—Rogue Hunters. Clever.

Plows scraped across the runways, trying to keep up with the storm. The jet's engines whined, deafening as they stepped out of the cab. A woman stood beside the boarding stairs, tall and beautiful in a dangerous, predatory way. Her plump red lips curled in the kind of sly smile a cat might share with a cornered mouse. She wore black slacks and a white fur coat that hung to her shins. A matching fur hat covered white-blonde hair that fell nearly to her waist. Slanted feline eyes, ice blue with vertical slits, watched her with disturbing intensity. High cheek bones—her face was arranged in angles and planes of perfect Slavic proportion.

Gabriella wanted to hate her. She glanced at Ian, not surprised to find him staring. A jealous heat flared through her, a feeling so foreign and distasteful, she instantly recoiled from it. Ridiculous. Ian didn't belong to her. This man, this immortal god, was not hers to claim.

"Sasha, what are you doing here?" Ian asked the woman.

She pulled a long drag from a cigarette and took her time blowing out a thin stream of smoke. "Erik called me two days ago, asked me to meet you here to accompany you on some little side trip. Don't you ever listen to your messages?" she said in a deep velvety growl.

"This was personal business. I wasn't paying much attention to the phone."

"Apparently not." Every word rolled from her tongue

with a seductive Russian accent. "He heard through our sources in France there might be trouble."

"Serious trouble, if he sent the likes of you."

Something dangerous flashed in her smile. "You weren't complaining when we captured those rapist pig rogues in America last spring."

"I wasn't criticizing you, just stating a fact. You're a lethal hunter, and if Erik sent you he must've been worried."

"And for good reason," she purred and took another long drag. "We are meeting him in Paris. The council has called an emergency meeting. From your call to the operations center, I assume your trouble still follows. Come, let's put aside our differences for now. We may soon have a common enemy for you to hate more than me."

Ian sighed and smiled with a weariness Gabriella hadn't noticed before.

"I don't hate you, Sasha. I am not fond of your methods, but I concede at times they are necessary."

He held out his hand to Gabriella and she accepted, following him to the stairs of the plane.

"That coat is beautiful," she commented as she passed by Sasha.

"You want to touch it, don't you?" She smiled, sharp points rippling over her teeth. She flicked away her cigarette and it hissed in the slush.

"She does not wish to pet your damn coat," Ian snarled, tugging Gabriella to the cabin door.

Gabriella bristled. Ian saved her tonight, she owed him her life, but that didn't give him dominion over her. She didn't want to make a scene in front of the other woman, so she bit back her retort. For now.

The cabin of the plane was paneled in rich red-brown wood, the leather seats were set up conference style. Near the rear were four reclining loungers that could be used for sleeping.

"The hides are snow wolf," Sasha explained, sliding into a seat across from them. She ran her hand down her arm, ruffling the thick white hairs.

"I've never heard of a snow wolf. Is that some kind of arctic wolf?" Anger rose in her, thinking of this woman wrapping herself in the pelts of some rare, beautiful animal.

The engine whined and the jet lurched forward. A moment later the pilot's voice came over the intercom. "We're just waiting for clearance for takeoff. It's shouldn't be more than five or ten minutes."

"A snow wolf is a rare hybrid of an everyday werewolf. They are found only in northern Russia and normally they behave themselves. But a small group of youngsters thought it would be great fun to travel to Moscow and start their own clan. They'd already turned twenty humans by the time I arrived last week. What a mess." She drummed blood-red nails on the leather armrest.

Gabriella's stomach did a flip. "So those are... werewolf skins?" She felt Ian tense beside her, felt him watching her reaction.

"Yes, darling. I couldn't just let such gorgeous fur go to waste."

"But I thought..." She glanced at Ian, not wishing to be chastised yet again for her ignorance of all things supernatural. "I thought when a werewolf died, it returned to its human form."

Ian's growl rumbled in his throat.

Sasha lifted her lip in a half smile, showing off an impressively frightening fang. "That is why you must skin them before they are dead."

It took a moment before Gabriella realized her mouth hung open, and she had to force her lips together. The cabin rolled in a slow spin. She thought she might pass out.

"Breathe."

She hadn't realized she'd stopped until Ian whispered the word in her ear. He grasped her hand, leaning closer until his scent calmed her enough to draw a steady breath.

"Remind me never to let you housesit my cats," Ian said to Sasha.

Sasha's feline eyes widened. "You have cats? I love cats. They are so soft and rumbly." She purred and curled her long legs up beneath her. "It's the doggies I do not care for. They should all be hanging in closets."

"Why must you say such things, Sasha? And you wonder why people think you're sadistic."

She shrugged. "I do not care what people think. I am told to stop the young Russian werewolves from wreaking havoc in Moscow, and I do as I'm asked." Sasha's eyes flicked to Gabriella. "And if it makes you feel any better, little bird. I only took skins from a few of the troublemakers and sent the rest home to their bitches with a valuable lesson about following the rules.

"I performed a valuable public service. The others, the

freshly turned, they were too wild to let them live, but I killed them very quickly. They did not suffer."

Gabriella nodded, too shocked to say anything.

The plane rolled onto the runway, the pilot instructing them to prepare for takeoff. Gabriella fastened her belt and dug her fingers into the armrests.

"Afraid of flying?" Ian whispered, his breath strangely cool against her ear.

"Seems silly after tonight." Her laugh sounded a little hysterical. She cleared her throat, trying to get a handle on her emotions. Why had she gotten on this plane? She let him lead her like a lamb, without questions. She needed to return to Chicago. As soon as they reached Paris, she'd arrange to get home. Only, she'd made a promise to Ian. After saving her life, she owed him.

"It has been a very strange night. You've handled yourself quite well, considering."

His words shook her from her thoughts. "Considering what? That I'm a girl?"

He grinned, his eyes dark emerald in the dimly lit cabin. She blinked to be sure, because she knew they'd been black earlier this evening.

"No, because you've been chased by vampires and you've been conversing with a shape shifter who makes coats out of werewolves."

Sasha stuck out her tongue and Gabriella noticed it was rather long and thin.

Shape shifters? Vampires? Werewolves? This was all too much. She pinched the bridge of her nose, taking a calming breath before meeting Sasha's unsettlingly focused stare. "What are you? I mean, what do you shift into?"

"I will tell you my secret if you tell me yours." Sasha lowered and raised long lashes in a slow, dreamy blink that would melt any man to a puddle of drooling goo.

How did Sasha know she had a secret? Gabriella ground her teeth. Her earliest memories were of games and chants she'd been taught to help hide her identity and of Grandfather forever preaching the importance of keeping their lives a secret. They'd lived an illusion, well crafted and well buried. But somehow this woman saw something beneath the facade. *How much*, she wondered?

Sasha grinned. "Do not look so shocked, little bird. I am sure even Ian is aware that you are... special. There is something about you. A glow, a purity I've never felt in any

41

human."

Leave it to a damn cat to out her.

Ian laid his hand on her arm. Its strange coolness sent a shiver through her.

"Sasha, you're making her uncomfortable. I'm asking you politely to leave her be."

Sasha's smile fell. "Or what?"

"Please don't fight. There's not enough room in the cabin and I have no desire to be caught in the middle of a...a cat fight," she said, unable to stop a burp of a giggle.

Ian arched a brow, frowning at her.

Sasha threw her head back with a snarling laugh. "I like you. You are very funny. Does little bird still want to see me as my true self?"

She yawned, but as her jaws stretched apart, her mouth expanded into a furry muzzle. Her nose widened and grew flat, black. Quickly, Sasha kicked off her boots and peeled away socks and slacks. She pulled the sweater over her head, freeing heavy perfect breasts covered in sprouting white fur.

Within seconds, she perched naked in the chair, her face more feline than human. Silky fur spread over her shoulders and down her belly. She lifted a striped, flaxen arm and ran her long cat tongue down its length to the tip of an enormous paw.

A little gasp escaped Gabriella's throat, belated by the surprise. A great blonde tiger with pale brown stripes sat in the leather chair, grinning at her through huge, sharp teeth—its fat tail sweeping the air beneath her seat.

She stared as Sasha thumped to the floor and sauntered up the aisle to one of the recliners in the rear of the plane. With effortless grace, the cat leapt into the seat and stretched out, her paws hanging limply over the sides.

Ian moved closer to Gabriella, no doubt trying to calm her. Looking away made her feel weak, but she was afraid to meet his gaze, afraid he would see the fear and confusion in her eyes.

How had she survived so many years without crossing paths with these creatures? She'd always considered herself an adventurer, striking out to remote places all over the world in search of rare books. But books seemed rather innocuous now.

Ian's face moved close to hers, his eyes searching. She drew in a breath, tasting the luscious spicy smell of him, like cloves and sage. Yearning tickled like seductive fingers around her stomach, igniting heat that swelled to her breasts, her mouth, and to other places she'd not even dared to imagine such invitations of pleasure.

She glanced again at Sasha, who lay in tiger form, her eyes shut and her breathing even.

"Is she asleep already?" Her voice sounded a little breathy. Would he notice?

"She's a cat, she naps all the time."

Ian leaned over to look around her. Solid cords of muscle brushed across her breasts.

She sucked in a breath and closed her eyes, gulping down the telling sigh.

He sat back in his seat and grinned. "Yeah, she's out."

Gabriella nodded, pressing back into the seat, as far away as she could get from his lithe body.

Did the man have any idea how sexy he was? She wanted to hate him for filling her with such futile, frustrating desire. The Order insisted she remain pure for her life mate, and that she would know him on sight and by the immediate bond she would feel to him.

But Ian couldn't be the man they had foretold. He was possessed by a demon, the very opposite of everything her people stood for.

Except, demon or no, that wasn't exactly true. Despite what her eyes had seen, her heart felt only goodness inside him, and bravery.

"How long have you known Sasha?" She gazed at his face, marveling at the gentleness in his eyes. If she had met him now for the first time, she would never believe anything evil could dwell behind them.

"We've worked together a few times. She's an incredible tracker. She's helped me rid the world of some very bad creatures."

"Huh," she said, watching his lips stretch and pucker as he spoke, wanting to touch them, to see if they were as soft as they promised.

"I know she's a little...harsh, but don't think too badly of her." His words pulled her attention back to the conversation.

"I'm too shocked she even exists to think badly of her. Why does she hate dogs? Is it...?" She bit her lip, feeling ridiculous. "Is it the cat-dog thing?"

Ian chuckled, but not in a patronizing way. "She had a

rough life. Her mother was a powerful witch and her father a shape-shifter. I hear they were very happy the first few years of Sasha's life, until the Yakutsk werewolves found them."

Gabriella swallowed, her stomach churning. "Yakutsk?"

"North-east Russia. It's the coldest city in the world. Sasha's family lived in a cabin in the forest about fifty miles up the Lena River. The snow wolves there were a feral pack. Most born into the life as pups, not humans."

"But why would they attack her family? They must have known they'd be harder to defeat."

"That's exactly why they chose them—the thrill of the hunt. Her parents could've escaped, but not carrying a child with them. Of course they stayed to defend her. They put up a hell of a fight. I've heard stories from some of the older weres—the ones who were born human and changed in their later years. The wolves had kept the child for sport, abused her in many ways..." He rubbed his temple.

"What happened?"

"She grew up. I suppose they believed her to be intimidated by the years of cruelty, but in reality, her rage only amplified with the passage of time. And they were so used to seeing her as a cowering child, they never noticed when she grew larger and stronger.

"Sasha always knew she had the power inside her, and the first time she changed, she exploded with it. There were thirteen weres in that pack and by the time she finished, she'd killed every one of them. She migrated to Moscow and made a life for herself, alone at sixteen. You've got to respect that kind of mettle."

"Of course. I can't even imagine," Gabriella said, suddenly missing her grandfather.

With its own will, her hand rose as if to push through Ian's tangled mane, golden in the light and copper in shadows against moon pale skin. His lips lightly blushed and pouting, tempted her to meet his with hers in moist caresses. Her heart pounded, a frantic knocking against her ribs as if begging to be set free. She closed her eyes, begging for what she wanted, what she desperately needed.

She raised her hand as if to touch him and his breath caught. He went rigid as her soft lids closed. Her lips gathered into a sensuous velvet bow.

He snatched her hand from the air and tenderly kissed her palm. Never in his life had he known such peace. After years of killing as a soldier, and then as a monster—he never felt he deserved it.

Sasha was right. Ian had sensed it too. There was much more to Gabriella than the sweet smelling blood singing across his soul like a sword over its sheath.

Her skin glowed softly in the darkened cabin. There was something about her—a purity that made his throat tighten and his soul crave to be near her. He basked in her silver-white radiance, drifting on a gentle current of serenity. His chest gripped painfully.

He could not tear his eyes from her, from her milky skin, her rose blushed cheeks, the flush lips. The deep dark warmth of her eyes drew him in with matching passion. If only he could read her mind, know what she truly thought of him.

More than anything, he wished to take her in his arms, to feel her breasts smashed hard against his chest, to find the warmth he smelled drifting up from her. How he wanted to touch her there, to slide himself deep inside her body and bathe in the pure rapture of this beautiful soul.

The beast stirred within his brain, the ever-present jackal. Ian blew out a breath, forcing himself to pull away. His heart ached for her comfort, his body ached for her heat, but he deserved neither, penance for allowing the parasite to share his flesh.

Her eyes blinked open, glistening in the dark. Their hunger turned to hurt and tore at his heart like nothing ever had. He knew he should turn away, move to another seat and free them both from this strange pull, but he was too selfish to let her go. Not yet. Instead he ran his fingers under the chain at her neck. She shuddered at the touch of his fingertips brushing her skin.

"What is this?" he asked, his voice hoarse with lustful desire.

She swallowed, pulling back a little further. She tugged the chain through his fingers, sliding it up from beneath the soft cashmere that suddenly felt like a silken glove caressing her body. Shuddering again, she laid the tiny silver cross in her palm.

"My grandfather gave me this, to ward off evil, he said. But to me it's just a pendant. It means nothing. I wear it to make him happy." She laughed. "Of course, after tonight I might change my mind about evil. Not that it kept any monsters away."

Ian stiffened and she quickly shook her head. "I meant the others—the ones that came to the Inn. Not you." *Never you,* her mind sang. "I know you get irritated with me, but after everything I've seen, I have to ask. The cross, it's silver. Does it bother you?"

"The demon cowers from it. I feel him trembling in the corner of my brain." Ian smiled sardonically, taking the cross in his hand, tracing it with a finger. "The silver, should it pierce my skin and touch my blood, would kill me. Sitting innocently in my hand, the cross does me no harm. My own sword is silver. 'Tis the best weapon to fight the others. We have guns with silver bullets, but sometimes it's difficult to carry them across borders, especially into countries where we have no alliance. Everyone respects the sword," he said, and allowed the cross to slip through his fingers.

He could have her, he thought, his breath quickening. As long as the cross lay on her breast, keeping the demon quelled, he could make love to her without fear of killing her.

He squeezed his eyes closed, turned his head away from her. How foolish to allow such indulgent desires. His only salvation lay in the book.

He glanced at her pack, askew on the table, the sharp corners of the box stretching the nylon. In Paris, he would find someplace, perhaps the catacombs, where they could perform the ceremony.

Erik would understand. If anyone knew Ian's pain, it was he.

He lifted the window shade and watched the moon sliding in and out of the clouds, squares of farmland and patches of forest glowing in its cold winter light far below.

Yes, that was the best solution for everyone. He closed his eyes, feigning sleep lest he be tempted to seek solace in her soothing voice or fall any deeper into the velvet softness of her eyes.

CHAPTER SEVEN †

Three Weeks Earlier, Paris, The Catacombs

Black smoke rose like dancing snakes from the seven anchored torches, the stench of kerosene thick in the air. Dim light flickered over walls built of skulls and bones, stretching feebly into the chamber, but not quite touching either floor or ceiling. Deep in the shadowed recesses, standing inhumanly still and silent, seven Conscripts awaited their sacred duty.

Lilith moved to the last of the granite tables and tipped the clay pitcher, pouring a wide crimson ribbon from head to foot, quietly chanting a prayer to honor the sacrifice of blood.

Thirst burned in her throat. She waved the bouquet beneath her nose, and her mouth filled with saliva, her tongue tracing the points rippling over her teeth. With a choking swallow she returned the pitcher to the marble altar and retrieved the urn. She closed her eyes, praying fervently until the craving passed. Retracing her steps, she sprinkled finely ground bones over the thick red puddles, praying to honor the sacrifice of the flesh.

She returned to the center of the room, setting the urn on the altar before raising the hood of her black velvet robe. Her hand worried the heavy silver cross resting against her breasts. With one last check of her preparations, she drew a breath and raised her arms.

"Bring in the Chosen Ones."

The girls wept and struggled against the disciples who led them through the lightless passages. They stank of filth—sweat, urine and feces. And blood, where they'd struggled against their manacles.

Her lips moved as she silently begged her lord for strength.

Seven vampyric disciples roughly shoved the girls to their places at the foot of each consecrated table, looping the chains of their manacles to the hooks.

"Remove their hoods and leave," she ordered, a thrill of

47

excitement shaking her with nearly orgasmic pleasure.

The vampires pulled the white silk covers from the girl's heads, bowed to her and quickly exited.

Seven girls shivered in virginal white dresses, their hair mussed, their eyes wide and hollow. The stench of fear reeked from their bony bodies. Golden torchlight turned tears into dripping honey on their cheeks. Beauties, all of them, well worthy of their calling. Two blondes, a brunette, and a freckled redhead—two dark skinned girls and one who appeared Asian, her black silk hair hanging in her face.

Unlike the others, whose fragile human hearts thundered with terror, hers remained only mildly quick. Her black eyes narrowed, staring at Lilith with raw hatred.

"Bitch." The girl spat, yanking hard against her chains. Blood dripped from raw wounds on her wrists.

Again saliva swarmed Lilith's mouth. For a moment she watched as warm thick drops dripped, dripped, dripped to the floor. She imagined lunging over the table, pinning the girl to the wall, and sinking her teeth into the flesh of her pale neck.

She blinked and looked away, praying harder for the strength that seemed to elude her tonight. "Control, give me control," she uttered, too quickly and quietly for human ears.

Composed again, she nodded at the girl, appreciating her spirit. The girl snarled, jerking the chain again and again, so hard Lilith thought her bones might snap.

She waited silently until the girl finished her tantrum. The girl's efforts left her eyes wild and her breaths ragged.

"Please don't be afraid." Lilith spoke softly. "For weeks my people sought out only the finest, purest candidates. This is a great honor, to be selected from so many to complete the lord's work. Three days ago my people brought you here and placed you in the cells. I ask your forgiveness. This was not meant to be a punishment. It was a necessary step to prepare you. Three days of darkness, to erase the evil you have seen in the world. Three days of silence to purify your minds with contemplations. Three days of hunger to awaken your soul. You are extraordinary, all of you."

But not as extraordinary as the one she truly sought.

She turned in a slow circle, making eye contact with each of them. They stared back, some listless, some hopeful, and the little Asian girl still very angry. How she wanted that little one.

"No!" she nearly shouted, startling herself and the girls. "Control, control, control," she recited the mantra until she suppressed the urge to tear open skin.

She clasped her hands tight, her nails digging into her palms. "You are the Chosen Ones. Chosen to do the lord's work. I assure you, your sacrifice guarantees you a place in heaven."

"What sacrifice?" A tall, pretty black girl asked, wiping the shine of tears on her shoulder.

Lilith frowned at the dirty smear on the dress, but she bit back her anger.

"We are at war. Fighting to cleanse the earth of evil, but we must build our armies. These new warriors must be special."

"Crazy bitch. Don't listen to her," the black eyed girl said to the others.

Lilith laughed and pushed her hood back.

"Look at my face. This scar." She ran her fingers over harp strings of flesh, stretching over the white bone of her cheek and jaw. Bumpy cords of damaged tendons held together the left side of her face. She tilted her head and pulled back a curtain of corn-silk hair for them to see.

They gasped. A couple of them retched.

Some time in her past—she could not remember when exactly, holy water had burned through her skull, sizzling away part of her brain.

"These scars are a blasphemy. *I* am a blasphemy. These wounds—they came from holy water and will never heal. This is my punishment for allowing this demon to dwell inside me."

She pulled up the hood, hating for anyone to see her, but it was necessary.

"The planet is a cesspool of sin. Humans wallow in pleasures of the flesh, destroying their precious souls with drugs and wars, raping and murder. It is time to cleanse the evil from the earth, but first we must rid the world of all those who would stand in the way of righteousness."

"She is crazy." A petite pale redhead laughed nervously and tugged at her chains.

"You are all wearing the crosses. They will keep you safe." Lilith went to the redhead. Her white fingers slipped beneath the crucifix, turning it once in her hand and dropping it against the girl's trembling chest.

"Safe from what?" A plump brunette shivered, rattling

her cuffs.

"Safe from the demons." She circled the room, touching each girl on the shoulder.

The tall black girl spit at her, her anger making her brave. The Asian girl lunged, gnashing her teeth, but Lilith ducked away with immortal speed.

Lilith returned to the altar and raised a hand bell. "Do not be afraid, you are blessed. You are the chosen," she sang in a monastic chant. "Take in you this seed. Bear the fruit of our lord's soldiers."

She rang the bell and the seven Conscripts stepped out from the niches. Tall, muscular and keenly intelligent with shaved heads and bodies. She had known their purpose from the moment she found them, as carefully selected as the girls.

Each wore nothing but the silver collars with spikes resting against their pale necks. Despite swearing their allegiance, trust went only so far.

She'd been betrayed before, she remembered bitterly, her hand moving to her cheek. They would live by the laws of the lord or die at her hand. One sharp tug...

Lilith raced from table to table, moving so quickly the girls barely had time to gasp before all seven of them lay flat on their backs. Theirs arms remained chained to the end of the tables, but now they were stretched out above their heads. Both ankles had been chained at the corners, leaving their legs spread. The blood and bones oozed from beneath them, staining their dresses scarlet.

"Lord, take these gifts we are offering and bless us with your bounty," she chanted and again she raised the bell, rang it once.

Lilith continued to chant over the screams and wailing as her Conscripts planted their special seed inside these sacred vessels.

Once finished, the Conscripts dropped lithely to the floor. She knew their beasts cried out in thirst, but fasting was a crucial step in the ritual. She now brought eight goblets from under the altar and filled them with blood from the pitchers stored there.

Though starving, the Conscripts accepted the offering reverently and bowed their heads as she unlocked their collars.

"Now go, feed," she whispered. Each emptied their cup and left it on the altar, bowing one more time to Lilith before disappearing into the passageway.

Every girl wept quietly, even the mouthy Asian girl, but raw fury melded with the tears of humiliation staining her cheeks. Her black eyes glared at Lilith, her jaw rigid, her teeth grinding. This girl's child would lead her armies, and Lilith's heart soared as the thought swelled to knowledge inside her mind.

Giddy with excitement, she moved from girl to girl, stopping at each one to lay a hand low on her belly, just above the pubic bone. She closed her eyes and listened, smiling as the first quiver of a heartbeat fluttered like moth's wings beneath her fingers. The girls would not feel movement for days. She pulled down their dresses and unlocked the ankle shackles.

Her throat tightened and a red film of tears swarmed her eyes. "You don't know how lucky you are," she said, smiling all around. "Such an honor to be chosen. To carry these children, to make this sacrifice to the Almighty." Blood ran hotly down her cheeks. "You shall be received with such love and admiration. I envy you. To be so welcome in your father's arms."

The girls stared at her in horror, and she didn't blame them. How revolting she must appear with her ruined face streaked with blood, speaking of glories they could not fathom. These girls were her only path to redemption, the only way she could prove her worthiness. She raised the eighth goblet to her lips, careful to tilt her head to the side, lest the liquid slide out the gaping flesh.

She clapped her hands and the seven disciples appeared from where they had waited in the passage. "Take them to the birthing suites." And to the girls she said, "I will see you in one month's time. I would not miss the births for anything."

"What the hell are you talking about?" The redhead looked like she might explode with fear, every muscle in her body coiled inward.

The disciples unlocked their wrists and gently helped the girls down from the tables.

"In four weeks each of you will deliver a precious, blessed warrior."

"In four weeks? You're crazy." The tall black girl tried to glare, but the earlier fire had flickered out. She looked to be the youngest of the seven, perhaps seventeen or eighteen, her body waif thin with sharp hips bones and shoulder blades poking through the dress.

Lilith went to her, cupping her soft, warm cheek in her cold hand. The girl shivered but didn't pull away. "I will see you in one month, dear one."

She turned to the disciples. "Take them now."

The girls still struggled, though with less vigor.

Lilith followed the passageway to the row of tiny cells. The iron door of the first creaked open, and she lowered herself to the filthy mattress. She rolled on her side, curling her knees to her chest and holding them with her arms.

Blood tears painted her cheeks as she sobbed and prayed. "Please, lord, end my suffering. Let me die for you. Please just let me die."

Someday she would prove her worthiness. She would bring the woman to her sacred chamber to be filled with the seed of the most ancient one. And what a treasure Lilith would have to offer, the greatest warrior—the child of Gabriella.

Then, surely, he would free her from this curse, from this pain.

*****

Amun waited for Lilith to leave the chamber before stepping from his hiding place behind a secret door in the fifth alcove. He drew a breath, shuddering in ecstasy at the heady smells of sex and blood flavoring the air like sickly sweet perfume. His plans moved forward with greater momentum than he had ever imagined and his sister, Amunet, played perfectly into his hands.

When he and she had been caught one night by hunters, he had used her body to shield himself from attack. The hunters used water from the River Styx, the only substance that could burn them, even kill them, and from which wounds could never recover.

Amunet had not died, but the water had eaten at her face and damaged her brain beyond repair. Disgusted with her appearance and the dullness in her once lively eyes, he had left her behind, sure the hunters would finish her off. But centuries later, he found her living off street waifs in war ravaged Paris.

She knew not her name, nor did she recognize him as her brother. After seeing her like that, an idea blossomed in his mind. He appeared to her, proclaiming to be a god from the heavens, and offered her freedom from her burden of shame. He convinced her she carried that shame, both because she murdered innocent children and for her sheer stupidity, as if he really cared.

She had cried at his feet for his slightest kindnesses. He told her that her name was Lilith, a small personal joke, since the demon Lilith ate small children. And he formed the Church of the Damned as a platform for his revenge against the humans who had reduced him, a great god of Egypt to a bloodsucking fiend.

And now his armies were strong, and he was nearly ready to unleash his wrath.

Excitement bloomed in his chest, spreading warmly to his groin, swelling in response. He thought of going to Amunet, for he knew her body and had once greatly enjoyed the way she had yielded to his thrusting power. She would be willing, overjoyed.

But how could he plant himself in paradise while staring into that wretched face from hell? No, the streets of Paris were ripe with sweet young things. Young men and women who would beg him to plant himself inside their secret gardens while drinking from their succulent fountains.

So he had turned his back on her sobs and disappeared into the deliciously dangerous Parisian night.

CHAPTER EIGHT ✝

Early Morning, December 9ᵗʰ, Paris, France

Gabriella checked the time on her cell phone, troubled to see she had missed several calls from home. "I've got to call my grandfather, he must be worried sick."

"Of course," Ian said, offering a tired smile before turning away to stare out the window of the limo.

Something had happened on the plane. She'd felt such a connection to Ian, and she'd been foolish enough to believe the feeling was reciprocated. That perhaps he really was the man she'd been searching for, for such a very long time. Yet at the last moment he'd pulled away, rejected her.

She found her grandfather's number and pressed send, tears blurring the screen. For so long she had guarded her heart. The one time she'd been stupid enough to share just a small part of herself, and she'd been humiliated.

Yet something still drew her to him. Was it only his vampyric power? She glanced at him as he stared out at the City of Lights, the sharp angled cheek and the strong square chin, his eyes weary as an old man with the burdens of the world upon him.

What had cut him so deeply that he would risk his soul just to be rid of the pain? Such a wound. She could almost taste his blood. *Taste his blood.* For just an instant, the strange, unbidden thought excited her. She swallowed hard against the welling panic. How could she think such a horrible thing?

The limo had been waiting at the executive hangar when they landed at the Charles De Gaulle Airport. Now they crossed the Seine, heading into the business district north of the Louvre and the Eiffel Tower. Sasha had chosen to ride up front with the driver, leaning very close to the man. Twice already Gabriella was sure she had seen a golden tail twitch above the seat.

Grandfather's voice rose as she recounted the night's events. She considered leaving out the part about the vampires, but he needed to know everything in order to warn her people. He demanded that she immediately return to the airport and fly home to Chicago.

"I'm sorry, I've made a promise," she said softly, turning her back to Ian, although she knew he could hear her.

"You've made a promise to The Order. You owe them, to keep yourself safe. The prophecy would die with you. Have you considered that?"

Anger heated her cheeks, but she kept her tone even, reminding herself he was an old man who was worried about her.

"Yes, of course. But my word is my oath, and I will not break it. Either I stay with the book, or I will return home without it."

He was silent for a long time. She could imagine him sitting in his study, chewing his pipe stem, his pruned face red with anger.

"You must stay with the book, but be very careful. What the vampire told you is the truth. The demon will be very dangerous while you are trying to exorcise it. I wish I could be there to perform the ceremony, but I don't dare leave my collections unprotected."

Fear squirmed in her belly. He'd never been so worried about discovery before. She wondered if he was aware of more danger than he shared.

"I understand. Don't worry about me, I can take care of myself."

"Call me later when you have some privacy. I know the vampire is listening, and he's heard too much already."

The phone went dead in her hand. Gabriella turned to find Ian staring intently.

"I understand his concern. I release you from our bargain," Ian said. "You should return home. I'll find someone else to perform the spell and the book will be hand delivered to you. I give you *my* word."

"No," she said a little too sharply. "No, I don't want to leave the book. I trust you, I do, but I'll feel better if I do this myself."

He smiled as if that pleased him. But why would he care if she stayed or left?

The limo stopped in front of a two story stone office building, brightly lit despite the late hour. Sasha wrapped herself in her furs before hurrying inside. Ian offered his hand to help Gabriella from the car. A cold wind swept swirls of snow from drifts along the street, but stars shown in the night sky, painting the winter night silver-blue. Ian took her pack and swung it over his shoulder. He looked a bit puzzled when she walked beside him to glass doors etched with the same insignia she'd seen on the plane.

"Your ankle seems better."

"Yes, it's much better, thanks." Stars in heaven, she'd forgotten about the silly ankle.

"Fast healer." He raised a brow. "Maybe Sasha was right about you."

"So tell me again, why are we here?" She quickly shifted topics.

They stepped into the warmth of the marble lobby, and she followed Ian to the elevators.

"I'll let it go for now, lass, but you will share your secret."

Her heart did a little flip at his rakish grin.

"First we must discuss the attack in Romania, see why the rogues are banding together, and find out what the hell is so important in this book."

Gabriella glanced guiltily at the pack on Ian's shoulder. Was it really wise, not to share the secrets of its pages?

They rode the elevator to the top floor. The doors slid open to a large rectangular room.

Several people looked up from a long oval table. Beyond them, a glass wall displayed a spectacular view of the Arc de Triomphe du Carrousel and in the distance, the top of the Eiffel Tower glowed above the skeletal trees.

She'd always loved Paris, especially in winter when its architecture caught the eyes at every turn.

"Ian, so good to see you." A dark haired man in a tailored black suit came around the table, his arms opened in greeting.

Ian didn't seem to notice his friend or the crowd. His eyes locked on those of a woman who sat in the seat beside their greeter. She stood now, tall and graceful, thick auburn curls spilling over a white silk blouse.

Ian trembled against Gabriella. Her arm slipped tightly around his waist as she led him into the room. She glared at the other woman, knowing she must be the one who had ripped Ian's heart to shreds.

"Ian, it's been too long," The dark haired man reached them, and Ian composed himself enough to share a brief man-hug.

The man turned his smile to Gabriella. "Who is your friend?" He sniffed the air and his smile faltered, though only momentarily. "Oh, she's human. Perhaps we should take her to another room."

She's human. The man's words struck Gabriella. She took a harder look around the table. Nearly two-dozen hungry vampires smiled politely back.

"Erik." Ian released Gabriella long enough to embrace his oldest friend, giving him the time to pull himself together.

Angelica. What the hell was she doing here? He gave her a nod, hating the hurt in her eyes when he couldn't quite bring himself to smile.

Then gripping Gabriella's arm again, Ian said, "I want her to stay."

Erik gave him a look, searching and hopeful, but Ian only scowled. No, Gabriella was no more than a companion. Though resisting the relentless pull of her blood made him wonder if even companionship was too risky.

"She is welcome as long as the others are in accordance."

Looking a little disappointed, Erik took Gabriella's hand for a gentle shake, but his brows pulled together and a question shaped behind the smile.

"Not that we wish you gone," he explained to Gabriella. "But we don't want any accidents, either. I'm sure you understand."

"Of course." She smiled confidently and lifted her chin to meets Erik's gaze, nearly a foot taller.

Ian grinned to himself, knowing that behind her bravado, her heart battered her ribs like a moth trapped in a jar.

"This is Ian's guest, Gabriella. Does anyone have a problem with her remaining for the meeting?" Erik asked. Murmurs circled the table and heads shook.

"Very well, please be seated and we'll get started. There's no time to waste."

Ian sat beside Gabriella, taking her hand in his. The bones felt so small, so fragile, yet a humming flow of power surged from them. He grasped the power, using it to give himself the strength he needed to meet his past.

"You have all heard about the attack in Greece?"

There were murmurs and Ian noticed Helena sitting across from him, dabbing her eyes with a bloody tissue. The seat beside her was eerily empty. She was a pretty woman, dark Mediterranean features, though the vampyric curse had turned her olive skin a dusty gray and her long black hair looked dull and un-brushed.

"Aeolos?" he spoke in a near whisper.

Helena sobbed into her hands, confirming his growing fears.

"They were attacked while they slept, during the day," Erik said. "Helena barely escaped with her life. If it hadn't been for their human servants, they both would have perished. They were able to awaken them from the death sleep. Unfortunately, not soon enough to save Aeolos."

"And they came to our home last week, and burnt it to the ground," said Ramos, the Spanish Council Leader.

His mate, Catalina nodded, adding, "We'd have been killed had it not been for our escape tunnels."

"During the day? They must be humans." Ian's mind reeled. Who would dare attack a vampire in its own home?

"They are not," Ramos said. "They are day walkers."

"Impossible," the Canadian councilman scoffed. "There is no such thing."

"There are now," said Helena. "And you'd best accept the truth before your ignorance costs you your life."

"If this is true, that day walker's really exist. How are they finding you?" Ian asked and everyone turned to Erik.

"We're not sure. There may have been spies watching when we met last quarter. We've never worried about such things before. I mean, who would dare to provoke a vampire? We now have guards on the streets outside, but it may be too late for that."

"Or perhaps there is a traitor amongst us," the dark Romanian leader, Nicolae, sneered.

"Please, we must trust each other if we are going to stop the violence," Erik said, taking his seat beside Angelica.

"And how will we stay safe?" Helena sniffled, revealing bloodstained cheeks and palms.

Ian felt Gabriella stiffen beside him, but to her credit she made no sound.

"I've called this meeting to propose the services of the shifters. They have agreed to keep watch over us while we sleep, in return for our protection. These rogues have been slaughtering them as well, calling them "blasphemous beasts against god". They've nearly annihilated the jaguar people in South America. The strike came very fast and hard, but once they realized the danger, they went into hiding. We've been in contact, and they are safe for now."

Sasha hissed from her seat.

Erik nodded to her. "That's why Sasha is here, as representative to the Council of Cats. Their leaders would like to meet with us. There have also been killings of the were-beasts in the states and in parts of Europe—mostly the wolves and the bears, but so far they haven't wanted to join in our efforts."

"Bears and wolves, they are too stupid to hide and too weak to fight," Sasha sneered. "Cats make themselves invisible."

"How did things get so bad so quickly?" He asked, staring at Gabriella's small fingers twined with his own.

"We weren't aware of the strikes on the other immortals until after we were attacked ourselves. You know we only monitor activity of the vampires," Erik replied. "Hell, until thirty years ago, we thought we were the only immortals."

Ian nodded. He remembered his own shock when the feline quorum had first appeared, killing a pack of werewolves that had cornered a young vampire in the Black Forest. Claiming to be the oldest race of immortals, they had educated the vampires in all things "were".

"Shape shifters are born that way, and they reproduce, have families. Their bites aren't infectious like were-creatures. Contrary to human legends, many were-beasts are animals that turn to humans, not the other way around, and some never turn human at all. The disease is spread through bites, like rabies, but they pass the infection to their offspring. I'm still tryin' to get a handle on it," Ian said to Gabriella.

She nodded, looking pale and stricken. He wished he knew what she was thinking.

"Are you sure all this killin' is bein' done by vampires?" Ian asked.

Angelica met his gaze almost shyly, as if expecting rebuke. After his curt greeting, he couldn't fault her.

"We're sure they're vampires, they've left their trademark everywhere. And we must stop them before this war spills out onto the mortal's streets. There has been too much bloodshed already."

A war, she called it. Ian mulled this a moment. "Can this be true, a cult so obsessed they would risk breaking the immortal codes?"

"It appears to be the case. They don't seem to care if they are discovered. We must be doubly cautious, and I believe it's time we take proactive steps," Erik said.

"What are you suggesting?" The Japanese leader weaved his fingers on the table.

"I'm saying it's time to form troops of our own. The random hunting we're doing now is not enough. Every council member from every country must unite their followers and band together—hunt down these killers before their numbers grow too dangerous. I'd like to put this to a vote." Erik glanced around the table.

Ian had no vote, he knew. He'd been offered his own territory, but he had no desire for that responsibility, choosing instead to live under Erik's jurisdiction in Chicago.

"All those in favor of declaring a preemptive war, please say 'aye'."

Ian was not surprised to see all twenty leader's hands rise solemnly in the air.

"And so be it. The vampires are at war."

"You said they're leaving a trademark?" Ian asked.

Erik nodded. "A blood-red cross inside a circle, and the name of the cult beneath it. 'Church of the Damned'."

Ian shot a glance at Gabriella. She stared back, her eyes wide.

"What is the Church of the Damned? 'Tis the first I've heard of them, and already I've heard the name more times than I care to."

"That's because you've been avoiding us for the past year. They've been terrorizing Europe for months. Killing humans here in my city. The people are disappearing from the streets," Raul, head of the Parisian Council snarled. "The same pattern of killing is happening in London and other European cities. Spray painting the murder scenes with those wretched red crosses. The cities look like cemeteries. The humans are close to a panic, demanding their police find these gangs and put an end to the blood spilling on their streets. They think it's the Russian mob," he glanced obliquely to the Russian councilman, who shrugged without offense.

"And there has been an increase in murders and disappearances in the States as well," Angelica added, her eyes flicking to him.

Ian sat in stunned silence. He'd been so lost in his own search, his own agenda, he'd grown oblivious to the struggles of his own people.

"One of us was followed to the Carpathians." Ian nodded to Gabriella. "We were attacked by a horde of vamps in Curtea de Arges. I think they were from that church. And I think they were after this book." He laid his hand on Gabriella's pack.

"You found it?" Erik asked, leaning forward in his chair.

Ian brought out the box of etched gold. More murmurs circled around him when he removed the lid and unfolded the volume from its wrappings.

"May I look?" Erik asked, glancing between Ian and Gabriella.

"Sure." Gabriella pushed the book across the table.

Ian watched his friend's face as he turned page after page, his expressions a kaleidoscope of shock and anger and grudging admiration.

"Hmm, the Church of the Damned would want this spell," he said at last, tilting up the volume for everyone to see.

Ian's jaw clenched. Everyone started speaking at once in angry tones.

"It's a spell to call demons up from Hell. Not an original idea, but this one is far worse than any I've seen. It binds the demon to a mortal body without the victim's consent. Can you imagine if the Church of the Damned were to get hold of this book? All of the demons we've cast into hell can be recalled and reanimated inside human hosts?"

"Sounds like what Ian explained as vampirism," Gabriella said in a small voice.

Erik nodded. "It is in a way, but we are shared, not possessed, and we always have control as long as the demons are fed. This spell gives the demon complete control over the host, and the human spirit is trapped inside."

Gabriella's grip tightened in his hand. Ian squeezed back and gave her a smile. She must think she'd tripped and fallen into some crazy alternate universe, poor kid.

"There are more, but some of the Latin is beyond my skill. There is a spell here that will free us from this curse." Erik closed the cover. "Any of you wishing to be rid of your demon may consider trying it. We'll have copies made of the spells before we turn the book over to Frederic de Chartres."

"Then who will protect the humans from others of our kind?" Gretchen, the Nordic council leader stood, wearing a wool sweater and jeans, her white blonde hair held back in a braid.

There were several sounds of agreements, everyone nodding their heads. Ian cringed beneath a stab of guilt. Was he a traitor for wanting free of this curse, for turning his back on not only his own kind but the mortals as well?

"Like hell we'll turn over the book. How can we let it out of our hands? Who knows what other spells are in there, and how much damage could be done if the book falls into the wrong hands?" Vanessa, head of the British Isles council spat. Her dark brown eyes narrowed as she curled her hands into fists.

Ian nodded, thinking of the death spell. A few whispered words and the target would drop dead. A shiver rushed down his spine.

"You can't keep it. I found it." Gabriella turned to Ian, pleading with her eyes. "I risked everything to find that book. My grandfather will keep it safe, I swear."

Maybe she should tell them the true worth of the book, the real reason the Church of the Damned would do anything to get their hands on it.

"We should place the fate of the mortals into the hands of an old man?" Sasha stood, pacing catlike in front of the glass windows, her ice blonde hair hanging to her waist.

"He's not just any man," Gabriella argued.

Ian tightened his grip on her hand and eyed the others. "I'm sorry, but right now that book is my property until Gabriella has completed the spell. I made a bargain, and the book is hers once she fulfills her end of it."

Protests mumbled around the table. Ian raised his hand for silence. "And as for her grandfather, Frederic de Chartres is quite capable of keeping this book safe. The security of his vaults is rivaled only by those of the Vatican, and only then because of their numbers. Not even one of us could break into them."

"How do you know?" Asked Vanessa, her soft cocoa skin shining prettily beneath the fluorescent lighting.

"I considered breaking into his library at one time, just to see if I could do it."

Gabriella swung around to face him, fear and anger trembling her hands. "Really? You tried breaking into Grandfather's vaults?"

"Aye, and it was no use. The security system relies heavily on combination, magnetic and biological triggers. Retinal scans and a palm scan, both designed to read blood constriction and pulse. You couldn't kill him and use the parts, they must be living tissue and they must be within certain parameters. If he were scared shitless, the locks wouldn't disengage, so even torture's not an option. Of course, I'm sure there're them who're more clever and devious than I, who might figure out a way."

"Like the Church of the Damned?" Her stomach roiled, thinking of her grandfather alone at his private library. Thank the heavens they had moved the scrolls of the Seven Sorrows to the Vatican.

"I am Scarlotto Genera, Council Leader for Italia," said an olive skinned man at the far end of the table. He wore a shiny gray suit, his coal black waves combed straight back, his eyes dark cobalt. "I was a Cardinal Bishop during the Roman Inquisition. A demon named Vlad changed me, thinking it great fun to inflict this curse on a man of the cloth. But it is that past that gives me the insight, and if I am correct, your grandfather is not only aware of this impending war, but he is already taking precautions to protect himself from our kind."

The room wavered a moment. She forced herself to breathe. "What do you know about my grandfather?"

Everyone turned to the Italian vampire. Ian still held her hand. She was grateful for his strength, but would he throw her out once he knew the truth? Knew she'd been hiding so much from him, after he'd been nothing but forthcoming with her?

"My job as Cardinal Bishop was to oversee charges of heresy brought by priests and lower Cardinals in much of northern Italia. I would hear the cases of the accused and mete what I considered justice. I had received information that two sisters were worshiping *Domina Oriens*."

"Moon worship? Witchcraft?" Gabriella asked.

Scarlotto nodded.

"Yes, I met with them at the prison where they were being held." Scarlotto stared at his hands on the table, turning his gold Cardinal's ring with long, thin fingers. "I am not proud of many things I did in my position. At the time, I believed I performed my sacred duty, but now in this modern world..."

He shook his head. "The sisters would not deny their faith in the occult. I had no choice but to order their execution. When it was done, I went to their home to collect their books of spells and such. Mostly just folk medicine, but in those days we were so afraid. I was to bring them back to Rome.

"But by the time I arrived at the cottage, there was a man inside gathering the books and writings into a satchel. The moment his eyes met mine, I knew he was a man of God—such a light shone from within him.

"He told me he was keeping the women's writings, to preserve them for their historical value. It was then he gave me the advice that I have carried in my heart to this day. He told me never be too harsh to judge, lest I be equally judged, that no God would send me to do the devil's work—the killing of another human. After that day I never convicted another wrongdoer. I used my position instead to help the poor and crippled and anyone in need of charity."

"And you think that man was my grandfather?" Gabriella tried to sound amused, but she felt it slipping away, the grand façade they had so stealthily hidden behind.

"I know it was your grandfather. We met again, during the Great War. I was vampire by that time, but Frederic's words still carried through into every deed. Since I had no choice but to kill humans to survive, I killed only the most evil I could find. I found evil very easily in that war and spent much of my energy hunting Gestapo officers and Nazi sympathizers, and then doing what I could to help the Jews escape occupied territories all over Europe."

Gabriella chewed her thumbnail, bracing herself as he gutted her ruse like an animal's belly, pouring her bloody secrets over the ground for all to examine.

"It was in France—in Bordeaux—that I met Frederic again. He was rummaging through the home of a Jewish family. At first, I thought him a looter and was prepared to drain the life from him, but immediately recognized my old friend. He collected the religious and historical texts from the homes of those who were taken away to the camps. I asked him if he was fighting in the war, as I was. But he said no, his charge was to preserve history, never to interfere."

Words he'd drilled into Gabriella her entire life. "Yes, that was Grandfather," she spoke softly, feeling a stab of guilt. She heard Ian's sharp breath beside her, but she was too afraid to look at him.

The joy of Scarlotto's smile barely touched the sadness etched in his face. The dichotomy of emotions profoundly touched her heart.

"He told me about you, and he spoke with such love. He carried a small photo of you in his breast pocket, for luck, he said. His Gabriella, woman of God."

Gabriella frowned and shifted in the chair. Never having shared Grandfather's faith, the name had always been a bane to her. Obviously she was different, but as a freak of nature, not some kind of saint.

"Your grandfather has been alive for centuries?" Ian asked.

She nodded, raising her eyes to his. She braced herself for his anger. No resentment showed there, only a wry, playful interest.

"Yes, he was one of the leaders of the Knights Templar. While in the Holy Land fighting the Muslims he was mortally wounded. He'd been left for dead on the battlefield, but he didn't die. His story is that a man appeared from out of the whirling sands. He told my grandfather he was his father, and they were immortal. He offered to teach him the ways of his people, to live a life of peace, and to use his time to collect and preserve the written histories of humanity. Books of every religion or belief, and their stories and legends, too. Everyone who knew him assumed he was dead, but he lived on."

"And on and on," Ian said with a laugh, and others joined in, though tension hung in the air. She felt everyone's gaze fall heavily upon her.

"So how old are you?" asked Sasha, looking delighted at this turn of events.

Her mouth went dry. She cleared her throat, licked her lips. "I-I was born in the early sixteen hundreds, in Southern France. We moved to America in the late nineteenth century. First New York and later Chicago."

"You're immortal too?" The red haired woman beside Erik asked in a soft voice. She smiled a warm, friendly smile. Gabriella felt herself smiling back in spite of the resentment she tried to hold onto, for Ian's sake.

"No, despite what the man told Grandfather, we are both aging and our kind can be killed. There are others like us in the world. They call themselves the Archivists." A half-truth. Archivist was their calling, not their species.

Ian snorted a laugh. "Archivists? Almost as scary as the dreaded Chess Club."

She shot him a glare. "Okay, so the name is lame, but

it's not like I had a vote, okay? We're not supposed to be scary. We're supposed to observe and collect written history, without interfering. We aren't truly immortal, not like you. There are very few of us remaining and there seem to be conditions. My mother lived for centuries, but she married a mortal man, and once I was born she began to age at the same rate as my father. She died a long time ago. No one is completely sure how this works, but my kind..." She shook her head. "They consider death an honor. They believe things exist across some veil between worlds that I can't imagine to be true."

She said no more, refusing to tell them of her fated life with some faceless, boring librarian. Some rubbish prophecy of the man whose heart and soul would call to hers and the whole pile of romantic crap that went with it. And of course, after Mister Perfect came The Kid, who would "save the world." A tired cliché. Ridiculous legend. She saw what happened to her mother, ravaged with age and dying a slow agonizing death for the love of a man who died in a car accident when Gabriella was only two. Forget having kids.

"Well, the book is yours once you've fulfilled your promise to Ian," Erik said. "Your family is apparently very capable of keeping it safe. More well suited than probably any of us." He turned to Ian. "Are you still determined to go through with this, old friend?"

Ian nodded. "But not until this war is ended. I won't be leaving you shorthanded."

"Thank you. You're the best warrior we have."

"If that's the truth, then 'tis a sad reflection on the rest of you," he joked, though his laugh sounded tired. "We'll send Gabriella home with the book. I'll call on her once things are safe."

"No, I want to stay with all of you. Maybe I can help. I'm good at translating in several languages and I..."

Why did she have such a strong desire—more than a desire—a maddening need to stay with him, to see this through? Her sensible mind screamed for her to be reasonable, go home to the safety of her archives. But her heart commanded her to stay this course, much louder and more demanding. She would not allow him to send her home.

"Absolutely not. You'll not be endangering yourself in a vampire war." Ian glared.

"I heal quickly. Maybe not as fast as you, but fast

enough." She fought to control the desperation in her voice.

"No," he snapped. "And what happened to observing, but not interfering?"

"I think you should ask the others." She looked around the table, her heart sinking at the looks on the beautiful vampyric faces. What use would these powerful immortals have for a woman like her? "Please, at least consider allowing me to stay. I can help, I know I can."

"We will consider it. We'll meet again tonight to take a vote, but for now we must excuse ourselves. Sunrise is nigh and we are all rather allergic to its splendor." Erik nodded. "The meeting is adjourned until nine o'clock tonight.

"Here," he said, sliding the book back to her. "Ian will stay with you today, to protect you and the book. We have special rooms at the Hotel Pergolese, just a few blocks west."

CHAPTER NINE ✝

Two Weeks Earlier, Paris

"I need you to go to Rome and fetch the scrolls."

Lilith knelt on the frigid stone floor, gripping the white robes of her savior. "Yes, my lord. They arrived yesterday, just as we were told."

"And you have spoken to your contact there?"

Lilith climbed to her feet, averting her eyes from her master. "Yes. The scrolls have been copied and the copies smuggled out."

"When is your meeting?"

She panicked, trying to remember. Meeting? She knew that sounded familiar, but there were too many things happening. Ah, yes. "Tonight. I leave at dusk, and arrive in Rome at eight."

"Very good."

* * * *

She made her way through the tunnel, climbing the winding stairs to the secret entrance.

Whenever anyone came or went, her disciples simply repaved the bricks behind them. The mortar rarely had time to set, but in the darkened tunnels, no mortals had yet noticed. And should one grow too curious and knock out the wall, her guards waited to greet them on the other side.

Anticipating her arrival, the wall had already been opened. She nodded absently to the guards at the top of the stairs before checking the outer chamber of the catacombs, half hoping a human might be wandering by. Her nerves made her thirsty. Although the lord frowned upon drinking unblessed blood, he would forgive an occasional slip. But sadly, there was no one in this rarely visited hollow. She'd have to find a snack later, she thought as she slid into the dimly lit tunnel, hearing mortar scraping over bricks behind her.

* * * *

Lilith spotted the priest in the rear corner table of the small café, just a few blocks from Vatican City. His eyes flicked nervously to the tinkling bell above the door, before refocusing on Lilith and her companion as they entered. She wore a long black dress and matching velvet cape, keeping the hood raised to hide her face. They had chartered a plane and drove straight here from the airport. Marcus, her most trusted disciple and former priest had accompanied her on the trip. He dressed now in a simple but stylish suit and held her hand to lead her from the Mercedes Limo idling for them at the curb.

It was very late, nearly midnight, and the young girl tending the place was sweeping floors, washing down countertops in anticipation of closing up shop. A very pretty thing, whose exotic pillow lips spread in a friendly greeting, wide hazel eyes crinkling at the corners. But no virgin. Lilith could smell a man on her, not too long ago, perhaps before she'd come to work. She wore her pretty peasant blouse off the shoulders and tight white jeans. Her heart beat with the steady strength of youth. Sweet coppery blood smelled absolutely mouthwatering.

Lilith swallowed the rush of saliva, working very hard to ignore the melodic rush of blood churning through the girl's veins.

Marcus held out the chair so Lilith could sit across from the priest, still fully dressed in his black garb with white collar. Sweat pearled over his forehead, beneath a shock of black and silver curls.

Lilith kept the hood raised, sitting with her ruined face to the wall, lest she frighten the man or the young barista.

"You have something for me?" she asked.

The priest nodded, licking his lips. From under the table he retrieved a cardboard tube and laid it on the table.

Marcus waited for Lilith's nod before shaking out the scrolled papers.

"What are you doing?" the priest hissed, casting panicked looks at the girl.

Lilith patted his hand, admiring the man's courage for not recoiling from her cold, pale fingers. Skin as thin as onionskin, blue veins flat beneath the flesh, she knew her appearance could be off-putting.

"Relax, monsieur. We are only inspecting the

merchandise before we pay." She smiled reassuringly.

He nodded nervously, tugging a handkerchief from his overcoat to pat sweat from his forehead. Marcus unrolled the papers, leafing through them.

"They are as he said." Marcus slid them back into the container and capped it, to the priest's obvious relief.

"I have kept my part of the bargain at great personal risk. Now I expect my payment," the priest said boldly, though the stench of fear hung thick on his clothing.

"You are a man of the cloth. Do you not fear retribution from your God?"

"Is this not the work of God, this immortality? Who else has the power to grant such a gift?"

Could it be true, she wondered. Was this not actually a curse, but a sacred calling? But her lord had told her otherwise, and was he not God's own messenger? Or perhaps God himself, in the flesh? Again and again, he told her she was nothing, a demon's plaything. And of course, the lord knew all.

"Of course we shall pay as agreed. Marcus?"

As she spoke his name, Marcus flashed to the front door, twisting the lock.

The shop girl looked up from her cleaning, fear flickering in her eyes. She glanced instinctively to the back door leading into the alley, and pretended to sweep while taking small steps in that direction.

Lilith lifted Father Vincento's hand, flipping it to expose the wrist. She bent over the table, running her nose over the coursing flow. She watched her own hand change, the knuckles thickening, the fingers curling into black nailed claws.

She opened her mouth and pulled back her lips. The priest gasped but did not pull away when she ran a tongue over the rows of razor sharp points.

Could it be true? That perhaps she was some kind of God? No, that couldn't be possible. That would make everything the lord said a lie. She pushed the blasphemous thoughts from her mind as she lowered her head to pierce the skin.

The priest sucked in a breath, reflexively tugging away, but she held fast. She groaned in near ecstasy with each long draught she pulled through her lips. His warm blood burned through her frigid veins, and she shuddered at the pleasure of it.

"Lilith!" Marcus said sharply from where he guarded the front door.

She raised her head, licking the crimson drops from her lips.

The poor little mouse still crept to the back door, pretending she saw nothing. As if she had any chance. Lilith's hood fell back, exposing the full glorious horror of her visage and the bloodlust—blood sliding through the damaged cords of her face and dripping off her jaw.

The girl screamed, dropped her broom and sprinted to the back door. But Marcus blocked her. He hit a switch, plunging the shop into darkness. One thick arm curled around the girl's throat so tight she couldn't utter a sound.

"Now you must drink from me," Lilith said to Vincento. She ran a nail along her own wrist and thrust it across the table. She had no desire to create more like her, but she had given her word. This priest had earned his price, smuggling copies of the Seven Sorrows right from under the noses of the Swiss Guard.

"God help me." He wrapped soft human lips over her skin, suckling like a toothless pup from its bitch.

"You are the god now." Lilith absently repeated words from a life that ghosted at the edge of her memories.

His belly, filled with her blood, had first been tempered with his own. Blood for blood, this was the only way to call up the demon.

Lilith felt the moment the beast arrived, felt the instant hardening of skin and bones. Sharp barbs erupted from his flat teeth, piercing her arm, latching onto the wound. She allowed him to drink only few moments longer before shoving him off her.

His beast stared back, looking quite macabre in its priest's clothing. Clawed hands curled for a fight. A devil's face of sharp cheeks and jutting brow snarled over bloodied teeth. Crimson coals appraised her hungrily from the black eyes. The new creature roared, born hungry and filled with a burning bloodlust, but it sensed he could not kill her.

Lilith tilted her head, raising her dripping arm, her finger pointing to the girl. The demon swung his head around, instantly catching the scent. The girl struggled, kicking and flailing her arms, eyes huge, a sickly noise gurgling from her throat. The monster ripped her from Marcus's grip and flung her to the floor. Her head struck the tile, knocking her unconscious. Just as well, Lilith thought, watching dispassionately as her newest recruit sated his need. She knew the young ones fought their thirst the hardest and needed to feed most often. She could go as long as a month without blood, though she preferred not to.

Finally the demon retreated into his new home, weaving through this man's mind and body. Vincento sat back on his heels, staring in horror at the girl's lifeless eyes. He buried his face in his hands, sobbing.

Lilith snorted and snatched the cardboard tube from the blood-spattered table. She nodded to Marcus, who helped Vincento to his feet.

They all cried the first time, as if the thirst came as some great surprise. Yet they all drank again, and again.

CHAPTER TEN †

December 9th Paris, France

Gabriella set her pack on the dining table before checking the refrigerator for water. She nearly gagged at the packets of blood stacked casually between cans of Coke and beer. The room was indeed special. A spacious living area built around a windowless bedroom, with a parlor and dining area complete with a well stocked wet bar.

"You wouldn't want me getting thirsty, lass," Ian said with a chuckle.

A little too amused with himself, she shot him a withering look that only made his smile widen.

"I'm fine." And to prove it she swallowed her disgust and grabbed a bottle of Evian from the door. She unscrewed the lid and took a long drink before wandering to peer out the French doors of the balcony.

"The view is gorgeous, but why is the room facing east?" She looked out over the city, bathed in artificial light. Everything dusted with snow, the trees barren.

"So when we awaken we can move around the suite without worrying about sunlight—it'll already be on the far side of the building. Otherwise we'd have to install steel shades on the windows, which would be a horrible shame. We enjoy a beautiful view as much as any human." He slid her a gaze that traveled over her body like sensuous fingers. Warmth flared up in her cheeks.

Ian grinned knowingly, damn him, and went to the foyer to flip a switch. Strange humming light filled the doorframe.

"What's that?"

"Ultraviolet light. It'll fry any vampires who try to break in while I'm sleeping."

Gabriella shuddered. "Are you expecting company? It's daylight, how could they—?"

"'Tis just a precaution, lassie. Of course if there are day walkers, this won't do a damn thing to stop them."

She sighed, trying to keep the irritation from her voice. "I wish you wouldn't call me that. I won't be saving Timmy from the well."

Ian's brows folded inward and she shook her head. "Never mind. Please, just call me Gabriella."

"Whatever you wish, Gabriella." He spoke her name in a slightly mocking tone that raised her ire, but she let it go. Perhaps it was lack of sleep and not his tenor. At the moment, she didn't trust her emotions enough to pick a fight.

Instead, she sat at the table tugging the golden box from her pack.

"Ian, I want to stay with you until this conflict is over with the Church of the Damned." She raised the volume from the table. "I'm sure they want this book for something more than calling up demons. I can help you figure it out." She prayed her face didn't betray her guilt.

Ian leaned against the back of the sofa, crossing his legs at the ankles. "'Tis a sound conclusion. There're some spells in there I cannot figure—the dialect's too ancient."

"What about the Church of the Damned? I mean, they came out of nowhere," she said, hoping to change the subject away from spells she was not yet ready to discuss.

"I have my theories. For decades our company has hunted the Rogues. They're vampires who murder for the sheer thrill of the carnage, and who offer the blood curse to the worst of humankind. They are the remaining children of Vlad, and I'm sure they've figured there's safety in numbers, banding together. I've got a bad feeling about this."

She'd heard the name already tonight. Scarlotto had said he was changed by someone with that name. "Who is Vlad?"

"He was the most evil creature I've ever met." The tremor in Ian's voice sent swarms of spiders crawling under her skin. She shuddered, running her hands up her arms to soothe her frayed nerves. "He killed his maker and hunted down the ancient ones. The civilized vampires, if you will—the ones with a code of ethics and who followed traditions that'd been passed down since man first walked the earth. The shifters claim to be the oldest immortals, but the vampires lost much of their history thanks to Vlad."

"What happened to him?"

"Erik killed him, more than twenty years ago."

"Erik, your friend?"

"Aye."

"Do you think they might try to bring Vlad back?" She glanced at the spell book, suddenly frantic to have it locked away.

"I'm sure 'tis a thought on everyone's mind, but no one wants to speak it out loud. If he comes back, he'll have a new body. We won't even know what he looks like."

"So you and Erik are close?"

"We're the best of friends. I've known him longer than any of the others."

"And the redhead...is she his wife?"

His jaw tightened, his eyes narrowed with pain. "Aye, Angelica."

He spoke her name with the same reverence that her grandfather spoke of his god. The sharp pang of envy surprised her.

She cleared her throat, cursing herself for mentioning the woman. Vampires seemed a safer topic than the true demon torturing his soul. "What are you going to do? How will you fight this war?"

Ian shrugged and pushed a hand through his long hair. "I have no guess. But if they've found a way to create day walkers, we'll be lucky to survive this war."

"And if you fail?"

"If we fail, there's nothing standing between them and the mortal population. There'll be anarchy, and civilization as we know it will fall."

* * * *

Gabriella returned to paging through the book, her mind swarming with too many thoughts to keep in order. She found the spell to free Ian from his demon, seeking refuge in the comforting complexity of the language and preferring to struggle through the translation of handwritten text rather than worrying about a possible apocalypse.

She glanced furtively as Ian tugged his t-shirt over his head, and watched muscles flex as he tossed it onto the arm of the couch. Was he torturing her on purpose? Didn't he realize how badly she wanted to run her fingers over the smooth granite curves of his chest? To feel the ripple of his stomach, the perfect contour of his arms?

She huffed a breath and shook her head to clear it. He'd

just forecast the end of the world, and she was thinking about sex. Yet every time she tried to think of anything else, every road in her mind led her back to him—his nerve tingling scent, his knee weakening body. With herculean effort, she forced her attention back to the book.

"Whoa, wait a minute," she whispered.

"What is it?" Ian stood behind her in a flash, leaning so close his waves of golden-red hair swept her shoulder.

"There's a weapon required to perform this exorcism ceremony—a knife. Supposedly, the blade was forged in the flames of hell and the shaft is made from...well, from Osiris's petrified phallus."

"His phallus? Isn't that...?"

Heat raced all the way to her ears. "Yes, that's his penis."

"Oh, I'll be excited to wrap my hand 'round that thing." Ian's voice dripped sarcasm as he pulled a chair up next to her.

"It won't be you holding the knife," she reminded him. "And let's hope this is figurative." He started to speak but she held up a hand, her heart pounding as she read on. "There's more. It says this knife is the key to many spells. These spells are the Requiem of the Undead, but there is another work by this same practitioner called the scrolls of Seven Sorrows."

She swallowed, not daring to meet his eyes. She knew she must reveal her knowledge of the Seven Sorrows.

"What?"

"Yes, and there's a caveat at the end of this spell regarding the knife. It can be used to open a crack in hell to free the Seven Sorrows. But if they're released all at once, it will be the end of humanity. For that reason the weapon was carried to the ends of the earth and hidden in a sacred place."

"Where is it? How can we find it?" He leaned close enough so that their foreheads nearly touched.

She took a deep breath of him, letting the vampyric aroma spread like soothing fingers through her tired, aching body. She glanced at Ian and ground her teeth—so at odds with her feelings, she had no idea which ones to trust.

For hundreds of years she'd been content to live as an observer. Rushing in to save the written histories, only mildly wondering about the lives of the people who had touched the tomes she collected, never dreaming she could change their fate.

Now, after one night with this vampire, she could no longer ignore the events. She had the power to change them while Ian had spent decades, maybe centuries protecting human lives. And still he called himself a monster.

Who was the real monster?

The answer crushed the breath from her.

"Are you sure we should try to find it? I mean, what if the Church of the Damned got their hands on the Seven Sorrows? Maybe it's best to leave the thing hidden." She rolled her lip through her teeth, half hoping he'd agree.

"Nay, if they have the scrolls, they'll be after the dagger, too. Maybe the dagger should join your grandfather's collection. Either way, I need the damned thing to finish my business."

"I thought you were waiting."

"I am, but someday this war'll be over, and I'll be needin' it."

"Fine then. Let me read this. It's a riddle of sorts." She ran a finger over the lines. "West of the Gates of the King, ride the path of Ra through the deadly sands to the tomb of they who guard the Field of Reeds."

"What does that mean?" His breath drifted like sweet honey as his hand flowed over the brittle paper, his fingertips brushing against hers.

"W-we shouldn't handle the pages so much. The chemicals in our fingers will damage the paper." She swallowed, all at once tingling and seething beneath this power he wielded so recklessly.

"Then let's not touch it." He slipped his hand beneath hers, pulling it back. His cool skin sent a wave of heat rushing from her crown to her toes.

"I think I know the answer. You know...the riddle?" She looked at their hands, then up into his eyes as pleasant desire slithered like a warm snake between her thighs. How badly she wanted *him* between her thighs. How badly she wanted to kick his shins, for making her swoon and melt like an idiot.

He closed the cover, tucking the book under his arm, gently pulling her to her feet. "The sun will be rising in a few minutes. I must be in the other room with the door closed."

Gabriella nodded, rising beside him, trying to decide if she hated him.

"So what about this riddle?" He closed the door behind them.

She frantically eyed the bedroom.

"There's only one bed," she blurted.

The flicker of a smile crossed his face. She ground her teeth. Why did she act like such an idiot around him? And damn him for enjoying it so much.

"I'll sleep on the chaise, unless you're afraid you'll be too lonely." He cocked a brow, raising his lip in a sly smile.

"Very funny. I think I can manage a night alone." Though as soon as she spoke the words, she caught her hand rising to touch his face. *No, no, no,* she scolded herself. Giving in to her libido was a terrible idea, yet allowing even that little thought sent a flood of warmth just south of her belly, making her shudder.

She sat on the edge of the bed and kicked off her boots, realizing she'd left all of her clothes at the Inn, back in Romania.

Ian watched her every move with hungry, predatory eyes. She worried, remembering his warning. The man may want her body, but the beast craved her blood. Could she stop him if he attacked? Then she cursed the part of her that wanted so very badly to find out. *Not good.* She glanced at the door, considering sleeping on the couch in the outer room. In the sunlight. But the bed felt so soft and her eyelids felt so heavy. Ian's brows pulled together, as if he were trying to read her thoughts, his lovely, pale lips set in a worried pout.

She would trust him, the man, to keep her safe from his beast. But she needed to clean up and get some sleep. Her body had repaired her ankle and all the accompanying bumps and bruises, but now it demanded payment in rest.

The bed was placed between two doors. One was slightly ajar. Inside she could see the glint of a mirror in the darkness. The bathroom, she hoped.

A sweeping chaise with a roll pillow sat in the corner, a colorful throw folded at the feet. Next to it was a heavy carved desk set up with a laptop and reading lamp. Another small refrigerator hummed beside the bed. In case the vampire guests grew thirsty during the day, she thought with a shiver.

The mirror and dark wooden dresser matched the night tables and scrolled headboard. She curled her toes into the thick Persian rug.

The book laying in her lap, reminded her she never answered his question. "The riddle is pretty simple."

"Hmm, to you perhaps." He went to the chaise, frowning as he tested the cushions.

She smiled, her body weary to the bones. "The Gates of the King...that translates to the Valley of the Kings in Egypt. Follow the path of Ra, the sun god, to the tomb of he who guards the Field of Reeds, the afterlife. It says to travel west from the Valley of the Kings to the tomb of Osiris."

"That's it? Could they be any more vague?"

She shrugged. "It says, 'If Osiris wills you to find the treasure, his tomb will make itself visible to you.'"

"And I'm supposed to believe all this mystic mumbo jumbo? That Osiris actually existed?"

She sat back on the satin duvet, sliding up to the head of the bed. "I'm supposed to believe vampires exist. And shape shifters, and werewolves." She arched a brow.

"Touché."

"And even if he was a myth, the ancient Egyptians worshiped Osiris and very well might have built a secret tomb in his honor."

Ian stretched his long body across the chaise, his feet dangling off the end. "Good point."

She watched with alarm as the color drained from his already pale face. In a flash of movement, he flipped to his feet, startling her.

"I remember now. The Scrolls of Seven Sorrows are seven demons to be raised from Hell and unleashed on the earth, each yielding one of the deadly plagues. Nothing as pleasant as locusts and dead cattle."

She clutched the book to her chest. She couldn't tell him the truth. Grandfather would never forgive her. "Ian, I don't believe those cultists have the Seven Sorrows. Scholars have been searching for it for centuries. I'm sure it's too well hidden." In the Vatican vaults, she thought.

Ian sat back on the chaise, his elbows resting on the knees of his jeans. A tangle of curls tumbled over his tired face, and he swept them behind his ear. He glanced up, his eyes dark beneath the shadow of his brow.

Golden stubble framed his strong jaw, and she felt the urge to cup his face in her hand, to learn if it was rough or soft, and to run her thumb across the cleft of his chin, his lips.

"I'll see what other spells are in here tomorrow. I think

I've had enough tonight." She set the book on the bed and pushed it away, resisting the lure of the pages. With a weary sigh, she stood and went to the bathroom. She took a quick shower and remembered she had no change of clothing. May as well hand wash her underclothes and hang them over the old fashioned radiator so she'd at least feel fresh until she could get more.

Ian appeared asleep when she crept into the cool room. The towel she had wrapped herself in fell to the floor as she slid beneath the satin covers. She sighed at the decadence of cocooning her body in such delicious softness. When she reached to shut off the lamp, Ian grinned unrepentantly from the chaise, his head resting in his palm.

"You were watching! Y-you..." she stammered, yanking the covers up to her chin.

"So sue me. You're beautiful, and I told you I enjoy beautiful things."

"Erg!" She snapped off the light before remembering he could see just as well in the dark. But before long the soft satin bed sheets stroked away her ire and she wondered if his hands would feel so luxurious, tracing down her neck and caressing her breasts. How would they feel sliding down her belly to the aching heat pulsing within the folds of flesh. Her stomach clenched, her hands fisted around the sheet. She cursed her traitorous body, the racing of her heart and the damn vampire. What a cruel trick he played.

In the darkness, she felt the bed give to his weight. "Please, don't," she said, her voice hoarse.

Her will to resist him waned, yet how could she let him take her, while his heart still ached for another? While her own fate lay so firmly cemented to another course?

"That chaise is too damned short. Don't worry, I'll stay on top of the blanket."

"Fine." She dared not say anymore. Rolling away from him, she squeezed her eyes shut and sighed. She willed sleep to sweep her away, but for the first time in her existence, hungry desires ruled the dark corners of her mind, and her scent rose in the air announcing her arousal.

Ian wanted her. Badly. And without hiding his interest, he inhaled a deep breath, letting her know he was aware that she wanted him, too.

Smelling her delicious scent and listening to the uneven thumping of her heart sent his need into overdrive. This desire infuriated him because he'd promised himself, he'd never again let his heart rule his head. Yet her smell bound him like silver chains. That and the blasted heat radiating from her soft folds beckoned him like warm summer rain.

He turned his back to her, staring into the room, still as death, hard as granite. Black outlines of furniture floated in a lake of gray darkness. He let the vampyric shields fall over his eyes and color returned to the walls and furniture. Shapes gained clarity and small details no longer hid in shadows.

Long after her breaths turned even and her heart beat the rhythm of sleep, he remained wide awake, his mind a whirl of thoughts, questions.

How could he travel in the desert? And in a place so vast, how would they ever find the tomb? Even with unlimited funds, the search seemed nearly impossible, like finding one particular shell in the ocean.

Afraid of awakening Gabriella, Ian rose and returned to the desk. Might as well make arrangements for their departure. He fired up the hotel's computer, searching Google maps of Egypt to plot a course. He was surprised to learn they'd be traveling through a mountainous region, as drab and arid as the desert.

After a while, he rubbed his eyes and glanced over at the bed. His body ached for sleep. Gabriella tossed and turned, moaning and sounding anxious as she fled whatever terrors haunted her dreams.

The time on the screen read nearly ten. Every vampire in Europe probably slept the dead sleep, except him even though his own demon struggled to drag him into unconsciousness.

Go ahead and twist in my brain, you bastard. Your days are numbered.

A door clicked so quietly, no human ear could have caught the sound. Ian tensed in his chair, listening as near silent steps crossed the tiled foyer. In a flash he held his sword, waiting rigidly by the door. Stealthy footfalls crushed carpet fibers, pausing just outside.

The bedroom door faced the north, but daylight burned through the outer room. Ian had no choice but to wait for the other to enter. He sniffed the air, shocked to smell not human blood, but vampire.

A day walker!

He glanced at Gabriella, lying still on the bed.

Warning her would alert the intruder. Right now,

surprise remained on his side. He dared not lose the advantage. Standing immobile as stone, he slowed his heart to the near death rhythm of vampire sleep and braced himself for battle.

The door exploded amid bursts of gunfire. Muzzle flash flared orange as bullets peppered the room. Wood splinters and goose feathers sprayed the air. Gabriella screamed and rolled from the bed, landing with a thud on the floor. Ian swung his blade straight down slicing the gunman's hands off at the wrists before he'd even emptied the magazine.

The vampire screamed in agony, silver poison instantly bubbling in his blood. As the beast dropped to his knees, Ian swept the sword sideways, taking his head.

But instead of exploding to dust, the body lay in mangled pieces, bleeding out on the expensive Persian rug.

What the hell?

The room hummed in the silent aftermath, a cloud of sulfur smoke curling through the air. Ian listened for any more intruders, hearing nothing but the drone of the refrigerator and the buzz of the light he'd set to protect them, for all the damned good it had done.

He rushed to Gabriella, his knees weakening with relief to see her climbing up from the floor. He sniffed the air. She hadn't been wounded. He would've smelled the blood. But she did look dazed. Her chest rose and fell rapidly with each breath.

"Are you all right?" he asked, staring through drifting feathers and wood dust at the small pert breasts, the smooth flat belly. His own breath quickened at the glint of a small hoop belly ring. Even if he wanted, he couldn't have stopped his gaze from traveling to the dark triangle at her cleft.

Then he realized how vulnerable she must feel and shoved his baser instincts aside. He snatched up the sheet that had slid off the bed, wrapping it around her body, and she took it, tying a knot above one breast.

"I'm fine, but I think he killed my pillow," she said, breaking the spell.

Ian nodded at the explosion of goose down on the bed, swallowing the first true fear he'd known in decades. He'd nearly lost her. The thought made him sick. Rage curled his hands to fists, set his teeth to grinding.

"Are there any more?" she asked him, rushing to the door. She grimaced as she stepped over the headless body.

"No, I don't think so, but I can't go out there."

"I'll check. You better call your friend, make sure the others are okay."

"Gabriella, I forbid—" Before the words left his lips, she'd snatched up the intruder's automatic rifle and settled it expertly in the crook of her arm before dashing into the deadly sunlight.

Ian dug his cell phone from his coat pocket, quickly dialing Erik's number. He blew out a sigh at his friend's sleepy hello. "Sorry to wake you, but I'm afraid we've got a problem."

Using a letter opener, he pried a bullet from the splintered bed frame.

"Damn," he muttered. Silver bullets. An angry awareness gripped his chest making him physically ill. If he'd been asleep, they would both be dead.

"Gabriella, come in here." He couldn't stand her being out of his sight.

"I'm right here. The door was unlocked. Someone must have given him a room key," Gabriella said, her staccato breaths made her words sound short and clipped.

The flush of blood in her cheeks stirred his beast, making it hard to focus on her words as she brushed her hair back from her face with one hand, cradling the gun in the other. "I checked the hall and down the next corridor to the elevator, but there was no one else."

"You shouldn't have run off like that. There could've been others waitin' in the hall."

"So we should just sit in here and wait for more of them to come?"

"Aye, that'd be better than me sitting helpless in here while I listened to them eating you for a snack."

"You're just jealous."

He narrowed his eyes at her. She shrugged, and he could tell she was trying not to smile. Stubborn woman.

"I didn't really believe it was true. Day walkers. How is it possible?"

Gabriella pushed the body with her toe. "Leather coat, jeans, boots. Maybe he just slapped some sunscreen on his face."

"It doesn't work that way. There's not a sunscreen in the world that will block out enough rays to keep us from frying."

"Why? I mean, if he's some kind of day walker, what does that mean for the rest of you?" Though as she spoke, he could see understanding in her eyes.

Ian pushed a hand through his tangled curls. "It's the silver that's got me worried. Something happens to our blood when we merge with the demon. Sunlight and silver become like poison to us. The sunlight literally boils our blood, and it turns our bodies to cinders. The silver should have done the same to him. He should be dust."

She tossed the gun on the dresser and retrieved the Requiem from where it had fallen on the floor.

Sighing wearily, she sat on the edge of the bed. Tears glistened in her eyes. He was nearly overcome with a strong urge to kiss them away, but he sensed this would embarrass her.

As he watched, the sheet fell away from her thigh, revealing the soft curve of her hip. Her skin glowed like a bright winter moon. He laced his fingers behind his back, forcing his eyes up to hers lest she notice him staring and cover herself. It'd be a shame to hide such a beautiful moon.

"So now what?" She leaned back on her hands. The movement tugged the sheet apart even further. He couldn't stop his gaze from following the flat plane of her belly, admiring the ripple of ribs, the crescent curve of half her breast. Fire flooded in his groin. His breath hitched.

How could she not realize she was torturing him?

He cleared his throat and turned away. "Once the sun clears that room, we'll meet the limo out front under the portico."

"No doubt you have a limo handy with UV glass."

He spun the desk chair around and sat, resting his arms above his head, across the back. A better view of what lay beneath the sheet from there.

"We have one ready in every city where we have permanent citizens, in case they have need to travel during the day."

"Sounds expensive."

Ian arched a brow. "In case you haven't noticed, we've got plenty of money."

"Ah, the perks of immortality," she shot him a look just short of hostile, puzzling him.

"Do I detect a note of sarcasm?"

"You detect a whole song, Mr. Private Jet. Every cent Grandfather and I earn is spent improving and expanding the storage facility. And we don't get a penny from any governments. If we want to eat, I have to work."

"I wasn't insinuating there's anything wrong with an honest day's work, but I'll not be apologizing for my wealth, either. Maybe you should ask for some help. I'm sure every government in the world would want to keep your documents safe."

Something flashed in her eyes. "They'd want to seize our collection, fight over ownership. Sell pieces off to collectors who don't know how to care for them. Or they'd want to display them in museums until the print becomes unreadable and the paper crumbles to dust. Can we risk them out in the world where we can't protect them or keep them safe from crazy whacked out vampires?"

He managed to stop his smile. No need to provoke her, but something about that venom in her tone made his knees a little weak. "If it makes you feel any better, I'll leave my fortune to you and Grandpa when I turn to dust. You'll have plenty to fortify your vaults and still live well."

She snorted. "I don't care that you have money, you just don't have to sound so smug about it."

"I am who I am, an old man set in his ways." He grinned his best wicked smile. "But not as old as you, now am I?"

"I knew I'd never live that down." She sat up straight again, pulling the sheet to cover her body.

Ah, well. It'd been a pretty sight while it lasted.

"How will we travel in the desert?" she asked.

"Erik's very creative. I'm sure he'll think of somethin'."

"But what about the daylight? You just said you're very allergic."

"We'll travel by night, and I'll have to stay inside during the day."

"Inside where? It's not like they'll have a Marriott out there."

"I meant a tent. Erik's havin' the plane packed with provisions. Tents and sunshields, food and water." What was with the tone? Was she trying to pick a fight with him?

"And clothes, I hope." She huffed impatiently. "Plus we'll need a guide."

"We're flying into Luxor. We'll try to find a guide when we get there."

"Try to find a guide? I don't like the sound of that."

"Gabriella, don't worry so much. Erik'll work out the arrangements before we arrive, I'm sure. No surprises."

"I've been on digs in Egypt. It takes months to arrange travel in the desert. They don't like foreign tourists just traipsing around, digging things up."

The demon clawed his soul as his patience waned. "I just said Erik is taking care of things. Why are you so set on arguing?"

* * * *

She curled her hands, digging nails into her palms until it hurt. "I'm a little tense. In case you haven't noticed, it's been kind of stressful."

What else could she tell him? That it infuriated her, the way each rise of his sculpted chest sent quivers down her belly? That she hungered for his pale lips pressed against hers, thirsted for his strange cool breaths in her mouth? She wanted to kick his ass for making her crave him this way. Stupid sexy vampire, she thought, staring at the floor.

"Aye, I've noticed well enough. And by the way, where the hell did you learn to handle a gun like that? I thought Archivists were pacifists."

"Grandfather says it's prudent to learn to defend one's self. We may never be the aggressors, but that doesn't mean we shouldn't be prepared to protect ourselves. Should we stretch our necks out on the chopping block?"

A wry smile flared all the way to his eyes. "Aye, no turning the other cheek."

She studied him a moment, feeling a pang of guilt. He'd saved her life and how had she repaid him? With whining and bitching. And still he kept his cool, his cocky good humor.

"I'm sorry. I know I'm being a pain in the ass. My nerves are a little raw."

"No need to apologize, muzzy."

"Yes, yes there is. I was just picking a fight."

"I don't have to be a shrink to figure that out."

Deep breaths, she reminded herself. "I know. We can move past that now."

His smug grin was getting on her nerves.

"Do you still want me to go with you?" A flutter of fear trembled in her heart. The sudden excess of emotions made her feel uncomfortably out of balance.

"After watching you swing up that gun and run around the place half naked, I wouldn't dream of leaving you behind."

"Did anyone ever tell you you're a sarcastic bastard?"

He looked playfully thoughtful. "More 'n likely, but it's hard to remember all the names I've been called in my life."

She felt the flush burn over her cheeks and she wanted to smack him. And kiss him. Damn vampire.

* * * *

As soon as the sun cleared the living room they left the hotel. A limo waited in the shade of the hotel's overhang, its windows smoky black. They drove into the waiting hangar and boarded in the shadows, just feet away from the blazing afternoon sun.

Dark shades were pulled down over the jet's windows and Ian opted to sit close to the aisle, his elbow now on the armrest, his stubbled jaw resting in his palm.

"I can't believe they made me bring Sasha," Ian growled as the jet taxied for takeoff.

"Someone has to guard your pasty hide while you sleep," Sasha said.

"Yeah, lucky me."

"I can't believe we don't have any guides secured." Gabriella gripped the armrests, sneaking a peek at the blurring French countryside as the jet rumbled down the runway. Her stomach clenched when the plane dipped before lunging into the air.

"I can't believe pretty bird is afraid to fly," Sasha purred.

"Knowing the physics behind flight doesn't make me feel any better about hurtling through the sky in a six ton metal tube."

Gabriella's thoughts drifted to her grandfather. She'd made a quick call to him before they left the hotel. He'd surprised her, telling her that two other Architects were coming to guard his vaults while he accompanied five members of the Vatican police and Swiss Guard to Vatican City. Grandfather would remain there, guarding the scrolls until the danger had passed.

The conversation had been short and cryptic. She'd fought back tears when she told him to have a safe trip, knowing there must be real and imminent danger for the Order to take such drastic actions.

Grandfather had promised to call once he reached Rome.

"Are you okay?" Ian watched her, his brows furrowed.

"Yes, just thinking about everything."

"You're worrying. Your pulse is quick and you smell wrong. I don't like it."

"This could get really annoying." She narrowed her eyes. "Tell me you can't read minds."

Ian raised his hands in mock surrender. "I swear, no mind reading. I'd be afraid to hear what goes on in that noggin of yours."

Oh, you have no idea. She should tell him. He had a right to know how deep this danger ran. He already knew about the Seven Sorrows.

She glanced at Sasha, who dug through a huge leather tote bag. Later, when they were alone, she would reveal everything.

"I can't believe I have to listen to you two prattling on for the next four hours." Sasha snapped open a Russian fashion magazine.

Gabriella blinked, laughing. "Is that you?"

The cover model wore a fur bikini and matching hat, her knees bent and her lips puckered in a kittenish pose. And she looked exactly like Sasha.

"Yes, it is, so what?" she said in a bored tone.

"Nothing, I think that's really cool. You're famous."

She snorted and turned a page. "So, because I was lucky to have pretty face and big tits all the *mens* drool over me. Like poor homely girls should be hidden away in rooms where no one has to look at them."

"And yet, you pose on the cover for all the "mens" to drool over you." Ian shook his head, drawing a paperback from his duster pocket.

"Makes me sick," she spat. "But if the *mens* are going to look, I might as well make the money. It pays the bills." She shrugged, her lip curling in a smile.

"I guess a girl can never have too many diamond studded collars," Ian said dryly.

"I dare you to try to put collar 'round my neck, vampire," Sasha sneered.

Gabriella glared at him. Must he always be so sarcastic? "Don't provoke the cat and then complain about the scratches."

"Sasha can take care of herself, little bird," she said, snapping her feline gaze back to Ian. "Just wait 'til you go to sleep, vampire."

"This is gonna' be a long trip." Gabriella massaged a

temple.

"It's not my fault. He wants to have sex with you, so he takes his frustration out on me," Sasha snarled.

Ian growled and Gabriella gasped.

"There are enough pheromones in the air to start a perfume company." Sasha waved her hand in front of her face.

Gabriella nearly choked. Was it true? He wanted to have sex with her? She glanced at Ian. What little color he had, had drained from his pale face. His eyes met hers and flashed away, sending her heart into little flips.

"In fact, I'll leave you alone so you can do as you please." Sasha retreated to the back of the plane, curling up on a recliner. More cat than human now, big paws curled under her chest. Her face seemed caught somewhere in between, patches of fur on her cheeks, her nose too wide for her pretty high cheeks.

Ian shifted in his seat and crossed his legs.

She tried very hard not to sneak a glance, to see if his desire was real, if it had spread to his jeans.

"Erik said there's a change of clothes for each of us in the backpacks by the bathroom."

"Thank God," Gabriella blurted, examining the backs of her hands folded white knuckled in her lap. She was trying not to stare at Sasha, looking like a botched genetic experiment in her semi-shifted state, though she provided a good distraction from Ian.

Absently, she unclenched her hands. A moment later she wriggled her journal from her coat pocket.

"What's that?" Ian stared curiously.

She opened to where her pen marked the page. "My journal. I keep detailed notes of all my fun and exciting adventures." She raised a brow at him.

His lip curled in a smile, his eyes mischievous.

"Hmm, perhaps there'll be a chapter in there about me? The dashing hero."

She snorted. "Maybe a footnote." An embarrassing blush crept up her cheeks. She raised the book to hide her face. One journal wasn't enough to write her feelings and observations about Ian.

She peeked over the top. He grinned and leaned back, lowering the seat until he was almost lying flat. "I'm going to catch a few winks. We've got a long night ahead if us."

"Uh huh," she said, pretending to lose herself in her

notes.

"You'd better be careful not to mix them up." His voice grew thick as he closed his eyes.

"What are you talking about?"

"The cover's are almost the same. That journal's nearly as beat up as the Requiem's."

"Go to sleep," she groused, but she closed the book and turned it over in her hands. Not exact, but they were close to the same size. He was right, both books had battered leather covers. At a glance, one could pass for the other. She flicked her gaze to the backpack on the table, bulging with the golden box, then back to the journal on her lap.

CHAPTER ELEVEN ✝

December 9th Paris, France

"You allowed Gabriella to escape, twice. I thought I could depend on you."

Lilith cringed beneath the sharp blow of words. She stared at the pitted marble floor of the chapel, littered with leaves and vermin droppings. Sunlight speared through the few unbroken stained glass windows, painting colorful prisms on the stone walls. She tried not to cringe away from the light, but vague memories of horrible pain worked to scurry her into the shadows.

"I'm sorry, my lord. The Scotsman was far more difficult than we imagined."

"My child, you know that I love you above all others, but how can I grant salvation to one who cannot obey such simple commandments?"

He loves me. Her heart trembled, forcing her to look away as her throat tightened with joy. Hot tears burned like acid. She blinked them away. The lord hated tears, hated weakness. She must be strong to earn salvation.

"We've figured how to work around his weakness, and hers. My disciples already await them in Egypt, in the desert away from prying eyes. I swear to you, we will not fail this time," she said, hating the quaver in her voice.

She glanced at the statue of Mary along the far wall, her arms open and beckoning. To be so wanted, so serene. The emptiness she felt inside pained her.

"Bring them both and keep him in the special cell. He will witness her fate."

"And the shape shifter they travel with?"

He paused a moment, allowing her to glance at his dark countenance, perched on the chancellors chair in the recesses of the nave. Such a humble throne for the King of Kings, though this choice only added to his grace. He pushed back the hood of his white robe, revealing thick golden waves and the perfect angel's face. So familiar, as if her heart had always known him. Intense sapphire eyes, so like her own. Soft pale lips forever bent in a beatific smile.

His beauty nearly stopped her sludging heart. She fought the instant twinge of sexual desire, the yearning that flared hot, twisting like a burning knife inside her, never to be relieved. The ultimate sin, he'd warned her. Sex was for procreation only, if she sought salvation.

Her followers tried to obey, but lust for flesh and lust for blood drove the demons with equal vigor. She did not hate them for their urges. Contrarily, she envied them their lack of faith that allowed them to act upon their nature. Her hand moved to her cheek, stroking the scarred cords. Herself, she had lost too much already.

She quelled the ache of her core, basking in the tenderness of his grin. Her own disciples cringed away from the hideous stains of her sin—the sin of sharing her mortal body with the beast who had infected her, and then sought to destroy her with holy water. Yet her lord stared at her like Mary stared upon the whores and thieves, with compassion.

"Obviously, the cat woman must die, but I've been reconsidering the werewolves. The shape shifters are taking sides with those who oppose my will. I am thinking we may offer protection to the werewolves in exchange for their loyalty."

"But they are unclean beasts."

"As are the Seven Sorrows, my child." He spoke in a patronizing tone that shut her lips. "Sometimes we must use our enemies for the sake of the greater good. That will leave only the vampires to oppose us. Rogue Hunters, indeed. As if our kind were the monsters. The humans are nothing but stupid beasts, no better than the apes they keep in cages. Sinful, vile, hate filled creatures. We must cleanse the earth of this scourge." He stood abruptly.

She nearly cried out in disappointment as he raised the hood, extinguishing the warmth of his glow. Without another word he disappeared through a side door that led to his chambers.

She pressed a hand to her stomach, sick with self loathing for disappointing him. For desiring him. Not again. Soon she would deliver The Vessel and the traitor vampire who protected her. And then the lord would restore her, relieve her of these horrid evil cravings. Flesh and blood, how she desired them, but salvation awaited her if she remained strong. All she needed was to capture the woman, and she would be freed from this curse forever.

CHAPTER TWELVE ✝

December 9th Luxor, Egypt

The sun set while they soared somewhere over the Dead Sea. Ian breathed the smells of the desert as they disembarked on the executive jet runway at the Luxor airport. Musty ruins and date palm trees amid dusty sand. He stayed close to Gabriella while the Customs agents searched through their bags and scrutinized their papers.

Gabriella followed the agents, digging through the canvas duffle bags as they dragged them from the cargo hold. "My God, look at this," she exclaimed more than once, holding up some gizmo, and he tried acting suitably impressed.

Four bags stuffed with equipment, plus four five-gallon jugs of water. She nearly started an international incident when they tried to take away her backpack, after seeing the treasure inside.

Several agents swarmed around her. Ian grabbed her raised fist before it connected with a jaw. He produced transport documents and a wad of American hundreds.

"You'd best take your money and go," he warned, fighting the demon that thrashed with the force of a crocodile in his brain.

His fists curled and his jaw clenched. What a mess. He'd have to stop them if they tried to take the book, and then they'd have to flee the country. Sneaking across borders to regain entry would be dangerous and time consuming.

He let out a breath when the Customs agents handed back her pack.

Moments later a truck arrived to take them and their baggage to the terminal. Inside several hawkers offered to load their luggage onto carts and to find them a cab.

Ian laughed to himself when Gabriella shooed them away with practiced competence. His laughter faded when she rebuked his help, too.

Stubborn woman.

Out front, an overly enthusiastic young man bobbed on his toes beside a stretch limo. He grinned a mouthful of teeth, his large black eyes bright in his russet face. His chauffeur's hat drooped low on his forehead and the arms of his suit jacket hung to his fingers. Unruly black curls brushed his collar, but he looked clean enough.

Ian studied the sign in the boy's hands with a frown.

It said "E. N. Mickshane Party".

Sasha laughed until the young man moved past the limo to a scratched and dented cab. At one time the thing must have been yellow, but now both front fenders were red, and the left rear quarter panel was painted primer gray.

The boy opened a creaking door, waving her in.

Her smile melted like snow in the rain. "You expect me to ride in that thing?"

The boy looked a little confused. "My name is Anpu. My cousin called me, said to pick up American photographers and sexy Russian supermodel for photo shoot in the mountains."

He wagged his brows at her. Sasha snarled.

Ian coughed a laugh into his fist.

"He also said to give you this." Anpu lifted an expensive backpack through the door, holding it out to Ian. A small key lock secured the zipper clasps.

"Thanks," Ian said, taking a deep breath. Fresh blood supply.

"But he gave me no key. Sorry." The kid shrugged.

Ian patted his bony shoulder. "No problem. I'll get it open."

"Your cousin is going to take us into the mountains?" Gabriella pushed the loaded luggage cart to the sidewalk, her cheeks flushed.

"Why didn't you just hire one of the hawkers?" Ian asked as she used her hip to push a slipping water jug back in place.

"There's some very expensive sensory equipment in these bags. I found a GPRS system and a couple of magnetic detectors. Along with more clothes. I owe your friend, big time."

She looked cute as hell dressed in the khaki jeans and t-shirt Erik had packed for her. Or maybe Angelica, he thought grudgingly. She'd be more likely to worry about their physical comforts, especially Gabriella's.

He rubbed his temple, realizing that thoughts of

Angelica had provoked only fondness. For a moment a little guilt nagged at him, as if not aching for her betrayed her somehow. He watched Gabriella, breathing hard, her heart thrumming like a bird's. Troubled, yet so strong and brave. Perhaps he'd been betraying himself.

"You could have at least let me push the cart." He reached for the push bar, but she grabbed his wrist with surprising strength.

"I don't want you to regret bringing me. I'm proving I can pull my weight."

"And everyone else's." He yanked his hand free and tried wrestling the cart away, but after a dangerous minute when everything threatened to slide off one side, he ceded her victory with a sigh. "You're a pain in the ass, you know that?"

She arched her brows and unleashed the power of huge copper eyes, so full of determination and...? Desire? Ah, he was such a bastard to want her, to know she wanted him, and to be too much of a coward to do the right thing.

Send her home.

No, he was much too selfish for that.

"I've been called worse by better men than you."

"I've no doubt." He scowled. Hopeless, he thought, trying with zero success not to stare at her lovely grin.

Such a tiny thing she was, swinging bags off the cart with strong efficiency and handing them off to the driver. She helped the boy arrange the bags in the surprisingly large trunk. Together they piled the rest on the luggage rack.

She whirled to face him as if she felt him staring and he smiled to deflect her suspicious glance. She returned the smile albeit begrudgingly, just as a gentle wind tossed her locks over her eyes. Maybe it was the desert air, the arid breeze rustling the fronds in the date trees along the road. Maybe it was the vastness of the night sky, the millions of stars twinkling with incredible clarity. Or maybe it was just *her* making the world around them more amazing.

Sasha sullenly studied her red painted nails while Ian blinked himself from his trance. He hurried to help finish unloading the cart before she rendered him completely useless.

Once the driver secured the bags, he again encouraged Sasha into the front seat.

"You sit up front with me," Anpu grinned.

Sasha glided like a predator over the sidewalk, stopping short of the door. She sniffed the boy, wrinkling her nose. "You smell strange. Like a dog, but different."

"Sasha!" Ian snapped.

But the boy just shrugged, his grin never swaying. "It's okay. We raise sheep. I am sheepherder mostly, and I sleep in the shed with the sheep herding dogs."

Sasha shook her head vehemently. "Nyet. Not shepherding dogs. I said, I smell something like a dog, but it is not a dog." She eyed him suspiciously as he closed her in.

Ian hesitated before opening the door for Gabriella. If nothing else, Sasha was an excellent huntress and for a good reason. Unequaled senses. If she thought this guy was off, he'd be a fool not to pay attention.

"Who sent you to pick us up?"

"I told you. My cousin."

Ian shook his head. "No, I meant who contacted your cousin?"

"A man, very wealthy. He lives in Jordan. He said he was an old friend of Eeon Mickshane. We do work for him sometimes. His name is Amun."

Ian froze. Even his demon ceased writhing. "And who contacted Amun?"

"I do not know. My cousin calls—I come. You want a ride or not?"

"Cheeky bastard," Ian muttered as he slid in beside Gabriella.

* * * *

Anpu sped out of the city to the north over a bridge that crossed the Nile River, and headed toward the black outline of mountains beneath a winking moon. Soon they left the pavement, traveling over a deeply rutted, dirt road.

Gabriella swore under her breath every time he hit a furrow, smacking her head into the roof. At first she worried for Ian and Sasha, being so tall, but both possessed some uncanny agility that kept them in place.

They drove for miles into the foothills until the road disappeared altogether. The car bounced wildly over the rocks and gullies. How could he find his way in the darkness? To her, the world looked like nothing but gray rubble in the headlights.

"Where are you taking us, dog man?" Sasha whipped a mean looking blade from the pocket of her white leather car coat. She pressed the blade to Anpu's neck just hard enough for a bead of oily black to well around the tip.

Gabriella had to give cat woman credit. In this bouncy car, she could have slit his throat.

Anpu grinned even wider, as if it were a great honor having a famous Russian supermodel poke a knife in his throat. "We're almost there. Look up ahead. See the lights?"

Gabriella's chin snapped up, trying to see past Sasha, whose tall, slender body took up much of the narrow front seat.

What appeared to be lantern light blinked from somewhere ahead. The foothills grew steeper, the small car's engine whining and balking, but they continued to creep up the incline.

Ian had been pensively silent ever since Anpu mentioned the name of his solicitor. Gabriella was dying to ask him about the mysterious Amun, but she sensed he would tell her in his own time. Perhaps later, when other curious ears weren't listening.

At last they reached a narrow plateau. The cab sputtered and shuddered to a stop, dust billowing around them. Out of the darkness, a line of camels appeared in the beam of the headlights. The animals blinked huge eyes in the sudden brightness, bellowing anxious nuuurrring sounds.

Sasha sniffed the air and wrinkled her nose. "Great. Camels. Can we not find guides who drive Jeeps?"

"Jeeps destroy the desert, and they are noisy. If you wish your enemies to no hear you, you ride camels," Anpu said.

A man followed the beasts, wearing traditional desert garb, a kaftan, light trousers, and a white turban on his head. He led a camel into the clearing, a long staff gripped in one hand. A compact machine gun hung on a strap from his shoulder.

The next seconds exploded in a blur. Gabriella barely blinked before Ian had the newcomer flat on his back. Sasha had dragged Anpu from the car, holding him in a stranglehold that could no doubt snap his neck. The camels groaned and paced nervously, but they remained close.

Gabriella climbed from the cab, keeping low while she tried to see into the darkness for any signs of an ambush. She closed her eyes, turning in a small circle, but nothing felt out of place. When she turned back to Ian, he was offering a hand to the newcomer and pulling him up from the dust.

Sasha released her death grip on Anpu with a threatening glare that would leave most grown men in need of fresh underwear. The boy laughed nervously when she patted his shoulder, saying something in Arabic akin to "didn't mean to scare the crap out of you, no hard feelings."

He answered in his native tongue, "You can touch me wherever you want on my body".

Sasha sneered at him. "I don't fuck dogs."

Anpu shrugged, answering in English. "Neither do I. Something else we have in common."

He winked. Sasha's eyes flared. She roared, sharp teeth rippling through her widening jaw. The camels bellowed, huddling together at the edge of the darkness.

That shut everyone up. But for some reason the Egyptians weren't freaked out. *Why not,* she wondered. This didn't feel right.

Gabriella shook her head, and hurried to join Ian who was speaking softly with the newcomer. He smiled as she approached, holding a hand out to help her up the rocky slope.

"Gabriella, this is Kafele. He and Anpu will guide us into the mountains."

She nodded, smiling unsurely. Her senses detected nothing strange from these two, but still she couldn't shake the feeling that they weren't what they seemed.

"You have a map?" Kafele asked.

Gabriella clutched her pack to her chest. "Not exactly." She looked to Ian. "We need to head straight west from the Valley of the Kings."

Kafele, an older, more somber version of Anpu, scowled. "That is all you have? West from the Valley of the Kings? Why don't we just put on blindfolds and wander aimlessly in the desert wherever the wind might carry us?"

"I have a compass, and I have an idea what we're looking for. If you don't want the money I'm sure we can find someone else willing to take us." She raised her chin and met his stare, hoping he didn't call her bluff. They couldn't exactly look up desert guides in the yellow pages out here.

Kafele shrugged, mumbling under his breath. "Idiots. There must be an epidemic."

"What did you say?" Gabriella said, seeing the alarm in Ian's eyes.

"An epidemic of idiots," Kafele repeated defiantly,

though he cast a worried glance at Ian, who towered over him.

"Why would you say that?" Ian demanded. Sasha dragged Anpu closer.

"There was another party seeking a guide into the desert. They said same as you, start at Valley of Kings and go west."

"When?" Gabriella hissed.

"This morning, early. They came in on first flight. They were asking around the marketplace—I have a stand there."

"Did they find a guide?" Ian stared down at Kafele, his brows pulled tight together.

"I-I do not know." Kafele took a step back. "I do not think so. No one travels with no direction into the desert." He gave Gabriella a look.

"We've got to get going, right now," Gabriella insisted.

Kafele's face twisted anxiously. "How may we find our way with no map? It is a fool's work, traveling blind into the mountains."

"I swear to you, we will not get lost."

"How can you say that?" Kafele asked.

Ian stared, his expression questioning an explanation. Gabriella swallowed. How could she explain in a way they could believe her?

"Take me to Al-Qurn and my..." She sucked in a breath. One more sacred trust about to be shattered. "I can lead the way."

"What?" Kafele looked skeptical.

She didn't blame him. Al-Qurn, a rocky peak of near pyramidal shape, looked down over the Valley of Kings.

Ian cocked his head, but he asked no questions.

Sasha appraised her with a hunter's intensity. "I think pretty bird has many talents. Take her to her sacred place."

"Sacred place? What are you looking for? I thought you came for a photo shoot," Anpu said.

Sasha slapped the back of his head hard enough to flip the chauffeur's hat to the ground. "Liar, you knew it was our cover."

Anpu shrugged, once again smiling. "Okay, so I know more than I say. That is trait of a good guide."

"Not true. The trait of a good guide is to share all that he knows," Sasha countered.

"Let us go now," Kafele said.

Exhausted, Gabriella stood back while the men loaded

the supplies onto camels. When Sasha tried to mount, the camel bellowed, his eyes rolling wildly, the whites showing. The beast tugged at its rope until she backed away.

"Fine, stupid beast. I walk." She slipped the spike heels from her feet. Was she really going to walk barefoot?

They rode single file into the hills with Kafele in the lead and Sasha watching their backs. She moved gracefully, showing no obvious discomfort for going shoeless.

The mood remained somber and heavy, but Gabriella tuned the others out. Her body hummed and the heat in her palms flared hotter with every step into the desert. But soon the camel's steady gait had relaxed her. Nothing but an endless terrain of sand and rocks stretched out ahead of them.

A hand on Gabriella's arm made her jump, her eyes flashing open. She'd been dozing in the high backed saddle, the camel's gentle motions apparently had rocked her to sleep. Ian's hand lay on her arm, gently shaking her awake.

She yawned and brushed off his hand. "I'm awake."

"We're here," he whispered almost reverently.

She sat up straighter, blinking away the sleep.

Her breath caught at the splendid sight below. She had visited the valley many years ago just after the Great War, but she'd never enjoyed it from this vantage point.

From atop the Theban Hills, barely visible in the ambient moonlight, a web of dirt paths and stone walls traversed the valley floor, leading to some of the greatest hidden treasures of Egypt—the most amazing being the Temple of Ramses, II.

"I've never been here before. It's amazing," Ian said and she nodded. He had pulled his beast up beside hers and they pawed the ground, mewling impatiently. "But we need to get going. We only have a few hours before sunrise."

"Of course." She looked around, gathering her bearings. They had stopped on the ridge just beneath the peak of al-Qurn. Power radiated from the crest of the peak. She scrambled down from the camel, her legs a little rubbery.

"Just give me a couple of minutes."

This was it. The end of centuries of secrecy. May Grandfather and the Architects forgive her.

CHAPTER THIRTEEN ✝

Predawn, December 10th Valley of the Kings, Egypt

"You think you can see your secret place from up there?" Kafele asked a little sarcastically from the base of the summit.

Gabriella ignored the urge to turn him into a burning pile of cat droppings. The rock wall crumbled under her hands as she struggled up the incline, but finally she managed to reach the uneven apex.

Oh yes, she felt it now. Standing straight in the hiking boots, she turned to the west and pushed up her jacket sleeves.

Thanks to the renegade vampires, she hadn't slept much since Romania. She'd used most of her powers destroying the shielding spell outside the cave, and with no sleep she'd felt drained ever since.

But magic swelled in pulsing waves from the ground beneath her, like water gurgling from a bottomless well. She closed her eyes, taking deep breaths in through her nose and blowing out through her mouth. The power of this place filled her nearly empty well. Each surge trembled her body with near orgasmic force, tingling through her hands, her legs, and through her torso, finally waking her mind.

Who needs a man? She thought wickedly, but Ian instantly filled her thoughts. The image of him inside her, filling her with the same slamming force this magic filled her body, the smell of him as he pressed against her, pinning her... She tried to force the fantasy from her mind, but it refused to leave.

Her skin burned with painless heat. She was shocked upon opening her eyes to find her arms alight with white heat. Maybe a man would be nice. But not just any man. Ian. That perfect face with the golden stubble, his muscled chest and rippling belly.

This isn't helping! Focus on the magic, not the man.

Finally the magical tingling ebbed, alerting her she had

reached her fill. She raised her hands, moving them in small circles, palms facing outward.

"Tomb of magic and myth, I call to thee. Buried under sand and stone, sing for me." She whispered the words three times. Each repetition sent stronger, louder vibrations through her palms until they hummed like tuning forks. She turned slightly to her left. The humming grew weaker. She moved her hands right of center, and again the vibrations lessened. Facing forward again, she opened her eyes, smiled, and pointed straight west.

"That way."

"Are you sure?" Ian asked, staring with wide eyes from the base of the peak.

Actually, all four of her companions were staring. *What?* They'd never seen a quivering, glowing woman before? *Sheesh.*

"Yes, I'm positive."

"How can she possibly know?" Kafele scoffed, leaning back in his saddle and crossing his arms.

She narrowed her eyes. *No burning the guide to ash. It might scare the camels.*

"I said, I know. Either you can accompany us and earn your fees, or we'll go on without you, which would suit me just fine."

"And you can take your little pervert with you." Sasha tipped her chin to Anpu.

The sudden earnestness of Anpu's face made Gabriella break into laughter. "I didn't think anything could stop his smile."

Sasha laughed her deep, throaty laugh.

"You may know the way, but I know the way of the desert. I gave my word. We will accompany you and assure you arrive safely to your destination," Anpu said quite seriously.

Gabriella bit her lip, so not to laugh again. As if. He'd seen only a flash of her power. She considered sending him and Kafele away, but it wasn't her call, and he might be right. These mountains were prone to flash floods and blinding sandstorms.

She watched Ian twitch a little as she slid down the slope on her bottom. She suppressed a grin knowing he was fighting his chivalrous impulse to race up the hill and carry her.

* * * *

Hours later, through narrow ravines and up sheer mountainsides no vehicle could have maneuvered, her hands continued to hum, leading them directly west. Her inner thighs screamed from squeezing the sides of the beast on the steep inclines. All around them, the sky lightened from deep charcoal to slate to dark cobalt. Soon the sun would roll above the eastern hills.

Kafele seemed irritated when Ian asked him to find a place to rest for the day, someplace mostly in the shade. Silently he led them into one of the narrow ravines, whose vertical walls would protect them from all but the midday sun.

Gabriella collapsed onto a boulder, too exhausted to help the men unload the baggage from the tired camels. The ravine dead-ended several yards further up, cradling them in a colorless sandstone bowl and leaving only one viable exit.

Sasha was obviously thinking the same thing, staring up the canyon walls that were steep but not terribly high. Springing off bent knees, she leapt effortlessly to the top. She dropped to all fours, turning a tight circle several times before lying on her stomach where she could watch the camp, hands dangling over the edge.

Gabriella giggled. Even human, Sasha looked like a cat.

Ian wrestled a tent from one of the duffle bags and had the thing set up in less than a minute.

The Egyptians didn't appear to notice or care about Ian's uncanny speed or Sasha's Wonder Woman leaping abilities.

That made her nervous. Most people would have been frightened or at the very least, amazed as she still was. But the two men busied themselves making a small fire and setting up an open sided tent beside a burbling spring.

"Come, you need to sleep." Ian raised the tent flap, holding a hand out to her.

She felt her own hand slowly rising to meet his, her breasts growing tight inside her skin.

"First she must eat."

Annoyed at Kafele for interrupting her fantasies, she turned to him. The man looked up from the fire and scratched his beard. Meat sizzled over the flames, skewered on two kabobs he held in one hand. Anpu turned a food-laden stick in slow circles, glancing up from beneath his long bangs, offering his friendly smile.

"He's right," Ian conceded. "Come to me when you've had your fill."

Come to me. Something in the way he'd spoken the words sent a shiver through her belly. Heat rushed to her groin and the virgin muscles clenched in anticipation.

She tasted nothing as she ate, her eyes drifting continually to the fluttering breach where Ian waited.

"Thank you for the food," she muttered and rose, her heart pounding against her ribs.

Her legs shook with each step. Could she turn her back on a millennia old prophecy, just to satisfy this crippling desire? How could she possibly continue this journey without satiating this fire?

She pulled back the flap, a little harder than she'd meant. Ian smiled up from an air mattress, stripped down to nothing but boxers. One hand cupped the back of his head, the other splayed across his rippled belly. Copper-gold curls tumbled like rays of sunlight around his perfect face—full lips, cleft chin beneath dark stubble, strong square jaw and sharp cheeks begging her hands to stroke their angles.

Quickly, before she could change her mind, she stripped off her clothes down to her panties. Ian's attentive appraisal only intensified the tingling crawling over her flesh. Every nerve sparked like a live wire. Her pulse thundered in her ears. Shallow breaths shook her breasts in uncomfortable ways. Ways that demanded attention.

Her thumbs slid beneath her panties. A large thick swell rose beneath his shorts in response. Her hands trembled as she squirmed the silk past her hips down to her knees. They dropped around her ankles and she kicked them away.

Knowing he'd already seen her naked didn't make her feel less exposed, less electric. His gaze was like silk whispering over her skin. Craving ached inside her, demanding relief.

Last, she moved to undo the clasp of her necklace.

"No, leave it on." Ian stood in front of her in a blur. His cool hands gripping hers, pulling them down by her sides.

"I don't—I'm not sure." A little late, she thought, standing naked before him, his erection pressed against her belly. She swallowed her groan.

Disappointment flashed in his eyes. How cruel, she

thought, to torment him.

"Ian, I barely know you," she whispered as her fingers moved over his chest.

"You're right," he said, his voice rough, the words simmered her blood. He lowered his head, and his breath washed over her, a cool breeze prickling her nipples.

"I-I'm saving myself for someone."

His eyes widened but he did not pull away. "Who?"

She felt ridiculous, embarrassed for having to explain herself. "I don't know. A prophecy of my people says I'm supposed to save myself for the 'one who is my destiny'."

Saying the words aloud sounded asinine. Especially standing like this. So close. So exposed.

His fingers slipped beneath her chin, lifting it as he brought his face close.

"What if it's me? What if I'm your destiny?"

She almost laughed, almost blurted "very funny," but his eyes were too serious, watchful.

"But we're so different—"

"So? Perhaps it's our differences that make us a perfect match."

She thought of the lines she had read, the most powerful spell in the book. "Between the dark and the light, seek ye salvation." Still, there was one thing that kept her from surrendering.

"What about the woman? Angelica?"

Her heart lurched, watching his eyes drift off thinking of her.

But when his gaze returned to hers, it was sharp, focused. "I can't see her anymore."

His hand cupped her cheek. "When I search my memories, I see only you. My beautiful, amazing Gabriella. You have restored my heart. You've made me whole again."

His Gabriella. How wonderfully those words rang in her ears.

She stared into his emerald eyes and saw the truth in them. Smoldering desire pierced straight through to her trembling heart, reassuring her he meant what he'd said.

Her hand slipped from his grip, moving from his chest to his neck. She pulled him to her, their lips smashing hard in open mouthed hunger. His taste filled her mouth like sweet honey and her body reacted. Her hips arched forward, grinding hard against the thick erection.

He lifted his mouth off hers just long enough to strip off

his boxers and again his lips were on hers like a desperate starving man. Strong hands explored, his cold fire burning over her hips, her back, squeezing her breasts. The velvet hardness of his erection pressed into her belly.

Her hand ran down the banded cords of his back, the firm roundness of his rear. Breathless and shaky, she slid her fingers between their bodies.

She cupped him. He groaned, a strange guttural noise choked in his throat. He took a half step away, his hands still touching her, but with less vigor.

She glanced up into his face and gasped, black eyes stared hungrily back at her and a quivering lip arched, showing off a dangerous fang.

The instinctive impulse to flee flashed through her mind. Yet, his hands held her lightly, allowing her a way out. If she were smart, she'd rip free of his arms, escape into the gray dawn. But in truth, flight was no longer a possibility.

Longing twisted her stomach, tethering her fate to his. The need in her womb demanded quenching.

"Look at the cross, Ian."

His jaw clenched. Cords bulged in his neck, lips curled from away from his teeth as he battled the demon. Slowly his chin dipped until his eyes averted. His gaze traveled down her face, to her neck and finally focused on the cross. Ian blew out a long breath. Muscles relaxed and the black eyes bled away to green.

Relief turned her muscles soft, and she fell into his arms. He lowered her gently to the bed, kissing her forehead, her temple, his cool lips whispering across her neck. The thrills of the unknown, fear and excitement sent tremors through her—to want something so badly, she would trade her life, her soul. At this moment, she wanted one thing only.

Ian.

He pressed his body against hers, pinning her beneath him. She squirmed under his welcome eagerness.

"You still have your maidenhood?" He slid the cross up from where it hooked her breast and laid it in the hollow of her throat.

She smiled at the archaic term. "Yes, I am a virgin."

He paused, brow furrowed. "I'll not pluck that precious flower, not unless you're completely sure."

"I'm sure of one thing. If we stop now I'll burst into

flames."

With a crooked grin, he stroked her cheek with his thumb. Strangely, his cool touch burned like fire. Fire, but with no pain, only heat.

She stared into gentle eyes that moments ago lusted for her blood. Fire and ice. Light and dark. Could he truly be the one? Could she really be so lucky?

Her hand slid between them, and she stroked his velvet shaft, empowered by the way it twitched at her touch. A low groan escaped him as she rubbed her thumb over the slippery bead at the tip.

"I'll be gentle, but I cannot stop m'self. Not now. I must have you, Gabriella—I cannot bear to wait."

"Nor can I." She stared intently as his hand traveled down her belly, sending a thousand birds to flight. Her breath caught when his cool fingers found her fleshy cleft and parted the opening. He rubbed across the swollen knot of nerves, sending sensations to every cell in her body, and she cried out in pure joy.

She raised her hips, rubbing against him letting him feel her flowing wetness. "I want you inside me. Now." She held him in her fist, squeezing him, demanding him. Teasing his hardness along the hot fold of flesh.

Ian poised himself above her, consumed by a hunger he'd never known. His lust for her eclipsed any desire for blood he'd ever felt at the demon's command.

Gabriella stared up at him, her cheeks flushed, her lips plumped from their heated kisses. He could no longer resist as she pulled him along with her need with such force. He could not deny this painful desire any more than he could deny his hunger.

He stared at the cross, afraid to take his eyes from it. His body was over-stimulated, trembling with unquenchable thirst. He wanted to drive himself deep inside her, to pound over and over into her sweet, wet warmth.

Fighting his need, he moved slowly, pushing gently past the unyielding opening. She gasped sharply. His eyes flashed to her face.

"Am I hurtin' you?"

"If you stop now, I'll hurt you," she hissed through clenched teeth.

He grinned and snatched the cross. He clenched it tight in his fist. Bending, his lips moved hers. His tongue thrust into her mouth each time he inched himself deeper inside her. He shuddered at the soft acquiescence of her tight crevice.

"Harder," she breathed.

The beast stirred restlessly, demanding release. Furious at his exclusion. Ian gripped the cross tighter, the corners digging into his flesh. He struggled to ignore the deafening rush of her blood, her rapid pulse, and the sweet scent of honeysuckle and lilacs—craved equally by the man and the beast.

This is mine. She is mine. I will die before I let you touch her.

He thrust his hips, hard, driving himself deeper inside her, breaking through the tissue barrier and claimed her. He looked down at her face but her eyes were closed and a sweet smile parted her lips.

Buried deep in the constricted fire of her core, Ian's body convulsed in violent delight. He drank the nectar of her breath until his mouth yearned to roam.

Her body shuddered beneath his. He cupped her breast in one hand, exciting her nipples with tongue and teeth. The other hand squeezed the cross so tightly, it burned his skin. The beast screamed and raged in his mind. Ian smugly ignored him.

She cried out once with pain and satisfaction, but the fullness of having him inside her felt better than anything she'd ever experienced.

Heaven.

She had died and gone to heaven. He filled her completely, and with each hard plunge struck some incredibly sensitive place deep inside her.

She raised her hips, thrusting herself upon him. Harder, faster, the tempo grew in unison as his every move matched hers. Every drive of his hips sent thrills of pleasure through her, spreading out in silky waves of satisfaction.

His tongue teased her puckered nipple. A moment later, he took the bud in his teeth. A bite.

She gasped as some primal part of her flooded with terror. A monster lurked behind her lover, a killer. But her carnal beast roared in pleasure as his mouth moved to the next nub, tongue flicking, teeth nipping, lips savoring.

Dizzying swells of pleasure spread into her belly, warming her body, flooding down her arms and legs. Her skin tingled, her nerves twitching. He moved more slowly now. Each plunge churned her insides to sweet butter, melting to warm cream around him. She wanted this feeling to last forever.

He was hers. She had no doubt.

The fates could not be so cruel, to give her this gift, this glorious man, his perfect fit, just to yank him away.

She felt something coming. A maelstrom boiled inside her. Building with such force she feared she might die from sheer desperation.

It hit her then. Pleasure. Satisfaction of such magnitude it was beyond comprehension.

"If you stop now I'll kill you," she growled in Ian's ear. She heard his husky laugh as he brought her to completion. Wave after wave battered her with shivering jolts of delicious orgasms. Once she'd spent the last body rocking spasm, his mouth moved to cover hers, to share her panting breaths.

Then it was his turn.

Ian exploded inside her, yanking her focus back to him. His jerking tremors reignited her orgasm. Every nerve pulsed electric, turning her bones to jelly. His skin blazed against hers. The smooth silk of his chest thrilled her breasts, every muscle of his belly grinding fire deep into her own.

She felt her release unleashing harder and stronger than before. Her bones twisted and writhed painlessly trying to be free from her skin.

She closed her eyes, exhaling a long groan of release. A strange tickling sensation spread down her back and over her shoulders. The silken sheets she lay upon squirmed with something warm and soft.

What was beneath her?

Ian's body went rigid. Even his breathing ceased.

What happened? Had she done something wrong? Was he angry? Worse yet, had he lost control of his beast?

Suddenly terrified, Gabriella opened her eyes.

Pressed tightly against her, Ian grew as still as death. He'd been focused on her and the need building in his groin, groaning with each spasm. And joy swelled within his chest. Joy as he'd never imagined. It was her. He belonged to her, inside her. He nearly wept from the wrenching heartache of this ecstasy. Of belonging.

But then the air quivered as if disturbed.

Something brushed his shoulder. A moth, perhaps. He'd barely noticed at first. Then another stroke, along his back this time. Long and soft like a cat's tail. He'd refused to drag his focus away from the moment, shuddering with aftershocks.

He barely noticed as white softness folded around him. Reluctantly, he raised his head. And froze.

What strange magic is this?

A cocoon of white feathers gently encircled him.

His head swung around, his body tensed. Predatory instincts demanded he break free from these bindings. With vampyric speed, he followed the patterns of feathers to bones and the bones to the source. *Gabriella.*

Wings. Feathered appendages unfolded from Gabriella's shoulders, binding him to her.

"What have I done?" His voice choked in his throat.

He had defiled—an angel!

He fought the horror, grinding his jaw. Of course, happiness was too much to expect. This would be the final curse upon his soul.

She stared up at him with wide, worried eyes.

He kissed her softly and pressed his face into her hair, too ashamed to look upon her majesty a moment longer.

"I'm so sorry." He sat back, gently pushing through the feathery folds.

She turned her head from side to side, seeming to notice them for the first time. Panic twisted her beautiful face. Her hands flew up, grabbing at feathers, tugging out handfuls in swift panicked movement.

At last, realization crossed her face. And then terror.

She kicked him square in the chest, flinging him against the side of the tent. Stakes ripped out of the ground, spraying dirt. The canvas molded to his body as he sailed through the air, slamming into the canyon wall.

To his shock, the force imbedded him inches into the rock. His demon exploded, refusing to remain captive when Ian's body, his host, was under attack. But Ian still clutched the crucifix. The demon screamed in agony as the cross burned the monster's skin. Flesh fried, sizzling and smoky.

The beast tore free of the rock wall, dropping lithely to the ground below. His head swung from side to side, sniffing air ripe with the sweet smell of pulsing blood.

The two men sat on rocks beside a fire, staring at him with a strange calm. Their hearts sped up, but not like the thundering beats of terrified humans. And their blood smelled...wrong.

He whipped around to Gabriella. Even subdued, Ian felt the beast's fury. But shock and fear overpowered the anger. The vampire turned away, and Ian felt the demon's terror.

He wanted—needed to tear his teeth into something. Hours had passed since his host last fed him and not nearly enough. Perhaps he would try the men, even though they were clearly not human.

A blur flew through the air, tumbling him over the ground several times. He flung his attacker off and leapt to his feet. A huge cat paced in front of his, snarling over long fangs. He knew this creature. The tiger woman. She held a pack in her teeth and flung it against his chest. He caught it, instantly smelling the blood. He shredded the canvas in half a second, ripping his teeth into the plastic bag. In less than a minute, he had sucked dry seven pints. Sated, he grew more aware of the pain in his hand. Flesh festered, the smell putrid. He could not release the cross; it had fused into his palm. He knew he must yield to his host or die. Silver poison boiled too close to the veins.

Ian exploded, enraged, his heart hammering in panic for Gabriella. The shimmering white of her wings spread to her skin, color bleeding away, even from her nipples. Her dark hair faded to the palest blonde.

She stumbled in a wild circle, naked, her face a grimace of panic as the wings flapped against the ground, sending up clouds of billowing dust. Handfuls of feathers scattered the rubble as she snatched at pinions like a cat clawing its tail.

He had seconds at best before she beat the air with real force, propelling herself into the sky, and out of his reach.

"Keep an eye on them," he ordered Sasha, pointing at Kafele and Anpu.

"Gladly," the tiger rumbled.

Ian lunged at Gabriella, carefully pinning her wings against her body as he tackled her to the ground. He held her tight until her trembling stopped. Slowly, her eyes regained focus.

"What's happening to me?" she questioned in a whisper.

"You don't know?"

She shook her head. Tears spilled down her frighteningly pale cheeks, glittering like liquid diamonds.

"Are you...an angel?"

Silky feathers rested inside his arms, and a strange power seemed to vibrate from her very center.

She looked at him crossly. "Do you see a halo around my

112

head?"

Ian laughed and kissed her tenderly. "That's my Gabriella."

His. How possessive he felt, yet he had no right to claim her. This revelation only widened the gap. Passion transformed her into this shining, beautiful creature, and he, on the other hand, turned into a hell beast.

He had no right to touch her, yet touch her he would. For as long as she wanted him. Whatever willpower he might have had disappeared the moment he'd joined himself with her.

"Don't worry, love, we'll figure this out."

He kissed her cheeks until he felt her relax. Beneath his hands, the bones cracked. Feathers shrank and withered. Color returned to her hair, spilling from the roots and flowing out to the ends.

At last her skin flushed pink, her cheeks growing warm. He breathed out a sigh.

She squirmed beneath him. He sat back to help her up, quickly untangling the sheet to drape across her shoulders.

His fingers brushed a strange rippling that ran down her back and curved around her sides. The skin felt conversely rough and soft. And then while he still touched her, the coarseness smoothed and disappeared.

She smiled ruefully and stood, wrapping the sheet tighter around her. She glanced to where Sasha paced before the two men, both of them sitting calmly beside their small fire.

"You have never looked more beautiful to me," Anpu cooed to Sasha. She roared fiercely, taking a swipe at the boy. He dodged the swing and laughed.

"Fool."

Ian ran a hand over his stubbled chin. "Sasha was right about them. I'm not sure what they are, but they are not human."

"What are you going to do?"

"You want I should gut them now?" The tiger growled through a fanged grin.

The breeze tumbled a curl into his face and he brushed it behind his ear. "Not yet, but keep an eye on 'em. They give you any cause, feel free to do as you will. I need to take cover soon."

He turned back to Gabriella. "But first, you and I need to talk."

"You might want to put something on." She stared at his manhood, which swelled in response.

He quickly, painfully zipped himself into a pair of jeans.

She glanced again at the men, then grabbed up a handful of the tent, shaking it at him. "I'm appalled at myself. How stupid, thinking this provided any privacy. They must have heard everything. I'll never be able to look Sasha in the eye again."

Ian gaped at her, for a moment wondering if she was joking. "After morphing into some kind of—flying creature—you're worried they heard us having sex?"

"Now the whole world knows I was a four hundred year old virgin."

"Four people hardly count as the whole world." Ian grabbed her elbow, tugging her along as he walked swiftly toward the mouth of the gorge, trying to understand her confused female logic, and this extraordinary miracle. "Besides, not one of us is truly human, so I don't think they even count."

He glanced at the sky, considerably lighter now. Instinctively he hugged the shadows of the eastern wall. He sat on boulder, patting the empty spot beside him.

His hand slid over hers, lacing fingers. "Gabriella, what happened to you?"

"I-I have no idea. But I'm not an angel, and don't call me that again. My people—we're the Architects. We're not angels or gods."

"Architects? I thought you were archivists."

She shrugged. "Keeping the archives is part of our work."

"So you design buildings or something?"

She giggled a little hysterically. "Not exactly. We design and we build—other things."

"What kind of things?"

She picked at a thread on the sheet. "Um—everything."

"So what do you build? Airplanes? Highways?"

"Bigger." She kicked a pebble with her toe. Scratched her arm.

He growled, frustrated. "Why are you being so difficult? Just tell me, damn it."

She raised her chin, and the flush in her cheeks deepened. "We're the Architects of the Universe."

"The universe? Like planets?"

"Yes, so they say. I was born here. I've never built

anything more complicated than a simple genetic code."

The demon perked up, interested. Ach, he wanted this beast out of his head! Private thoughts and conversations—how he took such a simple thing for granted in his human days.

"Genetic codes? And you're sure you're not some kind of god?"

She made a face. "Do I look like a god to you?" Their eyes met and she raised a hand. "Never mind, your judgment is warped."

Rare, strange heat spread up his neck and face. His thumb stroked the ridge of bone along the back of her hands. "Whatever's happening to you, I promise I'll stay with you as long as you want me."

"How about forever?" She laughed shakily.

"'Tis a serious request from someone you've known such a short time."

"I know, and I'll understand if you say no." Her lip rolled through her teeth. She raised her eyes, staring from beneath the feathery fringe of lashes.

He swallowed. So close to her, the connection was undeniable. Already it pained his heart to consider being separated from her. He yearned for her laughter, craved her body. As impossible as it seemed, she was a part of his life now.

"Yes," he said simply.

"Hold me."

He wrapped his arms around her, pulling her head to his chest. Kissed her hair. "I think you'd better tell me everything."

She nodded, her tears hot against his skin.

Am I going crazy?

Gabriella clung to Ian, afraid that if she let go she might fade into this dream. The passion, or perhaps the physical orgasm had triggered the metamorphosis.

Had Grandfather known this would happen? Wouldn't he have mentioned something this momentous when they'd had that awkward sex talk? Or was this some kind of punishment for choosing the wrong man?

No. Not the wrong man. No soul had ever touched hers like Ian's had. No man could ever fill her the way he did. Do those things to her....

He tightened his hold, mistaking her shudder for a chill. "Are you okay?"

She nodded, nestling against his marble chest. Seconds later she sniffed the air, then recoiled, nearly gagging.

"What's that horrid smell?"

The cross.

He tried opening his hand and winced. The skin of his fingers had fused to his palm, burned when the beast gripped the silver icon. Damn, it hurt.

Gabriella leaned closer to see, wrinkling her nose.

"Sun and stars, what happened?" She laid his hand flat in hers and tried to pry his fingers apart.

He yanked it back, holding the throbbing mass to his chest.

"When the demon took over, I was still holding the cross. Apparently his demon skin didn't take too well to touching something silver."

Something silver or something holy? He wondered now. Gabriella's confession had shaken everything he believed about faith and God. Unquestionably demons existed, creatures intolerant of silver and sunlight. Yet the ancient gods had existed long before the God of Abraham, so how did the Architects fit into all this?

Ian rubbed his temple, the ache in his head nearly surpassing the pain in his palm.

"Why didn't you say something?" Her eyes reflected her concern.

"We had more important things to discuss." The sheet sagged low on her breasts. Even now, in pain, confused, his body reacted. His body, his very core, hungered for her.

"Just let me see it." She grabbed at his arm, prying it away from his body, her delicate hands deceptively strong.

"What're you going do, kiss it and make it better?" He teased, though he felt little brevity.

She gave him a searing look. Still, he made her fight for it. Whatever she planned, he knew it would hurt.

With a final yank, she gained her prize. Mostly because he was afraid he might hurt her if he fought any harder. Stubborn woman.

Gabriella cupped the smoldering hand between hers. Instantly, heat surged through his palm. He tried to yank free, but she held on tight. Gold light glowed from his skin, flaring painfully through the muscles. He cringed, gritting his teeth. Skin ripped and pulled beneath his folded fingers. He trapped a growl in his throat, embarrassed to let her see how much it hurt. After a few moments, he relaxed. The fire scalded like ice over his skin—numbing it.

Soon the icy burn receded to tingles. He swallowed hard, uncurling his fingers. The cross lay in the slightly pinked skin of his palm. Phantom traces of pain skittered through regenerated nerves, fading as quickly as the stench of burnt flesh.

"How...?"

She lifted the crucifix, the broken chain dangling from her fingertips. "I told you. We're architects. We...build things."

"I know what ye said, love. It's just not the easiest thing to imagine."

Her eyes flickered away. She seemed uncomfortable discussing her powers. "Enough about me, already. We need to talk about the Seven Sorrows."

"What about them?"

"They're not exactly hidden." She looked up, biting her lip. "My grandfather delivered the Scrolls to the Vatican last month. He's traveling there right now under heavy guard, to make sure they remain safe."

"Scrolls? I thought they were a book."

She shook her head.

"He's had them all along?"

"I know I should have told you, I'm sorry. But I'm breaking the laws of my people by telling you this. Even the Vatican isn't sure what he brought them. They only know they are ancient sacred scrolls and that they are to keep them in their most secure vaults."

"Why'd he take them to Rome? His vaults are the most secure I've ever seen."

"The Vatican has more guards. It would have been too conspicuous, assembling a small army to protect the scrolls in Chicago."

Ian nodded, considering. He couldn't be angry at her for keeping secrets. Listening to her melodic voice was like a violin bow across the strings of his soul.

Watching her soft lips move, her worried eyes glancing at him, sent blood rushing to his groin again. The memories flooded his mind. The thrill of thrusting inside her, of her hips bucking against his. He wanted her now. He wanted her forever.

He cleared his throat, concentrating on her words.

"Obviously the vampires have figured out where the dagger's hidden, and they already know of its importance.

But there's another reason they want the Requiem." She worried the cross in her fingers, turning it over and over.

"Go ahead."

"In the back of the book—your friend skimmed past it yesterday—there is a spell to cast the Sorrows back into Hell."

Her shoulders heaved with a sigh. She picked up a stone at her feet and tossed it. "You know what they'll do to the Requiem if they get their hands on it, right?"

The demon's laughter echoed hollowly in his mind. "Aye. They'll destroy it."

He clasped her hand and lifted it to his lips, breathing in the mouthwatering sweetness of her flesh. Memorizing her scent. Blood pulsed through the thin blue veins at her wrist, quickening as he kissed her palm. He shuddered—disturbed that a part of him still thirsted so viciously for her blood—horrified, realizing how often his cravings meshed so flawlessly with the beast's.

"What other powers do you have, besides building universes and healing the sick?" He asked, curious, but also seeking a distraction. Saliva flooded his mouth. He willed himself to move her hand away from his face.

She laughed softly. "I can feel magic and bend it to my will. It's actually nothing more than manipulated energy. Once I've found it, I can either use it, absorb it, or dispel it, depending on what type of magic it is and if I have any use for it."

Ian nodded, pretending he had a clue what she meant. Ah, so much to learn about her, and he anticipated every lesson.

They lapsed into silence. He drifted deep into his thoughts, wondering how he'd come so far in one night. From wanting to end his existence, to vowing every moment of it to this woman he'd barely met.

Sunlight glinted off the far wall, painting sandstone dull beige. He must soon take cover.

"I've got a confession of me own." He glanced up the seam of the chasm. The giant tiger still paced. The men set out prayer rugs and faced the rising sun. He cleared his throat, bracing himself for her reproach. "It was no accident that your grandfather found that map."

"Are you telling me you put a priceless artifact inside that bible? That *you* sold him the bible?"

Unbelievable. Gabriella eyed him in awe. She could

hardly be angry at him, not after her own revelations. Not after that incredible, amazing explosion of orgasms. Just thinking about their encounter and her nerves sparked, sending tremors through her belly, firing lower. She swallowed the embarrassing groan that had begun its accent up her throat.

He nodded at her question, decidedly unrepentant. She started to protest, but he raised his hand to silence her.

"I found the map in Russia fourteen years ago. I taught myself Latin, but I knew even if I found the book I'd need someone else who could translate the spell. When I read about you and your grandfather, I came up with a plan. I hid that map inside a rare Gutenberg bible, and then advertised on all the sites for book collectors. I knew he couldn't resist. Remember, he purchased the bible from an anonymous seller in Rome? And I knew once you discovered the map you couldn't resist the challenge."

Gabriella's mind reeled. He'd set her up. And without the map, the Requiem would have stayed safely buried. But if the Church of the Damned ever got their claws on the Scrolls, her people would need the counter spell when things went badly. And they would go badly.

Did Ian have any idea of the danger he'd placed her in, putting her in the path of those crazed vampires?

"Grandfather said he received a note warning him saying those fanatics were after his greatest treasure. If they followed me to Romania, I can only assume they're after the Requiem."

Ian shrugged. "Maybe not. They might've been following me. I'm a Hunter, after all. Wouldn't be the first time they've tried to kill me."

"But he warned me before I left Chicago, insisting I go right away. Remember? I thought you were one of them."

She let her head fall into her hands. "How could she have been so foolish, to not have thought this through more thoroughly?"

"We'll have to stay a step ahead of 'em. And we need to lock up that book. If I'd known its importance, I'd never have let it leave Paris. We could have taken it to Rome."

"No! They can never be together, don't you see? And we're not a step ahead of them. Not if others arrived this morning."

"All the more reason we should've left it behind," Ian snarled.

"What I don't understand, is *how* they're always a step ahead of us. How can they know so much?" She glanced at Sasha, but Ian vehemently shook his head.

"Sasha's annoying as hell, but she's no traitor. She's had my back more than once."

The sun rose higher. Ian glanced again at the golden death creeping over the canyon floor. Sub consciously he rubbed the cool skin of his cheek, never again to be kissed by daylight. For all the years of languishing in the shadows, this no longer bothered him. He turned back to Gabriella and smiled, basking in the warmth of his own personal sun. And he knew his heart had given itself to her without his consent. Separating from her now would cause him actual physical pain.

God, he was such an idiot.

CHAPTER FOURTEEN ✝

December 10th Western Desert, Egypt

Moonlight washed silver over the desert sands.

Kafele and Anpu led them through the rough, rocky terrain. Eventually, mountains gave way to flatlands. Gabriella directed them, unfailingly pointing due west.

The men's continued silence worried Ian. Even if they were not mortal, they should still have been shocked after witnessing Gabriella's transformation. Asking questions would be a perfectly natural reaction, yet they'd asked none. They seemed unperturbed, with a single minded purpose. It was this secrecy twisting at his gut. Perhaps they should turn back, forget the dagger for now.

He rode up beside Gabriella, watching as she moved her hand. Fingers pointed to the ground like a witching stick. Her skin glowed soft white in the pale light. With closed eyes, she appeared to be in a trance.

The camels mewled nervously, and he swiveled in his saddle.

The huge Siberian tiger trotted along behind them. Since the cat was out of the bag, so to speak, Sasha had opted to remain in the predator's form. She'd growled something about not trusting their guides. Ian empathized completely.

If not for the burning thirst in his throat—and if Gabriella's blood did not smell do damned delicious—he would have freed his own demon to protect her.

Something wicked this way comes, he thought grimly. The beast squirmed ceaselessly in his brain. Every instinct, every sign warned him away from this desert, these strangers.

He leaned to Gabriella, whispering. "Let's just turn back. Right now."

"We're here."

Magic had been vibrating through her hands in a constant electric hum. Something had happened when she

121

climaxed. Okay, major understatement. Something in addition to the incredible mind bending, life altering, explosive orgasm, Ian pulled from her body.

Orgasm triggered dormant powers, making her grow wings. Wings!

She'd felt like she was about to explode out of her skin, like a butterfly tearing free of its chrysalis. The world appeared differently to her, as if she had just awoken from a hazy dream.

Even in the darkness, everything sparkled, clearer and brighter. Every grain of sand appeared separate, twinkling in the moonlight. Smells of things unseen wafted in the air. Desert flowers and water—an oasis many miles away.

She heard a spring bubbling up from the earth, goats bleating. The sound of the camel's feet treading over the desert sand. Sasha's heart thundered in her ears.

Contrarily, Ian's sluggish rhythm played a slow, exotic mating call. Lub-dub. Love me. Lub-dub. Fuck me.

She shivered, just thinking the words. Crude, yes. Still, she wanted to curl her fingers in his shirt and growl the words.

Ian. She had no words to describe how delicious he smelled. Like sandalwood incense—musky, smoky. Exotically sweet. As she thought of him, her mouth watered. And while her hand pointed away, her body leaned toward him, reacting. Craving.

"Gabriella? Are you all right?"

Ian stared as her, his brows pushed together, his pale forehead wrinkled with worry.

"We're here," she repeated, pulling her camel to a stop. She reached to smooth her thumb across the puckered skin between his brows. He snatched her hand, pressed her palm to his lips.

She noticed Kafele and Anpu exchange a dark glance. Ian was right. They should leave right now. Warnings screamed in her mind, shaking her from this distracting carnal hunger. But they had traveled too far, just to turn back now. And more importantly, they needed to protect the dagger.

"We're already here, Ian. We must retrieve the dagger and hide it from the others. The Seven Sorrows can't be stopped without it."

The night air was cool and dry and smelled of dust and animal dung. Ian stared out at the endless miles of dunes around them.

"I think your witches stick needs tuning, love. There's nothing here but sand and bones." And thank God for that, he thought. The faster they could get the hell away from the Egyptians, the better.

She gave him a withering look that made his sluggish heart falter. He slid from the camel's back, sighed, and dropped to the ground beside her.

"If it is around here, I'd say it's already pretty damned protected." He helped her unpack equipment from the duffels. "If we can't see anything then neither can the bad un's."

He stroked his hair back from his face. "Do you even have a clue where to start digging?"

"They could just as easily have the same kind of equipment." She assembled the underground sonar and circled a patch of ground. Indistinguishable from any other patch of ground as far as he could see. She stopped mid stride, her eyes snapped up to meet his.

"They've already been here. I can smell them."

Ian spun in a circle, scanning the desert. "You're right. I smell 'em, too, but very faintly. I think it's been a while."

How had he missed that stink? What an idiot, to let his emotions mess with his focus.

"They probably didn't find anything so they kept going. I don't see any signs of digging." She sat on her heels and stabbed a sharp spade into the earth. "But it's right here. There should be a door."

"Seriously, love, if they passed it up, don't you think it's well enough hidden? Some things are best left buried." He glanced meaningfully over at their guides hoping Gabriella took his hint.

Sasha trotted nervously around the men, snarling with unnerving frequency. He glanced obliquely at the Egyptians. They had also dismounted and were watching Gabriella digging away in the sand. Why this sudden interest when nothing else had fazed them at all?

Gabriella glanced up at him, smearing dirt across her forehead with her fingertips. "There's something here, Ian. I just need to find a way in."

She puffed an errant chunk of hair from her eyes, stabbing harshly into the hard earth.

Stone scraped over stone. Gabriella let out a surprised gasp.

Ian wheeled around to see her vanish into the earth.

He dove into the chasm behind her, leaping down the steep stone stairs to where Gabriella lay groaning on the sandy floor of a small stone chamber. The secret door loomed open above them, sand still spilling over its edges, the stars sparkling brilliantly in the night sky overhead.

She must have struck a trigger mechanism with her shovel.

"Are you all right?" He knelt beside her, helping her to sit up.

"You seem to forever be asking me that." She hissed through her teeth, her eyes squinted with pain. "But this time, no. I think I broke my arm."

He smelled her blood. Heard the drops striking the floor. *Plop, plop, plop.* The demon screeched with frenzied madness, flinging itself again and again at the steeled edges of his will.

He drew a breath through his mouth, tasting her on his tongue. *Stay put, you greedy bastard.* He seethed, fighting, fighting it back.

It seemed like an eternity before he gained control. At last he trusted himself to examine her wound more closely.

"Let me have a look." He gently tugged the arm from her side, not surprised to see the bone shard tearing through her skin.

"How bad?" she asked.

"Pretty bad. Can you do that thing...to heal yourself?"

"Probably, but the bone needs to be set first." She bit her lip, her eyes glistening. Her pain sent a stake through his heart.

"You want me to do that?" He offered, cringing inwardly. This would be painful for both of them.

She looked up at him gratefully. "Would you? Please?"

A snarl shrilled above them, followed by growls and yaps. Ian shot a look up the stairs just as something plummeted through the hole. He shielded Gabriella, taking the worst of the impact. A mass of bodies struck his shoulder and tumbled away from him.

He blinked, his brain trying to reconcile the ball of fur rolling over the floor—too many colors, too many bodies.

"Hold on, I'm going to set this, but I've got no time to be gentle."

She nodded and squeezed her eyes shut. "Go ahead."

He moved quickly, sliding the bone back through skin

and muscle. She bore the pain well, merely cursing softly through her teeth.

Her blood felt slick on his hands. He held his breath, afraid the sweet smell would send the beast into a rage he could not stop.

"It's done," he said, wishing he had time to comfort her when a single tear escaped her wet lashes. He wiped it away with his sleeve as she blew out a breath and slumped against the wall.

She wrapped her hand around the wound, looked up, and her eyes went round.

Sasha's angry growl had Ian swinging around, snarling in surprise. She sat back on her haunches, a clawed paw raised, her teeth bared, her ears flat against her skull like a circus cat.

Two black-furred creatures circled the tigress. The new beasts' heads and legs were those of jackals, with the torsos and arms of men. Temple guards, Ian thought. Like the ones depicted on Egypt reliefs. Only these wore boxers instead of loincloths.

Standing on elongated paws, their knee joints jutted backward, but human hands curled around wicked, sharp spears, and they stabbed at Sasha without mercy.

"Stay there," he hissed to Gabriella.

He hated leaving her side, even to move just a few feet away, but he had to help Sasha. The jackal beasts poked at her, slashing her skin and driving her down a narrow passageway.

Ian sniffed the stale air, muttering a curse for ignoring his instincts. Vampires. Their smell hung heavily in the air. They hadn't moved on after all. The entire trip through the desert had been an elaborate trap, arranged by their enemies and carried out by their guides.

His first impulse was to grab Gabriella and disappear into the night. He could do it, outrun them. But then he glanced back at Sasha standing against the guards. Bloody slashes dotted her breast and shoulders. His lip curled over sharpening teeth. "Gabriella, get the hell out of here. Run! Don't stop for anything, and don't look back. Just go." He prayed she would listen, but he gave it less than even odds.

With a feral shake of his head, he let the demon explode in all his hideous glory. Ian lunged into the passageway.

* * * *

Gabriella removed her hand from her arm, amazed by her own power. How quickly the bone had healed. She stood too quickly, a wave of dizziness staggering her next few steps before she regained her focus.

Shouts and snarls sounded from a chamber down the narrow passage where Ian had disappeared.

A growling screech sent terror all the way to her bones.

Sasha. She'd been hurt. Badly, judging by the awful noise she'd made. But she could heal Sasha's wounds, maybe save her.

Gabriella dashed toward the passage. A skin-crawling grating noise shuddered through the chamber. She slid to a stop, almost colliding with the stone wall that slammed down in front of her face. The slab crashed to the floor, sending up a cloud of dust and sand.

"No!" she screamed, pounding the barrier. She tried to will the change—her metamorphous into the greater creature. Her teeth grit, she grunted and strained. Imagined herself a winged monster. Nothing happened.

She knew of only one thing that would make the change happen.

She pounded until the soft bones of her hands broke. Blood ran from scraped knuckles.

Desperate, she tried her magic, raising her hands, chanting the words. The stone refused to budge. Her voice grew louder with her frustration.

Her angry shouts gave way to sobs. Finally, defeated, she slid to the ground, covering her face.

"You smell delicious," A lovely voice said.

Gabriella jumped to her feet, a scream caught in her throat.

A shrouded figure stepped from the shadows.

Gabriella pulled from the earth, drawing up the force of the raging fires at its core, feeling her body trembling with it. She swung up her hand, firing a blast of power, but the creature danced out of the way. Gabriella reeled in more energy, planning a wider, more powerful explosion. She flung spears of light again and again, but the hooded creature lithely dodged her magic.

Something sharp struck her neck from behind.

Her hand flew up, quickly finding and dislodging the source of the pain. As she stared at the syringe, the walls began to quaver. A swell of nausea washed over her.

She fell to her knees. Blackness closed in, narrowing her

vision. "Wha do ya want?" she slurred. Her tongue felt thick in her mouth.

A swirl of velvet ghosted across the chamber, stopping in front of her. Thin pale fingers lowered the hood.

Bile flooded Gabriella's mouth. She swallowed, blinked.

Obviously, once beautiful, the vampire peeled back her lips. Pointed teeth grinned from the skeletal jaw through strings of flesh on the ruined half of her face.

"I want you."

Icy hands gripped her arms, dragging her backwards, hauling her roughly up steps.

"Ian," she cried out, but she couldn't be sure she spoke aloud. She drifted in a dream of dark shadows and silken whispers. Her head fell forward, her chin resting on her chest. She struggled to stay awake, but it was useless. Whatever drugs they'd used had paralyzed her muscles.

Please live, Ian. Find me. She willed him to hear her with her last conscious thought.

* * * *

Through inches of stone, Ian heard Gabriella's cry. His roar shook the walls. Desperation drove him to the edge of madness, but demi-gods and vampires swelled around them. He could do nothing more than fight to stay alive.

With his back pressed against Sasha's, they battled beside a golden altar. The petrified body of Osiris lay wrapped clothed in rotting finery. The eternally erect phallus of the dagger stood straight out from his groin.

"You sought to steal our charge," a Jackal said in Kafele's voice. "These vampire's came ahead, warned us of your treachery."

"You're wrong. These vampires came to steal it. Yes, we were going to take the dagger, but only to hide it from them."

The tiger tilted a chin to the twisted pale monsters. Black eyes glared back in the dim torchlight.

Ian scanned the room, looking for any escape, but the chamber was small, its walls solid stone. Given time he could dig his way out. To save Gabriella he would claw his way out of hell. But he had no time.

"Liar!" Kafelle lunged at Sasha. She dodged the spear, leaping on top of the shrine.

She phased instantly to human, snatching the dagger

from the sacred body.

Screams of fury filled the chamber. Ian remained in a ready crouch.

"Catch," Sasha said, tossing him the dagger.

He snatched it from the air. Spears soared past his head.

"No!" he shouted.

Blade after blade pierced Sasha's body.

She screamed fiercely. The scream turned into a roar as she phased back to the tiger, lunging at her attackers. Sharp teeth ripped into a jackal's neck, tearing out his throat. She tossed him aside, shredding apart two vampires even as they tried to corner her.

Ian hurled himself at the closest vampire. His dagger swiped the air, killing the closest. He swung his sword, beheading one after another.

Sasha continued to slash and rip their attackers. Unstoppable, he thought. His heart surged watching her fight. Blood flowed from her wounds, snorting from her flared nostrils with every rasping breath.

No matter how many he killed, the vampires still swarmed him. He struck blow after blow.

He saw the trick a moment too late.

As others kept him busy, one slipped in fast enough to plunge a needle into his heart. His breath caught. Red fury swam in his eyes as his body froze and then fell limp.

Cyanide. It would take all of his demon's effort to purge the poison from his heart.

As he dropped to the stone floor, a sneering vampire pried the weapons from his hands.

Sasha continued to fight. A spear struck her mid-leap, the force throwing her back. Her body twisted, her back arched in pain. Ian never felt so impotent, watching as she struck the ground and slid, stopping just feet away from him.

Her ice blue eyes stared, unseeing, even as the cat gave way to the girl. She looked impossibly small and vulnerable. What a nightmare. Sasha could not be dead. But not one muscle flinched when she struck the floor.

The Anubis creature raised his hands to the vampire who held the dagger. "Thank you for your service," Kafelle said. "Your warning has saved Osiris from these evil plunderers and we are in your debt."

Fool. Ian thought and rolled his eyes up to Kafelle,

who'd obviously expected them to return the dagger.

They did. The vampire plunged the blade into the Egyptian's chest. More fighting ensued.

Ian closed his eyes, the pain spreading, burning like fire from the inside.

"What do we do with him?" A heavy shoe kicked his ribs, cracking several and puncturing his lung. Ian had no idea how much time had passed or where he lay.

"Enough. Lilith said to bring him back alive."

Cold hands dragged him into the hall. He caught drifting scents of blood—smelled ancient, musty air. They were still in the chamber. His captors dropped him brusquely onto the passage floor. He slipped in and out of consciousness, listening to vampire nails digging through sandstone.

Fresh night air blew over his face when the claws broke through the wall. Gabriella's scent hung like smoke in the antechamber, filling his aching lungs. He forced his lids apart for one last look at the chamber behind him. The smell of blood tainted the air like poisonous gas. One last look at Sasha and his eyes flashed a little wider. Anpu, now human and bleeding, knelt over her, tugging the spears from her body.

Perhaps it was the poison, or more likely, a trick of the heart. But Ian was sure he saw her blink.

Pain squeezed his eyes closed, and his thoughts disconnected. He fought to stay conscious, but the demon prevented him from shock by forcing him to sleep. Before he succumbed, he summoned Gabriella to his mind, wanting her face to be his last flash of memory.

With thoughts of her, came questions. How had this happened? How had she engrained herself in his heart so quickly?

She had. She'd restored his life. He almost laughed at the irony.

Won and lost in one night.

CHAPTER FIFTEEN ✝

December 11th The Catacombs, Paris

Gabriella gasped awake. Panicked, blind, she grappled to touch her face, but she couldn't move her arms. Something cold and rigid dug into her wrists holding them back.

She blinked, feeling her eyes behind the lids. A good sign, she hoped. And no pain. If they'd blinded her, there'd have to be pain.

She sat up, tugged her arms into her lap. Metal dragged over stone. Chains. She moved her feet, feeling the shackles around her ankles.

Where am I?

Memories flashed into her mind. She had no idea how she's gotten to this place, wherever she was. She moved to her knees, hoping to feel around, but the pain in her head nearly flattened her. Nausea roiled around her stomach from the effort of sitting up.

This must be the after affects from the drug.

The drug.

She'd been in a cave. No, not a cave, an underground room. Was she still there? No, it's too dark. There were stars in that chamber, she remembered the sky. And the smell of old air, dirt. This place smelled wrong. Like death. Death and filth.

She struggled to stand, but pain stabbed inside her head, dropping her to her hands and knees. She retched over and over, but only bile burned up her throat. She shivered violently, and realized she was naked.

"Where am I?" she screamed, but her throat was parched, and her voice came out in nothing more than a rasp.

Starving and thirsty, she felt around for her backpack, for its stash of power bars and a canteen.

Her backpack.

More frantically, she swept the floor, straining the

chains to their limits. She curled her arms around her knees and thought.

She remembered everything—Ian trapped behind that stone wall, the Requiem, and her journal.

Everything was lost.

Desperately, she flipped the filthy mattress that took up most of the floor. The straw stuffing reeked of urine and feces, and of course her things weren't there. Ripened by her stirring, the stench stung her eyes, bringing on a new wave of nausea. No air flowed in this stinking place.

Again she tested her limits, scraping her body against the stone and stick walls surrounding her on three sides. Such a small space, she couldn't even stretch out on this floor. Not that it mattered. She didn't plan on staying here very long.

Her hands struck bars, old rusted iron. She squeezed the rods, calling up her magic. Metal deteriorated under her hands with little effort. Some light would be nice, she thought.

"I wouldn't do that if I were you."

Gabriella gasped, stumbling against the wall. She recognized the voice. The scarred woman from the chamber. Had she been here since Gabriella awoke? Watching her while she lay unconscious? How incredibly sick.

"Where am I?" she asked, unable to speak in more than a whisper. Her fingers dug at the steel bands at her wrists. Heat flared in her hands, stretching the manacle.

A lantern blazed. She blinked as bright light burned her eyes.

"My god, this can't be real." But she knew it was, very real.

She'd not been scraping against stones.

From every wall, skulls grinned at her, resting atop their nests of piled bones.

The woman grinned through her shredded skin. A bizarre small boy gripped her robe with filthy, too large hands. He hid his face in the velvet folds, though Gabriella could clearly see his thick brow and a pointed ear. His clothes were tattered and two sizes too small. Blond hair sprouted in patches from his misshapen head.

What abomination was he? Clearly not human. She'd seen every disease, every deformity, but this was no mortal affliction. Yet, he was a child.

"If you continue to try to free yourself, he will die."

The woman swung the lantern around and stepped back. Light cast into the cell across the narrow passage.

"Ian!" She grabbed the bars, pressed her forehead to them.

The silver shackles that held his wrists, ankles and neck were lined with inward facing spikes. Pure silver, she guessed, or he'd have easily freed himself. Ian's demon held him in an unnatural pose, only his shoulders and buttocks touching the ground. The rest of his body lay rigid at twisted angles, keeping his skin from piercing the deadly barbs.

"I am Lilith, and you are my most precious chosen Vessel." The woman's voice coiled around her like a venomous snake. "You are strong and beautiful."

The woman's ruined face twitched at the words, as if it hurt to speak them. "I cannot have you escape, so I've added these safeguards." She swiped a hand through the bars of Ian's cell. A cranking noise sounded and the chain at his neck pulled tauter. Ian hissed, gritting his teeth as the spike bore a small hole in his flesh.

"No! Stop it. Leave him alone."

"You see how this works. If you try to free your protector, the chains will pull too far apart for him to hold himself like that. And if you escape and leave him behind, he dies. That simple." Madness and rage flashed in her eyes.

A madwoman held the fate of her beloved. Gabriella backed away from the bars, filled with crippling terror.

The boy at Lilith's skirt tilted a round cheek, one brown eye staring curiously at Gabriella.

"Don't...please, don't do anything. I'll stay, I swear it," she whispered.

"No!" Ian roared.

Lilith crouched, sharp tips rippling over her teeth. "Remember what I said."

Anger fired up from Gabriella's very center.

"Let me tell you something, hag. The only thing protecting you is his life. If he dies, you're next."

The child poked his head out, his lips raised over rows of sharp teeth. Despite his frightful looks, Gabriella felt sorry for the creature. Moon pale skin and pointed ears, his hands curled in oafish claws. Half child, half vampire, she guessed.

"Your idle threats do not frighten me, mortal." Lilith swirled away in a billow of black velvet. The boy nearly stumbled, working hard to hold on to the robes, but the woman moved as if she didn't notice. Or care.

The lantern went out, plunging them into darkness.

Gabriella sniffed the air, trying to gauge if Lilith was gone, or if she might be eavesdropping just out of sight. But there were too many smells, and her powers grew weak. She held out her hands, searching for energy. Nothing lingered here but death.

"Ian, they have the Requiem." She hung her head, sick with guilt. How could she have been so selfish, insisting she keep it with her?

"It's not your fault," he said, reading her thoughts. "They're well organized, and they seem to have eyes everywhere."

"A spy." It wasn't a question.

"Aye, afraid so."

"God help your friends."

"There's no god for the likes of us."

"Don't say that."

"Why not? 'Tis true enough. Our kind are killers. Every one of us is tainted by innocent blood."

"But it wasn't your fault. You have a demon inside you. There's no being in the universe who could judge you as anything but a good man, Ian. You have a hero's heart."

He laughed bitterly. "Some hero I am, eh? I can't even wiggle my toes."

Her throat tightened. She smiled through the ache in her chest, loving his humor. Loving him.

"Tell me where you come from," she said, desperate to know everything about him.

"I was born somewhere around 1520. My parents were casualties of the English—Scottish wars. I was too young to care for myself, and I had no choice but to live with a spinster aunt who wanted a child as much as she wanted a raging case of smallpox. Still, she fed me enough to keep me alive. As soon as I was strong enough to hold an axe, I ran off to fight. Joined the army of the Earl of Arran."

"Oh no, Ian." The words slipped out before she could stop them. She knew what must follow, and it pained her heart to hear him speak the words. But she had given herself to him, a life bond, and she had to learn all she could.

"'Twasn't so bad. I learned to use a bow and sword. As the older more experienced fell, I moved quickly up the ranks."

"How awful. Your whole life was centered around

death."

"I lasted longer than most. But in the end, it was an insignificant mortal death. We were outnumbered by ten thousand, our enemies armed with far superior weapons. Guns. I can tell by your reaction you've heard of it—the Battle of Pinkie Cleugh."

"Yes. It was a slaughter."

"Aye, and good feeding for a vampire who wanted nothing more than to end the sufferin' of dyin' men."

"But he changed you—Erik?"

"I begged him to change me. I wanted his power, his immortality. He obliged, and I cursed him every day after, though he explained well enough what I'd be getting into."

His affectionate chuckle stung her heart. Why couldn't they have crossed paths centuries ago? So much missed time. If only she'd met him before.

"What about the woman...Angelica?" She bit her lip, hating herself for asking, but she had to know.

His silence twisted sharp and gut deep.

"Gabriella, I'll not lie to you. Not ever, that's my solemn word. Angelica always belonged to Erik. He left us for a while, not by choice, and he made me promise to protect her. After a while, I thought he was gone from our lives forever, and I allowed myself..."

Gabriella sat back against the lumpy wall of skulls and bones, swallowing the painful thickness in her throat. She changed her mind. She didn't want to hear this. The urge to tell him to shut up grew so strong, she curled her lips between her teeth to stop the words. She'd been the one to ask, now she'd listen.

"I thought I was in love with her. But it was a sick obsession that grew inside me, took me over, made me crazy. Almost killed me. Until I met you. And now I'm sure, what I felt for her was never really love."

She sucked in her breath, straining to listen. Surely, she must have heard wrong.

He laughed his throaty chuckle. "I think you had a cupid's arrow in that gun."

She smiled at the memory, which seemed like it happened weeks in the past.

"You cast a spell on me, Gabriella. And you broke a spell. Years of self imposed exile for nothing but an infatuation. How clearly I see that now. I know we only met a few days ago, but you cast a net around my heart, rescued me from a sea of despair, and laid me out on sands of joy, warmed by your radiant love." The last words faltered, his voice growing hoarse. "You saved me from myself. I can only hope I've given you a fraction of that happiness."

Her throat swelled with emotion, choking off her words. A fraction? How could she tell him without him thinking her insane? How trite, how cliché to tell him he was the one she'd been waiting for, searching for. But the truth remained. Her soul had bonded with his. He was as much a part of her as her breath, her sight, the beating of her heart. To lose him now would shred her into irreparable pieces.

"You must free yourself." His voice broke through her heartache.

"What?"

"Gabriella, do you really believe they'll allow us to survive this torture? Save yourself, now. I order you!"

She lunged forward, clenching the bars. They crumbled in her hands, metal flakes pouring like sand over her bare feet. "If I were in there, would you leave me behind?"

"The situation's not reversed," he bellowed.

She flinched at his inhuman roar, stumbling back and landing hard on her ass.

He growled, "Whatever your destiny, are you willing to let it die here in this—this hell pit?"

"Ian, I can't leave you." She curled her knees to her chest, wrapping her arms around them.

"Then, you've betrayed us both."

"No," she choked out. How could she tell him? How could she not...? "You saved me, too. Ian, you are my destiny."

She could not leave him. If he died, she would follow him gladly into the next world.

CHAPTER SIXTEEN ✝

December 12th The Catacombs, Paris

Lilith knew divination had led her to these secret chambers. At first she'd grown despondent exploring the catacombs, finding them much too public for her use. She'd nearly lost hope until the night she passed a bricked archway near the Innocents Cemetery. The dead had cried to her from behind the wall. Following the wails of despair, she knew without doubt her lord had led her to the mortared bricks.

Behind the wall, rose steep winding steps through passageways lined with bones. Within the honeycomb of twisting tunnels she found seven small cells. All had creaking iron doors behind which plague victims undoubtedly spent their last miserable hours. They were small spaces with barely enough room for a person to lie down in a fetal position. The key to the door-locks hung from a skeletal hand protruding from the wall. And beyond the cells she discovered the chamber with its center altar and the seven niches along the walls. Truly the lord's work, this place had been created for her purpose.

Her lord awaited her there now.

She set the lantern on the altar, lowering her eyes as he stepped from the niche on the furthest wall of the rounded chamber.

"You have done well, my servant."

"Thank you, my lord." She dared a glance, her sluggish heart quickening. His blond waves glowed golden in the torchlight. His face, beaming and brilliant, was almost blinding in its stellar beauty.

Vague memories plagued her—recollections of a face, just as stunning, smiled back from a looking glass, memories of a time when she cast her eyes down for no one, a day when she boldly would have offered her body and her blood for his pleasure, expecting his in return. Like smoke, the images floated apart and disappeared.

Had she once been that beauty or were these visions of what she could become? If only she could remember.

She ran a hand along the harp strings of her cheek, cringing at the sudden recollection of white hot pain, the burning smell of melting skin and muscle, flesh that could not heal. The stench still fouled her nostrils and burned her throat with every breath.

"Lord, will you not take pity upon me, and restore me to my former self. My mind is thick mud, sucking down my thoughts. I could be so much more useful to you."

He drifted toward her, raising a hand. She flinched as if he might strike her. Although he never had, she felt she deserved his punishment.

Instead, he smiled lovingly and pitifully. She closed her eyes as his fingers closed over hers, drawing them away from her face.

"Your restoration is promised with the Rapture. Soon, my dear one. Be patient. Right now your service is still greatly needed. Please understand."

The tenderness of his voice drove her to her knees. She clung to his robe, burying her face in the sweet smelling fabric. "What may I do for you, my lord?" she gasped between sobs.

He knelt before her and lifted her face in his hands. "I believe you have something for me."

Panic. What did she have for him? Had she stolen something? Was he angry?

The boy stepped from where he'd drifted into a niche, raising up a scuffed leather knapsack. Ah yes, the bag she had taken from the girl.

The lord smiled, snatching the satchel from the child's clutches.

"Ah, here it is." He lifted out the golden box, and flung the bag at the boy with such force it knocked him off his feet. The boy fell hard, striking his head against the wall, and he started to cry.

"Shut him up or I shall quiet him permanently."

She rushed to the child, helped him up, and kissed his head. He smelled neither human nor vampire. Almost animal, like a pet pup she'd had once in another life.

"Didier, go to your cell." She gave him a shove toward the passageway.

The lord thought the child a blasphemy. He would take any excuse to kill him, but Lilith couldn't bear it. They were alike, in a way—she and the boy. Misshapen outcasts, condemned to hiding in the catacombs.

The lord placed the box on the altar, running his hand over the etched gold. "With this book, no one can stop us from releasing the Sorrows." He raised the lid and lifted out the battered leather-bound tome. Opened the cover.

He went very still for a moment, his white marble face paling to sickly gray. Then his eyes flashed up. Lilith flinched at the fury he flung at her.

"Is this a joke?"

"What do you mean?"

He ripped out a handful of pages and flung them at her.

She dropped to her knees, scrambling to pick them up. She read line after line, not believing her eyes. They were pages from some kind of diary. No spells, no magic, just boring words of some expedition. "She wrote them. The girl, Gabriella."

"My, aren't you the bright one," he said through a clenched jaw. "I couldn't have made this any easier for you unless I'd gone to fetch this book myself. And somehow you've managed to let that woman outsmart you?"

"I'm sorry, I'm sorry, I'm sorry." Lilith's fingers coiled tightly around a handful of hair, yanking it out by the roots. Pain burned over her scalp. She deserved this pain for her stupidity. Worthless, she was worthless. How could He tolerate her? Despair drove her closer to madness.

She ripped out handfuls until a heap of golden silk piled in front of her. And just as quickly, follicles tingled and new hair sprouted, growing out full and lush. This only upset her more. Why would every wound she inflicted upon herself heal, every hair she tore from her scalp grow back, yet her face mockingly refused to repair its hideous skeletal grin?

"Go through her things, find the book." His voice broke through the fog.

She glanced up, her hands gone still beside her face, fists clenched. "Certainly, my lord. Right away."

And then he smiled at her.

She could not stop the sob, turning her face away. "Please, how do you suffer me? I do not deserve your kindness."

"Lilith, my child, I have always loved you. I have faith in you, for what you lack in focus you more than make up for with persistence. I know you will find me that book, but you must be quick about it. We have but a fortnight."

She threw herself to the floor, prostrating at this feet. "I swear, you will have it in time."

In two weeks, on the eve of the new moon, they would raise the first of the sorrows.

CHAPTER SEVENTEEN ✝

December 12th Paris, The Catacombs

"Ian, are you okay?" Gabriella's voice drifted through the bars, penetrating his focus.

He'd had no choice but to surrender to his beast to keep his body still and alive. And as long as Gabriella remained in this pit, he would live...for her.

In the endless darkness, he had no concept of time passing, though every moment he remained suspended, he thought of nothing but her. He listened to her soft breaths— her heart's even rhythm when she slept, times which happened more often.

She had crushed the bars of her cell to dust, and freed herself of all but one ankle shackle, allowing her to venture to his cell door. He was sure she could free herself from the final chain, but the stubborn woman ignored his arguments.

His gut twisted as fear and filth slowly eclipsed the sweetness of her skin. He cringed every time she knelt in the corner of her cell, retching from her empty gut. That bitch, Lilith, had not even given her water.

"I'm here," he growled in the voice of the demon. "But why are you?"

"Please, we've been over this a thousand times. I'm not going anywhere until I figure out how to free us both."

"Gabriella, why do you torment me? You've not eaten in days. You've been trapped in that horrid pit as your power dwindles—I see the glow fading from your skin. You have no idea how that pains me!"

"I think I have a clue, Ian. Remember, I saw you laying there almost skewered on those damned spikes of death."

She wrapped her hands around the bars that separated them, staring blindly into the darkness, but his demon eyes saw as clearly as if they stood in daylight. He turned to see her face, hissing through his teeth as silver barbs snagged at his skin.

What were their captors waiting for? Every moment in

this place drove him nearly mad with fear for her. Mad with the last memory of Sasha's lifeless, staring face. Mad with fear for this incredible woman, the woman he'd loved; probably even as she'd shot him in the chest. If he'd never sent that map to Gabriella's father—

"What are you?" he asked.

"I told you, I'm—"

"I know what you've told me. 'Archivist or Architect.' We both know those are just covers for something else. Tell me the truth. We owe each other nothing less."

Her heart beat louder, the frantic rhythm throbbing against his eardrums.

She sighed, swallowed. "They, my father's people—they really are Architects. They design and build galaxies, and keep watch over the life forms that evolve, recording their histories."

"Your people are gods?"

"They don't see themselves as gods. They created the deities that exist on this planet, gave them more powers than normal mortals, to keep order. But their powers were contingent on the faith of their followers and how they treated those who believed in them. It was a test of sorts. A test the Greek gods failed miserably. They were too in love with themselves to care much about the humans under their care."

Anger flared, but he tempered it. "Playing games with humans? Creating demons?"

"Ian, vampirism and demons were an unforeseen side-effect. And these were my ancestors. I wasn't even born yet. Remember, only my grandfather is pure, my mother is only half. I'm more human than not. My grandfather chose to come to earth, as a Guardian and collector of histories."

"Is that all we are to them? A swarm of ants?"

"No...I don't know. My grandfather hasn't told me everything. Obviously. Sasha was a shock to me."

His snarled at the mention of his fallen friend. "She's dead, you know. She was killed trying to defend the dagger, and me, against the mutant creations of your manipulating super race."

He heard her gasp and regretted his harshness.

He closed his eyes. "Forgive me, that wasn't fair. This is a lot to take in. I know you're not like the others. I know you. I felt your heart, your purity of purpose. I don't deserve the likes of you."

"Ian, don't say that. Don't make me feel more like a freak, please."

"That was never my intention—"

"The only thing I've ever been sure of is you."

"Gabriella, I don't care who or what your people are. I love you, and if you're fool enough to have me, we'll figure our way out of this." How easily the lie rolled off his tongue. Swearing, ordering didn't work on this stubborn woman. Perhaps she only needed some hope. He closed his eyes, imagining her face. Recalling the sweetness of her lips.

"Ian!" Gabriella hissed. "Someone's coming."

His lids flashed up. Unable to turn his head, he could only stare at the soft gold shadows of the grinning skulls above him. Grinning, as if they knew he'd soon be joining them.

Gabriella scrambled up from the floor, but quickly fell when her tingling feet refused to hold her up. She bit her lip as blood rushed painfully into her cramped limbs. Something skittered over the floor, down the passageway. She crawled back to her cell, slipping through the opening she had made. The chain clanked noisily as she dragged it in behind her and pressed herself into the corner.

Feet scraped unevenly over the stone floor. Her heart sped up as the noise grew closer, stopping just outside her chamber. Her sight had improved at her awakening, as she'd come to think of her lovemaking with Ian, but sharper vision would require more light. Did she dare?

"Hello. Anyone there?" she asked tentatively.

No answer, but she heard a snuffling noise near the floor. She closed her eyes, drawing up from the deepest wells inside herself, until her skin cast off a silver glow.

"Oh," she exclaimed.

The deformed child creature stumbled back from where he squatted by the iron frame. His limbs were long and thin, his joints exaggerated as he spider walked, naked, out of sight.

She blew out a breath, unsure if she should go after him. *Wait*, her instincts warned.

After a few moments, a pale hand appeared near the entrance of her cell. Seconds later an eye peered at her from a face still half hidden. The child's feline nose sniffed at her, his strange black eye blinking curiously.

She reached out, tentatively. The boy hissed, baring rows of small sharp teeth, but he didn't draw away.

"It's okay. I won't hurt you," she said, scooting closer to the iron frame.

The child snuffled at her hand, his tongue hungrily licking his lips.

She fought to keep the disgust from her face. This child was obviously some kind of mutant, caught between vampire and human. He seemed more shy than dangerous.

"My name is Gabriella, what's yours?"

The boy's hairless brows pushed inward. "Di-Didier," he said in a scratchy voice, as if he didn't use it much.

"Didier. That's a nice name." She smiled, her mind working madly on an idea. She glanced around her cell, but of course it was empty. Finally she pried a skull loose from the wall. This would work.

"Do you like how my blood smells?"

The child nodded.

"Would you like a taste?"

"What are you doing?" Ian bellowed, sending the child scrambling into the shadows.

"Trust me," she said firmly. "Please, Ian."

She heard him growling as she leaned into the corridor. "Didier? Are you here?"

She knew he was, she could smell his strange dirt smell and hear his sluggish heartbeats.

Patiently, she waited by the door of her cell. The naked child crawled on all fours, his bony spine nearly piercing the waxy skin of his back.

She slid her foot into the aisle. "Did you want a taste?"

His colorless tongue slid over his lips. "Mère says unblessed blood is bad."

"Just a taste. What will that hurt?"

Ian growled. The child looked nervously at his cell. Gabriella cleared her throat, nudged the child with her toes. He swung back around. Hunger, craving glistened in his eyes.

"Just a taste," he rasped.

Gabriella gasped as his teeth pierced her ankle. She let him suckle a few seconds before snatching her foot away. The child lurched after her, his blood smeared lips looking black in her dim glow.

"No more," she said firmly. The boy cowered, pressing himself against the far wall near Ian's cell. But his face had changed. He stared hungrily, his eyes pleading and predatory. Mutant or not, she couldn't help but feel sorry for

143

him. The poor thing was starving.

"More," he said, raising his lips in a sneer.

"I will give you more, in a moment." Her heart slammed her ribs as she grabbed for the skull. Whispering under her breath, she commanded her skin to part. Flesh bloomed at her wrist like the parting petals of a rose. She nicked the exposed vein with her nail. Blood sprayed in pulsing spurts, but still it seemed to take forever to fill the base of the skull.

"Seal," she said, and the wound curled in on itself—the vein repaired, the skin meshing.

The boy mewled, pacing in front of her cell.

Snarls shrieked through Ian's bars, sending the boy skittering up the corridor. In her palms, she felt the warmth of the blood through the thin bone.

"Didier, wait. I'll let you drink as much as you want, if you feed this to him." She held out the skull, nodding to Ian's cell.

Didier shook his head, curling his small, clawed hands against his chest. "Mère will beat me if I feed him." But his tongue flicked around his lips.

"I won't tell, I promise." She held the skull to him again. She could feed Ian herself, but if she broke this last chain at her ankle, Lilith might kill him to punish her. Her only chance of saving them was to give Ian the strength to save himself. Even then, she wasn't sure. But without trying they had no hope.

The boy snatched the skull and started to raise it to his lips. Her speed surprised her as she snatched it back, sloshing precious drops over the edge. "No, this is for him. Once you've fed him, I swear you can drink from me again."

His head swiveled from her cell to Ian's and back in quick, animal jerks.

He held out his hands. With a sigh, she gave him the skull again. The door to Ian's cell creaked open without a key. There'd been no point in locking it, with Ian secured as he was.

Gabriella heard Ian snarling at the boy. Worried, she dragged her chain into the tunnel, watching as Didier sloppily poured the blood into Ian's gaping mouth. She cringed, turned away. It hurt her soul to see Ian this way, so waxy pale and malformed by the demon. Even worse was watching that child, who would never be anything but a half monster mutant. She wondered what these creatures had done to create him. What his life must be like, condemned to live in these hideous tunnels. By the way he moved so deftly through the dark, and how he'd blinked at her glowing skin, it was clear he rarely, if ever, saw any light. What a tragedy.

Didier returned moments later, carelessly dropping the skull as he eyed her ankles. "More." His eyes sparkled with excitement.

"Yes, I promised." Gabriella snatched up the skull, shoving it under her mattress before she sat and raised her leg for him. Cold fingers gripped her foot. She cringed as teeth tore through muscle. Slurping noisily, the child drank as if he were starving. She had promised to let him drink as much as he wanted, but now she worried that might be more than she could spare.

The chamber was starting to spin. Gabriella moved to push him away when a light cast over the walls of the tunnel.

* * * *

"Didier, stop," Gabriella whispered urgently. She doused her glowing skin, leaving them in darkness. Still, the child suckled her blood. She tried to kick him away, gently the first time, more violently when his teeth remained latched to her leg.

The light drew closer, blinding after her skin's dull glow.

Gabriella blinked, the brightness stinging her eyes.

"What are you doing?" Lilith screamed. She ran the last few steps, snatching the boy up by his scrawny neck so quickly, that Gabriella was yanked into the air before he had a chance to let go.

Lilith slammed the child against the wall, smashing several skulls. The boy cried out, raised thin arms to deflect her blows.

"Shut up! Shut up!" she screeched.

He crawled to his feet. Lilith backhanded him so hard, his neck cracked. He fell, motionless to the floor.

"What are you doing? He's a child, you killed him."

"He defiled the sacred vessel."

"What are you talking about?"

"You, my dear, are the sacred vessel."

Lilith roughly tossed a white dress at her naked chest. Grateful for having something to cover with, Gabriella snatched the garment and turned away, quickly sliding it over her head. Her stomach cramped, smelling her own

145

sweat, but the dress was loose and warm after shivering naked so long in this damn cell.

In the lantern light, Gabriella saw Lilith was a tiny woman, almost fragile. She figured she could take her. Yank her by the hair, pound her head against the floor until her brains came out her ears. But not yet, not with Ian trapped.

"You are quick to obey." Lilith's serene smile made her want to punch her face.

She forced her arms against her sides, lest one of her fists found its way to the bitch's mouth.

"I've been freezing my ass off in here. Of course I'm wearing your ridiculous dress."

"For three days you have been kept in darkness, to cleanse your thoughts..."

Three days? The drug had left her exhausted. She'd been drifting in and out of sleep since the first time she awoke. The nausea grew worse over time, but that was from hunger and thirst, she was sure. And poor Ian, lying so still all that time. She prayed her blood had helped him.

Lilith droned on, but her own thoughts roared in her mind. She had no idea what this lunatic was ranting about, but she knew she wouldn't like whatever was coming.

"Bring her out of the cell," Lilith instructed the boy.

To Gabriella's shock, the vampire child sat up, rolling his neck until it cracked. He stood with a stoop, taking the offered key from Lilith. He wouldn't look at Gabriella as he unlocked her chain from the wall.

She wanted to apologize. She'd never meant him to get in trouble, but she feared speaking to him might make things worse for the boy.

"She's staring at me!" he whined to Lilith, and he hissed at Gabriella.

Watching him, listening to his childish speech made her heart ache for him.

Lilith grinned at Gabriella. "Didi was an experiment. We wanted to see how children handled the transformation. Unfortunately, at this age, they have little control over the demon. But he's a good boy." She slid a finger under his chin and lifted it. "Aren't you, my pet?"

Gabriella stared in horror as his demonic features smoothed into a cherubic smile, hair growing into thick gold curls, his bony body full and flush. How easily this one could lure his prey! In his human form, he was beautiful.

"Come, the lord awaits us," Lilith said. The child tugged

her chain.

The lord? She already knew this woman was insane, but what madness had she planned?

"I'm not leaving here." She crossed her arms, trying to keep her heart steady, afraid to betray her terror. "I won't leave Ian. He's the only reason I've stayed so long."

"Oh, do not worry, precious one. We could not imagine sharing this experience without your vampire protector."

My vampire *lover*, she almost corrected, but some instinct told her to keep their intimacy secret.

Lilith exposed a hidden panel in one of the skulls in the wall. After hitting a few buttons, a harness around Ian's chest pulled snug. A motorized crank whirred, pulling him to his feet. Once he was standing, she opened the door to his cell.

This is very bad, Gabriella thought. Lilith would never have let her see the panel if she planned to return them here. Maybe they were being moved to a new location. But she didn't think so. She would play along for now, until she saw a chance to save them both.

Lilith removed the shackle from her ankle before snapping a chain to the collar at Ian's neck. She tugged him like a dog into the corridor, though she took care not to pull hard enough on the spikes to pierce a vein.

Gabriella shuddered at the barbed restraints hanging loosely against his ankles, wrists and hips, their sharp tips making dents in the flesh. So sick with terror, it took her several moments before she realized Ian was no longer in vampire form. A new wave of panic almost knocked her legs from under her. Was the demon too weak to protect him? Hadn't her blood helped him at all?

Filled with despair, she barely registered when the child vampire slid a cold hand into hers and pulled her into the death-black tunnel.

* * * *

Gabriella's blood had changed him. He had yet to decide if that was good or bad. The moment he had swallowed from the skull, he'd felt a shift in power. Though his body shifted to its human form, his skin was still impermeable, and his sight as acute in the dark as in light. The demon howled furiously, but no longer in the foreground of his mind.

Hmm, this was a good thing. For the first time since the

possession, he wielded all the demon's powers without the demon being in control. This could be very useful, and right now, they needed a damn miracle.

Ian's mind worked furiously, knowing if they didn't move soon, they would never escape. He suspected they were somewhere in the catacombs of Paris, though this place held no familiarity. Places like this existed under many cities in the world, but Paris had its own scents of cafes and patisseries, French perfumes and cigarettes, all which clung to Lilith's robes.

The path sloped deeper into the earth, the air growing thin and stuffy. Ahead, more lights flickered into the passage and other scents struck him like a blow. Kerosene torches, blood, sex, and vampire. An ancient vampire, one whose scent he knew very well.

CHAPTER EIGHTEEN †

December 13ᵗʰ The Catacombs, Paris

"Amun," Ian snarled. "I should have known."

The Ancient One stepped from the shadow of a wall crevice. A hood rested on the cowl of his snowy robes, his feet bare on the stone floor. Ram horns pierced high on his forehead, curling back into thick golden curls.

"One cannot expect a god to sit idly by while man destroys the world around him."

"You're no god, Amun. You're a demon, just like the rest of us."

Lilith hissed, snapping the chain. Spikes pierced the skin of his neck. He clenched his teeth, sure the next tug would end him.

"No, Lilith," Amun snapped. "He is to live, to see this." His gaze flicked to Gabriella and back to Ian.

"I am a god of Egypt. I remained in power long after my fellow gods faded into evil, bitter shadows of the great beings they once were, fading into obscurity in the shadow of the God of Abraham. But I knew that someday I would return to power, and reclaim my throne."

"By killing off the humans?"

"They betrayed us with their fickle allegiances. And now they worship money and power, and kill each other in the name of their gods. They are a scourge in need of cleansing."

Clearly, he was insane. He had to keep Amun talking while he tried to find of an escape. "Why kill the shape shifters? They're of no harm to anyone, except maybe the were-beasts and the snow wolves," Ian asked.

"The shifters would challenge my authority. Best kill them off before they can prepare for war. And the humans? Look at what they've done to this world, and their precious God of Abraham is nowhere to be found. He gives his children free will, and they use it to destroy the planet."

"But they've done much good, too. Medicine and technology. You can't tell me you haven't enjoyed the fruits of those discoveries. Electricity and telephones? Cars and airplanes?"

"And pollution and genocide. Weapons so vile they could destroy every living thing on earth."

"Are humans not your food source?"

"I would not kill them all."

Ian sighed. He'd learned centuries ago that arguing with a madman was useless.

"Did you know that I am the first true *day walker*? Father to Alexander the Great, the first day walking, half human warrior."

Ian's chin snapped up. "But how can that be? His mother was very much alive."

"His mother was not Olympia's. Her son was stillborn, and she feared losing her position as principal wife to King Phillip II of Macedon. I was counsel to the king and came to her in the night with my plan. Create a warrior like no other, gain her power and position, and then I would rise in favor among men once again.

"I impregnated one of her servant girls, kept her locked away for a month until she gave birth. Olympia's remained secluded during this time, keeping a pillow beneath her gown so those bringing food would believe her still with child."

"What about her midwife and her attendants?"

Amun's wicked smile answered him. Of course, he'd had them killed so they couldn't betray the secret.

"You fathered a child with a servant, and he lived? And became a student to Aristotle and the conqueror of the Persian Empire?" Ian remembered Vlad's compound, how the previous ruler of the vampires and his minions would impregnate young girls for the sheer pleasure of watching the children rip apart their mothers. Afterward, they would slay the infants. If only Vlad had realized their potential power. Thank the stars, he hadn't.

Ian loathed the practice.

"I can see by your expression that you've witnessed the births first hand. I heard of Vlad's compound, and that he would not tolerate the halflings to live. I discovered all one must do is suckle the children."

"Aye, but do they drink milk or blood?"

"They seem to require both. We find nursing mothers and bring them to our estate, to feed the children. The babes take milk from the nipples and blood from the breast."

Ian heard Gabriella's heart thudding against her ribs.

"And that's what happened with Olympia's? She nursed the child?"

Amun nodded. "On the night of his birth, I brought the babe to the queen. He grew quickly, and later he was stronger, faster than any human male. I fought by his side many times. His battle helmet was engraved with ram's horns." He ran a hand over one rough horn. "The fear those horns instilled upon his enemies was so great—it's the reason the devil is depicted with horns and ram's feet. The rest is history."

"You are a day walker?"

"Yes, all the Ancient Ones were—the original Gods of Greece. Only vampires infected by our bite cannot walk in the daylight. When the gods possess you—"

"They are not gods, Amun, they—and you—are nothing more than demons driven to damnation by your petty jealousies. And no one possesses me," Ian snapped.

Amun waved a hand. "The lesser gods and demons are more than happy to join with the bodies of humans to share your pleasures. But this union changes your physiology. You are no longer able to tolerate sunlight, and silver is..."

"I know the effects well enough, I just didn't know the history," Ian said. "But Alexander died. What could kill the son of a god?"

"Wouldn't you like to know that secret?"

Ian shrugged. "What secret? Who am I going tell? Seems safe enough to pass it on to a dead man, eh?"

Gabriella gasped beside him. He dared not look at her, afraid his resolve might crumble.

"How have you known our every move? You knew we were going to Egypt. If I'm to die anyway, at least tell me who betrayed us."

Amun's golden brows pulled together. "Let's make a deal. I will answer one of your questions, so choose wisely. What is more important to you? Knowing the secret of killing day walkers, or knowing who betrayed you?"

Ian thought a moment. Which information would be most useful to his people, if he were to survive?

"Who's the viper in our den?"

Amun laughed, clapping his hands together. The noise echoed loudly in the small chamber, startling Gabriella's heart. He wished he could pull her close, whisper lies to calm her fears. But he wasn't an idiot. Death awaited him at the tips of hundreds of silver spikes. He could barely turn his head to see her staring at him. When at last his eyes met hers, her mouth turned up in a trembling smile. So brave. He returned the gesture as best he could.

"Ramos and Catalina."

The names snapped Ian's head back so fast he almost gored himself.

"That's not possible. They were attacked, their house burned down. They barely escaped..." But as he said the words, they uncovered their own truth. Once a vampire fell asleep, it was difficult to awaken them. He knew if he'd been asleep when he and Gabriella were attacked at the hotel, he at least would be dead. The Greeks, Aeolos and Helena had to be awakened by their human servants, and she had barely escaped.

"Ramos and Catalina had no servants. They didn't trust humans," he said in a whisper. His stomach wrenched and his knees nearly buckled. "They destroyed their home to make themselves look like victims, so no one would suspect them."

A sinister laugh bled from Amun's lips. "Yes. They've been very helpful. But as much as I've enjoyed our little chat, we have more pressing business to attend to." He nodded to Lilith. "It is time. Put her on the altar."

Lilith handed Ian's leash to the child. The boy looked up with an impish grin, yanking hard enough to make him wince.

Gabriella stared at her feet as Lilith led her to a stone table prepared with blood and ground bones. Lilith put her hands on Gabriella's waist to lift her, but Gabriella slapped them away.

"I can manage myself." She sprang onto the table, sitting in the center and laid herself out. She pulled her hair over her shoulder before resting her head in the gore, then waited, unmoving, for her fate.

Ian trembled with rage, his teeth grinding, yet he stood helpless at the hands of this monster child.

Lilith bound Gabriella's hands and ankles. After feeding the greedy little mutant, Ian doubted she possessed the strength to free herself. Not that she would, knowing an attempt to escape would cost his life.

Ach, how could he bear this, knowing she'd sacrifice her life to prolong his for what? Seconds? Minutes? Didn't she realize he had no desire to live if she were to die? If death were their plan for her.

Amun stepped to the foot of the table, leaning to push the dress above Gabriella's hips. She whimpered, turned her head away and closed her eyes.

"Don't touch her! I'll kill you!" Ian tensed. If he lunged at Amun, could he kill the other vampire before the poison killed him? Was he strong enough to kill an Ancient One with his bare hands?

Amun smiled, bemused. "Why do you threaten me? It is you who brought me the one I sought."

"What?" Ian flicked his gaze to Gabriella.

She looked back at him now, eyes wide.

"My spies knew of your quest to find the Requiem. We found the map within the Vatican archives. I had it planted in the Madaurus family papers, and fed you clues to find it. I knew your Latin was weak, and if you remember, it was Ramos who mentioned Gabriella and her grandfather to you in passing. Planting the seed."

Ian shook so hard, the spikes rattled over his skin.

"You thought yourself so clever, concealing the map in that Guttenberg. I knew where the search would lead you. I've lived long enough to know what spells the Requiem contain. Did you know it was I who had Osiris's tomb built beneath the sands and replaced the Phallus, making him whole again? Three thousand years ago, I spent four decades creating his shrine in the desert. Yet for all the work we Ancient Ones did to preserve our histories, we were cursed. Condemned to drink blood for our sustenance.

"But we Ancient Ones had a code. Knowing what had happened to the other gods, what their hatred had turned them into. We drove them out, down to the netherworld, to keep mankind safe.

"And how did man repay us? Lusting after power and immortality, they could not wait to spread the plague of demons. Look at yourself. You are an abomination, a human living as a god."

"But if you knew where the book was, and the Phallus..."

The pieces fell into place with perfect precision, the scale of betrayal so clear. His heart sickened, his rage building. "You were after Gabriella all along. That's all this was ever about."

"Her, and putting into motion the events that would lead to the scrolls being sent to Rome." He bent to retrieve a roll of papers from the shadows. "The Seven Sorrows."

"No!" Gabriella cried out, yanking hard against the chains. She ripped the hook from the stone above her head, freeing her hands. She sat up and tugged at the chains on her ankles. "Ian, we have to stop them."

In a flash, Lilith jabbed a needle into her neck and shoved down the plunger. Gabriella's eyes rolled back. She fell limply over the side of the table, blood and ground bones smeared across the white dress.

Ian dropped to his knees, rage ripping through him with the force of an explosion. This was his fault. He had led her into this trap. More than anything he wanted to impale himself on the spikes—to die, and go to whatever hell awaited him. But his death would not save Gabriella. He would do nothing to harm himself as long as she still breathed.

"Why her?" he asked. "What is she to you?" But in his gut he knew.

Lilith roughly shoved her back on the table.

"Enough of this talk. We will do what we came to do." Amun threw open his robe, his erection hanging large and heavy.

Ian trembled with such force, the chains clattered. The child vampire took a step back, looking at Lilith for direction, fear in his eyes.

Good. He must do something, now. He would not let that beast defile the only pure creature he'd known in his long, dark existence.

"Just hold the leash," said Lilith to the boy.

"It is time," Amun said. In one move, he leapt on top of the table, poising himself between her creamy pale thighs.

"This child will be the most amazing day walker yet. With the Architect's powers combined with my own, this child shall rule the world and lead my armies."

Lilith kissed the flesh of Gabriella's belly, stroking it lovingly. She pressed her ear against the womb. And froze. Her head jerked up, her ruined mouth yawning in a scream. "No! This can't be."

Amun, his hand on his member, guiding it forward, paused. "What is it?" he asked, looking annoyed at the alarm on Lilith's face.

"She is already with child. But that's impossible. She is a virgin." Lilith whipped around, glaring at Ian. "What did you do to her?" she screeched. "You have defiled the Vessel.

Now she is ruined. Ruined!"

She lunged at him. He stood, shocked, helpless to defend himself as her harpy claws raked down his cheeks. Fury spent, she crumpled to the ground, sobbing.

Ian slowly raised his head, his stringy hair hanging over his eyes. His heart thumped heavily, the pain of his wounds barely registering. Gabriella was with child? His child? But how could that be? It had only been that once. Of course, he knew once was enough. Why hadn't he considered this a possibility?

Amun jumped from the table, his face dark with rage.

Lilith glared up, eyes bulging wide and wild with madness. A dagger appeared from beneath her robes. She stood, and Ian braced himself. But she turned away from him, crossing to Gabriella and raised the blade above her head.

"No!" shouted Ian. "You can't kill her." He yanked against the chains, stabbing deep gouges in his flesh. Pure silver leaked beneath his skin. He roared against the pain, gritting his teeth as liquid fire bubbled over his skin.

Didier clutched the chain, staring in panic at Lilith. Not that Ian cared. He would gladly die, but if he punctured deeper, he'd never reach her before the poison killed him. Still, he must try.

He coiled himself for one last lunge as the blade arced downward. Before he leapt, Amun grabbed Lilith's wrist, stopping the deadly blow just inches from Gabriella's heart. Ian checked himself, snarling out a breath.

"He is right, we cannot kill her. She will bear this child, and he will have the powers of his father and his mother. This one will be the strongest of our kind. He will believe me to be his father, and I shall raise him as my son. Now take her to the compound and leave me to deal with him." He glanced at Ian, his eyes narrowed.

Ian's fists curled. Never. That madman would never raise his child.

We can escape, my host, the demon hissed inside his head.

What? He thought, surprised how distant the voice sounded.

Yes, we can flee him, but you must trust me.

Trust you? How can I possibly trust you? You've ruined my life—taken my soul.

Yet as Lilith lifted Gabriella from the table, her arms

and legs dangling limply, her head lolling, he knew he would risk anything to save her.

What can I do? I can't escape this silver poison. He rattled the chains.

You cannot escape, but I can. Let me free. Give me control, complete control, and I will save us.

No. Never. I'm not an idiot, demon.

A hollow laugh echoed in his head.

And so, what shall we do? Bow our head and wait for his final blow while they make a slave of the one you love, and turn your son into an evil warrior? Are you a warrior or are you a coward?

I am no coward, sneered Ian. *But I'll not give myself over to you, so that I'm never seen again. I can do Gabriella no good if I am gone, either by his hand or yours.*

You give me too much credit, my host. Your mind is your most valuable asset to me. Without your senses, I feel nothing. I am trapped inside an empty shell. My body is long dead, only my ka remains—my spirit. I cannot make these limbs move without your help.

Now I know you're lying. Demons never had bodies. That's why you're so fast to take ours.

Demons all had bodies once. We were gods, loved and worshiped by men.

Of course, Amun had said as much. *Then how do you expect to save us, if you need me to make this work?*

I am able to take control, but only for a short time, and it will take much of our energy. We would need to feed immediately after. There would be a danger of losing control and killing innocents. I know how much you loathe doing so.

Ian considered this. Already he was starving, the thirst for blood burning in his throat. Even Gabriella was beginning to smell tempting, the taste of her blood still sweet in his memory. *But there's a chance?*

Yes. Escape from these bonds I can assure you, but what happens after that will depend solely on your actions.

This could be a trick. What if the demon kept him trapped inside his own body? Did he dare take the risk?

Yes. This was his only chance to save Gabriella. He loved her and now, she carried his child. He could do no less than risk his life to save them.

All right, have your way, but you best hope that you're telling me the truth. I'll fight you to my death, if you betray me.

Close your eyes, my host and let your mind go free.

Ian obeyed, forcing his mind to drift to nothingness. When the change began, it startled him. Without thinking, he fought against it.

Relax, the voice ordered.

Ian emptied all thought, ignoring the strange flow of his body, the constriction of his muscles, how they gathered and bunched at his core. He fought panic when first his hands turned to tentacles, shrinking back into his wrists. His arms lost their bones, waving about like thin vines before sliding up through the manacles and disappearing.

He felt a tingling sensation as his toes fused together and his feet became like dancing snakes, slipping easily through their bonds. When he dared to open his eyes, he gasped, only it was not a gasp. It was a hiss. Wound loosely through his chains was the body of a snake, thick muscles sliding over the floor.

Heavy black scales covered its body, protecting Ian from the deadly silver barbs. He pulled his head through the collar that had held his neck, coiling away from the harness and the chain at his waist.

Amun screeched in fury.

"You will not escape me. I will not allow it."

The snake rose up until its eyes met Amun's.

"You have no power over me," said the sibilant voice, flicking his tongue.

The vampire child rushed to Amun, eyes wide with fear, clinging to his robes.

"Get away from me, you abomination. Go sit in your cell and wait for your mother's return. If it were my choice, you'd be dead." Amun struck the boy's head, knocking him away.

The child skittered into the corner, wrapping thin arms around his knees, blood tears streaking his round cheeks as quiet sobs shook his chest.

Amun swung around, pulling the Phallus Dagger from his robe. "You are no match for this weapon. It was forged to kill demons such as you."

The snake swayed from side to side. "You are quite mistaken, Amun. I am no demon. I never gave myself to the darkness. I was still a god when I was murdered. I drifted in the underworld, awaiting my revenge, hiding inside this human until we chanced to meet. It was you who killed me in Egypt, not my brother Set. I am Osiris, and I have a long memory. The dagger you hold belongs to me and will obey my commands."

His words filled Ian with horror. A god had resided inside him all these centuries? And now he'd allowed him to take over his body? Not good, not good at all.

Four long strips of flesh peeled away from the snake's body. Writhing muscle took shape, and bones grew, forming elbows, wrists and fingers. The legs followed quickly and it was seconds before the creature stood on two legs, though the beast still rested on its coiled tail.

Amun struck out, jabbing over and over again with the dagger, but the snake-man easily dodged each strike.

"I grow weary of this dance," the creature sneered. He struck hard and fast, sharp fangs sinking deep into Amun's wrist. Iron jaws bit down. Amun cried out. His fingers uncurled from the Phallus. The dagger clattered loudly to the floor.

The beast withdrew its fangs and reared up, its neck spreading in a wide hood around its face.

Amun rushed to snatch the knife, but the snake struck faster, snapping his wrist.

"You have no power over me. I am a greater god than you. You could never defeat me." Fangs lashed again, striking Amun's jugular.

Ian witnessed through the snake's strange eyes, feeling the body's twists, the spine bending and curling in a way no man could move.

It's certain death to drink from another vampire, Ian protested.

Not to the Ancient Ones. His blood will only strengthen you.

Riding along as a powerless passenger both amazed and terrified him. Ian fought to take his body back, feeling the god struggling for control.

Let me back, or I'll toss you out, Ian warned, somehow sensing he could take back his body. Gabriella's blood burned in his veins, her power becoming his. Changing him. And now the blood of this ancient one fed him.

Ian felt the creature's tentacles loosening their hold on his brain.

Amun screamed, grabbing the snake's head, trying to tear the fangs from his neck.

Ian twisted his fingers through Amun's hair, shoving his head against the wall to still him while he drank and drank.

Osiris fought bitterly for control, but Gabriella's blood

worked like a shield. Now Ian controlled the beast inside him. And no matter how much Osiris professed to never giving in to the dark side, Ian knew better. The rage and thirst for revenge had long ago demonized this once great god.

Power from Amun's god flowed into Ian's body, filling him with a dangerous strength. Yet the more he drank, the more his thirst worsened. His throat grew parched, as if he swallowed desert sand. Bloodlust consumed him, and his body screamed with hunger.

It was the child who ended his madness.

"Leave father alone!" The boy shrieked.

Something sharp pierced Ian's back. He uncoiled and swung around to find the boy had flung the collar at him, holding it by the leash. A spike had snagged his skin like a barb. Had he not been half snake, the strike would have killed him almost instantly. Still, the barb had lodged between scales, piercing skin, but not too deeply. It hung from where his shoulder blades would be if he'd had any bones in his back.

He twisted nearly full around to yank the blasted hook free. But the barb went deeper, nicking a vein. Acid-fire burned through his body. Sweat poured off his face, which quickly morphed to its human form.

The boy whipped the leash back for a second strike, but Ian snatched the blasted collar from the kid's hand and flung it into the passageway.

He swung around to see Amun stumbling along the wall, blood dripping through the fingers clenching his neck.

"You are mine now," Ian said, fully manlike once more.

"You may have a god inside you, but you are no match for me with your mortal shell." Amun laughed, raising the scrolls triumphantly from the shadows.

The damn scrolls! He'd nearly forgotten. How had Amun managed to get his hands on them?

Ian listened for the voice inside his mind. For the first time in more than a hundred years he was met by silence. His body ached from the silver poison, but either Gabriella's blood or the blood he'd drunk from Amun seemed to have slowed its dispersion. Still, he watched death climb the veins of his arms like black vines. Once the poison reached his heart, his life was over.

"If you survive, we will meet again on the eve of the waxing moon. I'll personally introduce you to the greatest

159

Sorrow. Mind Bender," Amun said haughtily. "On that night, you will kill your beloved, and then yourself. And I will carve the child from his mother's womb and teach him to kill anyone who opposes me. Can you imagine his power, with Vampire father and Architect mother?"

How did Amun know about the Architects? Ian snarled, crouched for the attack, the Phallus dagger tight in his furious grip. Amun backed to the crevice. Fine, Ian thought. Let the coward corner himself.

Amun faded into the recess. Ian lunged behind him, the blade arcing down. Sparks flew as iron bit into stone. The niche was empty.

"No!" Ian shouted, banging his fist against the limestone.

A secret door. Ian had no idea how to trip the lock, and he'd waste precious time and strength digging through. He knew he must stop Amun, but right now he could only think of finding Gabriella.

He dashed into the passageway, sniffing the air for her scent.

Sing to me, my love.

As it had that first night in Romania, her blood played a hot, sweet melody in the stilted air. Still naked, his limbs burning from the poison, Ian raced through the tunnels, following his destiny, not caring where it led him. As long as it led him to her.

CHAPTER NINETEEN ✝

December 14ᵗʰ The French Countryside

Ian. Her mind adrift, the name came to her like a flashing beacon through the fog. His face appeared haloed in light. She grabbed hold of the memory as if it were a life preserver, clinging on for dear life as the image dragged her up through the blackness.

Ian, the voice in her mind insisted.

She sat up with a gasp, his face hovering a moment before fading away.

The haze left her brain, and she blinked to clear her vision. A wide-eyed stranger stared back. She screamed, then laughed shakily when she realized the wild haired woman was her own reflection.

She smoothed down the tangle of curls, examining the spartanly furnished room in meager light. Was it early morning or evening? A door opened to a small bathroom. She could see a toilet, shower stall and a plain porcelain basin on metal legs. Bars covered the window behind her and another door she assumed led to a hallway.

She was sickened to see some stranger had washed her naked body while she lay unconscious, and dressed her in a soft white flannel nightgown.

How long had she been out? Her stomach rumbled hungrily, and her throat ached with thirst. It had been days since she'd had even a sip of water.

A small tray sat on the nightstand beside the bed, offering a pitcher of juice, some saltines and a bowl of fruit.

Her mouth watered at the thought of food, but she trusted that bitch, Lilith, about as far as she could pitch a car. Still it pained her to dump the juice down the bathroom sink.

She refilled the pitcher with tap water, drank every drop, and refilled it again. Her stomach cramped at the sudden assault. The room spun, forcing her to grab the sink for balance. For several seconds she thought she might throw up. Once her stomach settled, she sat on the bed and

161

nibbled a few crackers, then she drank more water. Finally, the cramping eased and truly famished, she ate a handful of grapes.

With her hunger sated, grief slammed like a bullet into her heart. What had they done to Ian? Had they killed him quickly or tortured him first? She couldn't bear to think about it, yet she couldn't shake the images of him in that chamber, the barbs hooked in his skin.

A small flutter tickled her womb. What the...? Her hand flew to her belly. Was it really true? Was this Ian's baby inside her? She choked a sob. The prophecy foretold a child, but it also promised a long and happy life with her destined mate. Had fate not considered these monsters and their insanity?

Ian's friends betrayed him, setting him up to bring her to that maniac, Amun and his twisted servant, Lilith. She could see the creature's face, the crazed eyes as he poised over her body, framed by the golden halo of hair.

And that beast had her backpack. Panicked, she searched the small room, but of course, her things were gone. Had they found the Requiem? She had to get out of this house, warn the vampires about their betrayer.

She needed to warn her grandfather, too, and make sure they beefed up security at the Vatican. Not that it mattered now that Amun had the scrolls.

But grandfather might know something about this vampire who claimed to be a god. Perhaps the Architects would help defeat him, if it meant saving this planet. Hadn't that been why she'd saved her virginity all these centuries?

More than anything, she had to protect this tiny life growing inside her, the part of Ian she could hold forever. The light and the dark.

Through the barred window, she saw a tall stone wall surrounding immense snow covered grounds. Beyond the wall, forests seemed to go on forever, dark and foreboding in the gray predawn.

Where was this place? Was she still in France or had they smuggled her out of the country?

A Mercedes sedan was parked in a gravel drive, in front of a converted carriage house. If she could only reach that car.

As if hearing her thoughts, a man dressed in black fatigues came around the corner of the house, an automatic rifle resting in the crook of his arm.

Gabriella snorted. Inside the catacombs, layers of death had deflected the earth's natural energies. In this place, magic swelled up through the floor like heat from a vent, and she'd already absorbed plenty while she lay unconscious.

A thug with a gun might as well be a kitten holding a feather. And heaven help the next jackass that came at her with a needle.

In the filthy, stinking cell, Gabriella had taught herself many new tricks. In fact, if she'd had enough power, she might have even been able to save Ian.

She swallowed the lump in her throat. No time for grieving, not until she and her baby were far away from this place.

"Hello? Is somebody there?" A voice called in French through the wall by the bathroom.

Startled, Gabriella knelt on the floor, pressing her ear to the plaster. Should she answer? This could be a trick. But if they wanted to spy on her, they'd just hide cameras in the room. She glanced suspiciously at the ceiling vents.

"This is Gabriella," she answered in English.

"My name is Anya. You are an American?" the girl said in heavily accented English.

"Yes. Were you kidnapped, too?"

"Yes, they grabbed me outside a café one night. Put me in some horrible dark place and..."

"How long have you been here?"

"Almost four weeks."

"Are you okay? Can you travel?"

There was a long pause and Gabriella worried she might have frightened the girl.

"I-I'm pregnant," the girl's voice broke.

Gabriella heard quiet sobs.

"Don't cry. I'm sure your baby's okay."

"Fuck the baby! The damn thing is trying to kill me. I want it out of me!"

Gabriella flinched at the hostility. Then she remembered the chamber, the altars and she swallowed down a rush of bitter bile.

"How far along?"

"I'm huge, like I swallowed a damn melon patch."

Gabriella lovingly caressed the small bump in her abdomen that had appeared literally overnight.

"I can't wait to meet you," she whispered to the flutter,

feeling almost guilty for the joy of her own baby. How horrible, to be raped by a beast and forced to bear its child.

"I'm so sorry. I'll get you out of here, we'll get you to a doctor."

"I can't leave the others."

The others? "How many are here?"

So much for a simple escape plan.

"There were seven of us, but I haven't talked to anyone in days. Monique had your room, but they moved her, to punish us for talking."

Gabriella again scrutinized the vents. Were those bastards watching and listening?

"Are they all pregnant?"

"I think so," Anya said softly.

"Where are they?"

"I don't know. There's someone on the other side of you. Marion is her name. And I think there might be more across the hall. I hear doors opening and closing when they bring us meals."

Gabriella sat on her heels, her back against the wall. What kind of a mad house was this? Like some damn puppy mill for vampires.

She returned to the window, glanced again at the Mercedes. They hadn't all driven here in that sedan.

"Anya, do you remember how you got here?"

"They had us in those horrible cells...and then those monsters..." The girl sobbed louder.

She sounded so young. Gabriella wished she could hug her.

"They blindfolded us and put us in the back of a van. We had to sit on the floor. I didn't see anything until we arrived here."

Maybe the van was parked in the carriage house.

"Do you know how long you drove?"

"About an hour, I think. I'm not sure."

That meant they were still in France. Gabriella froze as footsteps sounded on the stairs.

"Hush, someone's coming," she whispered and climbed back in bed, pretending to be asleep when the key rattled in the lock and the door swung inward.

"Don't bother pretending, Ms. DeChartres. We saw you."

Gabriella opened her eyes to find the vampire woman from the catacombs trading the tray of crackers and grapes for one covered with a linen napkin. The woman moved carefully, avoiding the light from the window.

The smells of soup and warm bread made her mouth water.

Two guards in black fatigues trained guns on her, one aiming at her head, the other at the tiny lump in her belly.

"Oh, like I believe you'd hurt the baby." She glared at the men as she sat up.

Headshot guard clicked off his safety.

"We know all about your powers. If you try anything, they will shoot you."

Curious, how could *blondie* know about her powers? She was just learning them herself.

"Why would I try anything while you're standing there? You think I'm a fool?"

Lilith set the tray of crackers on the dresser and tugged the napkin from the new one. Steam rose from some thick cream soup, and pats of butter melted on pumpernickel rolls.

Gabriella's stomach grumbled in loud betrayal.

"Eat," Lilith ordered.

Gabriella lifted the bowl and sniffed. The chemical smell stung her nose. A narcotic. If she ate it, she'd drug herself.

She opened her hands and let the bowl fall. Glass smashed on the floor, splattering soup everywhere. Lilith and the guards reflexively jumped back.

Gabriella's pulse drummed deafeningly in her ears. She had less than a second to make a move.

CHAPTER TWENTY †

December 14ᵗʰ Paris

Ian awoke to the sound of murmuring voices. He was instantly alert and on his feet. Pain ripped through his body like a flash fire, nearly knocking him unconscious again. Silver burned in his bones. White hot lava seared through his veins. And yet for some reason he still lived.

Brick walls surrounded him on three sides, and a tall wrought iron fence faced the street, where an elderly couple bundled in coats and hats stared as if he were a zoo exhibit. A tiny dog dressed in a plaid coat bared his teeth, growling bravely and straining against his leash.

In that moment, Ian realized two things. He had fallen unconscious outside the catacombs, behind the locked gate at the entrance. And he was standing naked on an icy walkway in winter.

He sniffed the air, clenching his fists. Whatever trace of Gabriella's scent might have lingered had stolen away on the breeze while he lay useless on the pavement.

The old man brought a cell phone to his ear, probably calling the police. Ian couldn't be caught here. Already the sky slipped from dawn gray to purplish orange, and soon daylight would trap him.

He jumped the fence, snatching the man's phone from his hand. The yipping dog whined and scuttled behind his master.

"I need to make a call," he said, racing off in a blur. By the time he realized he should have covered his privates, he was well out of their sight.

"Erik!" he shouted into the phone. "I know who the spies are."

He told his friend of the traitorous Spaniards, and the hell hole prison the Church of the Damned kept beneath the catacombs. "Meet me at Chez Tristesse," he finished and then tossed the phone into an alley.

166

* * * *

Ian had bought the townhouse in the trendy 12th Arrondissement neighborhood shortly after Erik married Angelica. He'd been deeply depressed and to ensure no one could find him, he'd titled the property under a new alias, Armand Tristesse. An intentional irony, since Tristesse meant sadness in French.

With no handy key, he ripped the iron grate from the back door and punched out the glass to reach the lock inside. After entering a code to disarm the flashing alarm, he made his way through sheet draped furniture, taking the stairs in one leap. The master bedroom closet held several changes of clothes. In his line of work, pants and shirts rarely lasted through more than one assignment, especially with randy girls firing bullets at his chest.

Ah, Gabriella. He tried to imagine them on the sofa by the hearth downstairs. A happy, smiling couple with arms wrapped around their child, holding the tiny babe as if he were priceless. Instead, he stood in the cold darkness surrounded by thick layers of dust.

Such dreams were not for the likes of him. He only hoped to live long enough to save her and the baby. Perhaps that would be penance enough to save his soul.

Speaking of souls, he hadn't heard one whisper from his hitchhiker since their fight with Amun. Strange. Lines of black poison snaked up his arms, now stretching across his shoulders. He had little time left, and he needed to spend every minute of it finding Gabriella.

A car stopped out front, a door slammed. Familiar footsteps rushed up the front walk. He'd flipped the deadbolt on his way through to the stairs, and now he heard the gentle creak of hinges.

Still buttoning a flannel shirt, he headed into the hall to meet Erik.

Fire exploded up his leg as it stepped onto the first stair. His knee buckled, tumbling him down the steps. He slammed hard into the wall by the door.

Ian blinked, finding Erik kneeling over him, dark hair hanging in his friend's eyes. "Ian, are you okay? Ian, stay with me..." A hand slapped his cheek, but the pain felt muted, the voice muffled as if his senses lay buried in layers of cotton.

The fire razing his insides reminded him how

completely he'd failed Gabriella. Every muscle gripped against the pain, and he could only lay rigid on the floor, dying. Agony shattered his heart. Was this his end? Would his last moment on earth be as insignificant as his life now seemed?

"What happened to you?" Erik said from the other side of the burn. Ian felt his lips move, but the world faded into blazing blackness.

CHAPTER TWENTY ONE ✝

December 14th The French Countryside

White light exploded from Gabriella's hands, sending Lilith and her goons crashing into the walls. Guns clattered to the floor. The men lay still, but Lilith rolled up on her side. She groaned, her dazed eyes trying to focus on Gabriella.

"Ha, and you thought you knew so much." She grinned at the vampire.

With a sweep of her hand and a few murmured commands, invisible wards bound her captors from mouth to toes in cocoons of magic, rendering them incapable of movement or speech.

She snatched up both guns and ran to the door, glancing briefly back at Lilith, who stared at her with such unveiled hatred, it made her cringe. What had she done to make this psycho bitch hate her so much?

The day walkers remained unconscious, but the vampire struggled against her bonds. Gabriella knew the wards wouldn't hold her forever. She had to move quickly.

Standing in the hallway, she took a moment to stretch out mental feelers, searching for the Requiem. A new talent born to her on a wave of carnal awakening, she could sense anything magic, in the same way she had the Phallus in the desert. But the pages weren't in this house.

Quickly, she went to find the voice in the next room, opening the locked door with a flick of her wrist.

"Hey, Anya."

The petite Asian girl looked up from where she still sat on the floor. She leaned against the wall as if too tired to move, her white nightgown pooled around her. Gabriella hurried to help her up, hugging her for a long moment. Sharp bones poked out from everywhere. The girl was barely more than a living skeleton, except for the huge round abdomen. Would her belly look like this in four weeks time?

"Didn't they feed you?" But she knew the answer, seeing

a tray on the nightstand with crumbs from a hearty breakfast. The child was literally draining the life from its mother.

"We've got to go. Can you walk?"

Anya nodded. Frightened eyes blinked from the dark hollows of her gaunt face.

Gabriella helped her into the hallway, carefully propping her against the wall. She concentrated, sweeping her arms in a gentle arc. Every door along the corridor creaked open. In the rooms across the hall, she found two pretty black girls. Both were frighteningly thin and hugely pregnant.

"Are you some kind of witch?" The shorter girl leaned against her doorframe.

"No, something else. I don't have time to explain right now. Come on, we have to get out of here." Gabriella held out her hand.

The girl hesitated.

"I don't have time for this. Stay here if you want. I'm leaving."

"I'm Stephanie, and this is Camilla," The taller girl stepped forward, cocking her head to the one who still watched Gabriella with distrust. "What's your name?"

"Gabriella. Now let's go before those three get loose." She nodded to the now conscious guards and Lilith, all struggling against their bonds. Furious snarls muffled behind the vampire's sealed lips.

In the next room, they found red-haired Marion lying on her bed. Like the rest of them she was dressed in white flannel. Her tray of food was untouched. Her chalky face worried Gabriella. The girl was obviously ill.

"I cannot move," she said in a Scottish brogue. Ian's face flashed in Gabriella's mind.

Blinking back tears, she slung the gun straps over her shoulders before bending to lift Marion from her bed. She carried her into the hall, propping her against the wall.

"Move as slowly as you need to, but keep moving," she said.

Stephanie hurried to put an arm around Marion's waist.

At a turn in the hall, Gabriella signaled the girls to stay behind her. She took a breath, digging deep for courage. Too many lives depended on her. She must save these girls, but her first priority was the child in her own belly. She formed a fireball between her palms, keeping the throbbing energy ready to fling. She took a breath and leapt around the corner.

Wow, this place must be huge, she thought, staring down an empty corridor. Her hands tingled, absorbing the energy back through her skin.

The hallway overlooked an opulent marble foyer, with a wide winding staircase and a fancy wooden railing. Colorful prisms painted the upstairs walls from the stained glass window above the double front doors. Somewhere in the house, she heard a television and children's voices.

Children. This place was not only a nursery, but a day walker daycare. All these children raised to hate and kill. Anger sent sparks spraying from her fingertips. She drew in a deep breath, forcing herself to relax before she gave them away with a fireworks display.

Five more doors ran along the wall, meeting another corner at the end of the hall. She splayed her fingers, sending out sensors, but these rooms were empty. If there were others, they must be down the next corridor.

"Wait right here," she ordered the girls, who waited, huddled out of sight against the wall. "There might be guards making rounds, and there's definitely someone downstairs."

Gabriella dashed to the next hallway. Six more doors waited around the corner. Pushing energy in the air, she flung them wide open. The stench of blood hit her instantly, so strong it nearly gagged her. Dashing inside the first bedroom, she found the source.

"Aw, damn."

Once beautiful, the girl's face was forever frozen in an agonized scream. Blonde hair tangled over her pillow, matted with dried sweat. A terrible sight, but the true horror was the girl's belly. Skin had been shredded from the inside, tearing apart the flesh. Blood soaked the bed, pooling on the wooden floor.

Shock and panic nearly immobilized her. She placed a hand on her own belly. Would that happen to her in a month? Would her child rip itself free from her womb? Oh, stars, it couldn't be.

Something squeaked beneath the bed. If she hadn't been frozen in place she might have fled. Instead she took a moment to collect her nerve, setting the guns against the wall before dropping to her knees. She kept a shaky hand filled with fire, ready to blast any boogiemen. Cautiously, slowly, she lifted the bed skirt.

In a puddle of congealing blood, a baby lay on its stomach, struggling to lift its wobbly head.

The epiphany was a sickening confirmation of what her heart already knew. This was how Amun was getting his Day Walkers. And this was the key—a mortal mother.

Streaked with blood, its hair plastered to its tiny skull, the child looked at her and smiled. Gabriella cringed, half expecting rows of fangs, but toothless gums filled the baby's mouth, like any other infant.

Despite the obvious impossibility, this child appeared to be a few months old.

It squealed excitedly, wiggling so hard it rolled onto its back.

Gabriella retched, covered her mouth with her hand.

The baby's belly appeared painted in blood. A gray-purple umbilical cord sprouted from its naval, attached to a gory bulb of membrane. Of course, there'd been no one here to cut the cord.

The child looked at her, upside down now, and cooed.

So sweet and seemingly harmless, tiny arms waved and legs kicked. Yet obviously the baby had killed its mother to escape her womb. How could something so small be so strong? And why hadn't anyone been here for the birth? The girl must have been screaming.

Gabriella knew she should gather the others and flee this house of horrors. But what about the baby? Could she just leave it here for those monsters to find? This child's future had become her responsibility the moment she stepped inside this room.

"Damn it," she muttered, pulling the infant from under the bed. She had no time for this.

The baby, a little boy, continued to smile as she rushed him to the bathroom, setting him in a pile of towels in the sink. She flipped open the cabinet and searched the linen closet for something sharp. Of course there was nothing sharp enough the girl could have used to kill herself. Finally she snatched up a small pair of grooming sheers and went to work. Unlike TV shows where cutting the cord looked as easy as snipping a grand opening ribbon at Wal-Mart, the flesh was tough and rubbery. It took a good deal of strength to cut through it with the dull blades. She wondered if this was normal, or if it might be something unique to these half vampire babies.

Gabriella took just a moment to wash away most of the blood from herself and the child before wrapping the boy in a fresh towel. She stooped to collect the guns and headed back to the hall. What a fright she must look, barefoot, with crimson streaking her nightgown. Her nerves already frazzled, she nearly screamed when she collided with two young girls in the hallway.

The girls did scream.

"Hush! You'll have the guards running up here." Gabriella cocked her head, listening beyond the hall, but she heard nothing except the television somewhere below.

The girls cowered from her, arms hugging each other, their swollen stomachs pitching violently.

"Do you speak English?"

The girls, a blonde and coffee complexioned brunette both nodded.

"I'm getting us out of here. We'll get you both to a doctor. Is either of you Monique?"

The blonde girl shook her head, tears streaming down her hollow cheeks. "That was her in there." She pointed to the room Gabriella had just bolted from.

"Is she dead?" The dark girl asked.

She nodded. "I'm sorry. She's gone."

The baby fussed in her arms then, his face turned to Gabriella's chest, mouth moving, trying to suckle.

Gabriella closed the bedroom door, sparing the girls the grisly scene inside. "Come on, let's get out of here."

"I-is that Monique's baby?" The dark haired girl asked, glancing curiously at the squirming bundle.

"Yes."

"Why did you bring that thing? It's a freak. It killed her." The blonde girl said.

Gabriella tried to be patient, but she'd wasted too much time already. "I couldn't leave him here. These people would turn him into a monster."

"It killed its own mother," blonde girl snarled. "It's already a monster."

"I'm not arguing about this right now." Gabriella peeked around the corner and over the rail, into the foyer. She listened and sniffed the air, let her magic feelers unravel, but she detected no one downstairs.

She waved her hand, signaling the girls at the far end of the hall.

All six of them waddled to the stairs, holding walls and

railings to keep themselves steady. Excited whispers swirled around when they saw each other, followed by quiet sniffles and resentful glares at the towel in Gabriella's arms. She held the baby tighter. What happened to Monique was terrible, but she could hardly believe the child would intentionally harm its mother. She had to believe with proper care, a doctor could have saved them both.

The lack of guards worried her. But how many guards were needed to watch over seven pregnant girls locked in rooms? Seven girls and her, and they knew she had powers. Plus there must be other staff to cook and keep the place looking so immaculate. Yet she sensed no one moving around downstairs. Except...in one room. The children, she thought. Six or seven young heartbeats drummed in her ears.

"Can any of you use a gun?"

"I can," Anya said.

Gabriella smiled, not surprised.

"I could try," said Camilla.

"Are you strong enough?"

Both girls assured they were. Gabriella gave them brief safety instructions—how to unlock the safety, warning them to brace themselves for percussion, and the most important advice—don't aim at anything they didn't intend to kill.

"Are you sure you're up for this? If you hesitate, it could get us all killed."

Camilla nodded, though not with the same angry vigor as Anya.

"Okay, let's go."

A little mouse of worry gnawed her stomach. This was too easy. Had her wards really been strong enough to hold Lilith this long? Escape would have been easier on her own. For the briefest moment she resented these swollen girls for slowing her down. Just as quickly she chastised herself. Their danger was much more dire and immediate than her own.

Young voices sang along in French to some children's show. Should she find those kids and bring them, too? No, there were too many already. She'd help these girls to safety and come back with Ian's friend, Erik and his people. Ian. The thought of him tore her heart with a sadness she couldn't afford.

Blinking at the sting in her eyes, she sent Anya to the rear to watch behind them while she led the way around the side of the house. The girls shivered in the frigid morning air, walking barefoot in the knee deep snow. Wood smoke scented the fresh winter air.

They just had to reach the garage. Gabriella was sure the van must be inside.

She turned the corner.

"Arrettez-vous!" The guard she'd seen earlier shouted in French, pointing his gun at her head. "Noisy bitches, you think I didn't hear you coming? Like a damn herd of cattle. Don't move," he ordered.

Before Gabriella could react, Anya stepped out from the others, firing several rounds into his chest. The guard's gun fired, wildly spraying bullets as he fell. Gabriella threw up a shield, deflecting the assault. The impact battered against her power, and then it stopped.

The dead quiet hung heavily after the noisy burst. Even the baby was quiet. She quickly peeled the towel back from the tiny pink face. When their eyes met, the baby cooed and waved his arms, as if the shootout had been some exciting adventure.

"What a funny little boy you are," she whispered.

She looked around, sure the gunfire would draw more guards, but still no one came. Hairs bristled on her arms. Something was terribly wrong.

In the forest, crows cawed. Cars crunched over snow on distant roads.

"Come on," she hissed, hurrying over gravel to the carriage house. A chain looped through the door handles, held closed with a strong padlock.

"As if." She smirked.

One quick flick of her hand crumbled the lock to dust. She stripped off the chain and closed her eyes, searching behind the door for any life forms. A strange energy pulsed around her. Not just from the garage, but there on the driveway, too. The birds had gone silent, the winter smells stripped away. The air stood deathly still and hollow, as if they were trapped inside an invisible bubble.

"Something's happening, isn't it?" Anya looked around, chewing her bottom lip.

Gabriella didn't dare answer. "Let's get out of here. Stephanie, can you hold the baby?"

The girl's eyes went wide, but she held out her arms.

The garage doors creaked outward. Inside, the white cargo van sat beneath a thin layer of dust.

"Everyone, get in the van." She hurried to the driver's seat, but hesitated. Magic required her hands. "Does anyone want to drive?"

"I'll drive." Anya, of course.

She eyed the girl's belly skeptically, but Anya managed to climb into the seat.

"Where're the keys?" Anya looked panicked.

Gabriella concentrated on the workings of metal and plastic, sending out a wave of will. The motor roared.

"I need to ride shotgun. The rest of you, I'm afraid you'll have to sit in back. Keep your backs against the walls and brace yourself with your feet." She helped them in and hurried around front, climbing in beside Anya.

Anya pulled down the gearshift and pressed her foot on the gas.

Nothing happened.

"What's wrong?" Anya's voice wavered.

Snow from the yard lifted and whirled into a glaring white funnel, thick and blinding. Gabriella climbed from the van. "Anya, when I tell you, I want you to drive like hell. Don't stop, don't look back..."

"What about you?"

"Don't worry about me, just go." She gave the girl the address of Erik's offices in Paris. "Go there and ask for Erik or Angelica. Tell whoever's at the reception desk it's an emergency—tell them I sent you. If anyone can get you help, they can."

"We can't just leave—"

Gabriella slammed the door and stepped into the whiteout. Snow rushed around her, scraping her cheeks, turning her hair into stinging whips. With raised arms, she listened to the voice of the storm, using her own magic to speak to it. The winds ceased abruptly. Snow fell heavily, all at once in a circle around her.

"Leaving us so soon?"

Standing with her in the piled snow were Lilith and Amun. Lilith, wearing her black cloak pulled tightly around her, eyed the breaking dawn with raw terror. Amun seemed unconcerned. Behind them stood half a dozen more guards, their guns trained on the van.

Amun took a step toward her, smartly dressed in an expensive dark suit, his topcoat unbuttoned, looking beautiful, stunning. No wonder so many followed him, she thought resentfully. His golden ringlets nearly glowed in the half-light, his face seductively handsome.

Gabriella stepped back, keeping her hands raised, her mind whirling. Now what? He claimed to be a god. How could she possibly defeat him?

But she didn't need to defeat him. She only had to keep him and his minions engaged long enough for the girls to escape. Someone had to get to Paris, to warn the other vampires.

Energy crackled at her fingertips, awaiting her command. She flung out her arms, sent a wave pulsing outward. Windows shattered. Guards flew through the air like leaves in the wind. Half of them struck the stone house, falling still in the snow. With nothing to stop them, the others catapulted over the grounds, landing hard. They rolled on the ground, groaning. Lilith lay sprawled on her belly halfway across the driveway, her fingers digging into the ground. She glared up at her, lips pulled back. She looked like a smiling skull, Gabriella thought, shuddering.

Amun hadn't even flinched.

Gunfire exploded from behind her. Gabriella cringed instinctively.

Three crimson stains blossomed over Amun's crisp white shirt. His expression changed inhumanly fast from shock to anger.

"Anya, no!" Gabriella cried, too late.

Before the words left her lips, Amun pulled a dagger from his coat and flung it at the girl.

She watched helplessly as the deadly blade spiraled past her.

"No!" she screamed, but her voice sounded miles away— an echo of itself. In that fraction of time, a surge of power erupted from her core, firing through her body, her legs, arms and hands. Wings unfurled instantly, and the blade glinted harmlessly off the feathers, landing with a soft thud on the snowy drive. White light cast from every inch of her, erupting with volcanic force, percussion waves visible as they changed the very atmosphere around her.

Amun, still on his feet, stood several yards further away as if he'd slid backward on ice. He stared at her with a mix of rage and awed disbelief. Behind her, she felt the girl's eyes on her back. What they must think, she couldn't even imagine. She heard their whispers, their prayers. Heard the ceaseless thumping in their bellies, the rapid beating of tiny hearts.

"Anya, get in the van and drive," she ordered without daring to look away from Amun.

A door slammed and the motor revved.

Anya stopped the van beside her, rolled down the window. "Aren't you coming?"

"Just go where I told you. I'll keep them from following."

The van didn't move.

"Go!"

Already the guards were climbing to their feet, shaking their heads and brushing snow from their clothes. Even the guard Anya had shot now rose, poking at the holes in his shirt. These guards were not human—they must all be day walkers.

Anya saw them too, punching the gas, spraying gravel from the icy driveway as she sped toward the road. A scrolled iron gate blocked their exit. Its wicked spikes stood higher than the eight-foot wall surrounding the property.

Lilith struggled up from the ground, her cloak streaked with mud where she's slid along the ground. Her teeth grinned through the shredded cheek, though her lips were pressed in anger. She glanced at the eastern sky, back to Gabriella and to the sky again, now bleeding bright pinks into the purple. With a snarl, she fled into the shadows of the house.

Amun smiled. The gesture made him look almost angelic. As much as she loathed him, she felt herself responding to his physical beauty. He radiated such appealing self-assurance. His scent, like Ian's, instantly aroused. She felt his gentle pull as he unleashed the full power of his godliness. She ground her teeth, ignoring the silky warmth that falsely promised peace, comfort. Perhaps it was her own fury, but at this moment, surrounded by creatures created at the cost of so many human lives, everything about him disgusted her.

He traveled over the ground to where he'd stood before the blast, his feet never moving. Gabriella forced the fear from her face, standing tall and defiant.

"What are you?" he said in a deep, smooth voice.

"I was about to ask you the same thing."

He ignored her question, cocked his head to one side. "And here I thought you were some kind of sorceress, but my dear, you look much more like…"

"Don't say it. I'm not an angel, okay?"

He laughed and his voice wrapped around her like

spider silk. "I was going to say you look like a fae queen."

"Ha, a fairy queen? Yeah, that's even better. Enough of the small talk. Let the girls go, and I promise not to destroy you. Today." Such tough words when her insides quaked like a shivering kitten. Her strongest blast had barely moved him a few yards.

He turned to the guards who had brushed themselves off and now lingered restlessly nearby. She was surprised to notice as many females as male.

"Go get them," he nodded in the direction of the van.

"Wait!" Gabriella shouted in a voice completely unfamiliar to her. Strong and resonating, sending out tremors that flattened the guards to the ground.

Amun clapped his hands as if delighted. "Well done, Miss ...."

"Where are your human followers?"

"Everywhere," Amun said through that maddeningly calm smile.

"Everywhere on this estate? In Paris? France? Europe?"

"Everywhere in the world."

She swallowed her gasp, glancing at the van. Anya had climbed from the van and was yanking futilely at the gate.

"How many?"

He shrugged. "Our numbers grow every day. Hundreds of thousands."

She nodded. "I thought you wanted to kill them all."

His laughter felt like spiders on her skin. "Not everyone. Who would remain to serve me if all were dead?"

"You've got your own family plan going." She glanced at the guards who once again climbed to their feet.

They glared back at her.

"And my creations need human blood to survive. Besides, I am not seeking total annihilation. We will rebuild the world, the right way. Free will is so overrated. Time for a new start, a new leader."

Gabriella crossed her arms. "And that would be you."

"Of course, young one."

"Young my ass—"

"Compared to me—"

"Whatever." She had one more question. "How long does it take those mutants to mature?"

Amun's smile changed and a cold darkness flashed in his eyes. "These here." He swept his arms, turning from side to side. "My soldiers in training are two human years old."

Gabriella's hand flew to her belly. Amun didn't miss the gesture.

"Ah, yes. My greatest soldier yet." He pointed down the driveway. "Get them, bring back my property."

The guards raced toward the van. Anya tugged futilely at the gate, her eyes wide, watching the approaching assault.

"No!" Gabriella shouted again in a foreign voice—loud, echoing with layered power. The force of her words drove the guards to their knees. They screamed, covering their ears.

Her wings trembled behind her, an extension of her shoulders, muscles flawlessly seamed. She felt their strength, willingness. White feathers rose above her head, catching the breaking dawn in a blaze of blinding colors.

Amun raised his arm, stumbling back. For the first time, his calm face bent in fear.

The wings stroked down hard, instantly sending her upward.

"Whoa," she muttered. Streaking skyward, she instantly remembered how much she hated flying. The wings wobbled, battling the wind and for a few seconds she thought she might nose dive into the side of the house. But after a few scary dips, she managed to hold them steady.

Maybe she could do this. Maybe.

Daylight crested the eastern forests, and the sun struck her skin, reflecting brilliant whites and gold. Radiance blazed like swords from her fingertips.

Amun glanced up with shaded eyes, his face slack with shock as her shadow passed over him like a giant bird of prey.

"You three, stop her! The rest of you," he shouted, pointing down the lane, "bring back the others."

"Leave us alone!" The command trilled from her throat, shaking the earth.

The half vampires screeched and fell to the ground. Blood ran from their ears. Her heart pounded against her ribs.

What the hell was with her voice? She glanced down at herself, a glowing creature in flapping, bloodied white. What had she become? She didn't have time to start guessing, she had to save the girls. Already the guards climbed to their feet, shaking their heads. A few glared up at her before racing after the van.

She could shout again, stop them, but she needed

something more permanent, something that would last more than a few seconds. This metamorphosis drained her power faster than she could draw more from the earth.

No time to waste. She soared toward the van. The girls had opened the back door and were watching with terror filled eyes. Anya looked defeated, standing just outside the open door.

"Get back inside!" She shouted again in that commanding voice.

Again the guards fell screaming to the ground. Even Amun covered his ears, his lethal teeth bared at her. She could feel the hatred spearing from his eyes.

She raised her hands, swept the air with them, firing a blast of power at the guards who raced after the girls.

She expected a blast of energy as before, but instead, blades of light speared from her hands. Day walkers screamed, severed like hot steel through wax. Torsos fell in half, tumbling as feet tripped over their own chests. Diagonal cuts sliced from shoulder to waist. Heads hurled from bodies, their momentum spiraling them forward.

"No! My babies!" Lilith screeched from the shadows.

Gabriella nearly gagged at the carnage. The girls shuffled into the van, slamming doors.

Guns fired behind her. She felt their report in the still air. Ting, ting, ting. Bullets bounced off her wings. She felt the impact, felt the lead deflecting away. Was she invincible?

A bullet struck her shoulder with a solid thud. A pain like the flames of hell exploded through her bone and muscle, answering her question. Another thud, another bullet shattered her ribs and lodged in her lung. Blood pumped up her throat, swarmed her mouth.

She spiraled toward the earth, the pain unbearable. She was going to die and the gate was still closed. *All this for nothing.*

No. She would not give up, not until the girl's were free. Someone had to warn the vampires in Paris. Ian's friends.

She forced the pain back, deep into her mind. She soared past Amun and the remaining guards. Wings folded across her back to protect her from more hits. Spears of light shot from her fingertips, severing the iron hinges. Seconds later, she slammed into the gate, tumbling end over end with the metal bars before crashing into the trees on the far side of the road.

Anya stared at her through the windshield, her eyes wide.

Gabriella struggled from beneath the twisted wreckage, frantically waving her arms. "Go, get out of here!"

Anya shook her head.

"Go! They're right behind you!"

Anya glanced in her side mirror, her face ashen. Tires spun, spraying gravel as the van lurched onto the plowed country road. Gabriella nodded encouragingly as the girl sped past.

"Go like hell," she muttered under her breath.

She glanced up the driveway, nearly gasping. Blood soaked the pretty white quartz where severed bodies had melted the snow. Guards charged her - two year olds in the bodies of grown men and women, raising their weapons. Lilith stood in the shadows, screaming and ripping handfuls of hair from her head.

Amun had vanished. Her head whipped sideways, watching the van growing smaller in the distance. Gunshots slapped the air. In a flash, her wings wrapped her body like a cocoon. Bullets pinged from the feathers and flung away.

She closed her eyes, willing herself to heal, terrified the wings would disappear and she wouldn't be able to bring them back. Bullets slid out through the wounds in her skin, becoming like pebbles beneath her wings. Arteries sealed off the bleeding, but the bones would take more time—time she didn't have. She had only seconds before the guards reached her.

Drawing up what power she could, she leapt into the air, unfolding the great appendages. A cold gust swept her upward, and she took off after the girls. She saw him then, moving too quickly for a human eye to catch. Amun nearly flew down the road. He'd almost reached the van.

A flutter in her belly gave her pause. She could escape, save herself and her baby. Ian's baby. But how could she live with herself, leaving the girls at his mercy? The girl in the bedroom flashed in her mind—so young, her belly ripped open. All that blood.

She flew fast and low, catching him from behind, just feet from the van's rear bumper. They collided hard and tumbled over the asphalt. By some stroke of luck, she found herself straddled on top of him.

"Get off me, you whore." He shoved her mightily, sending her flying up and back, but her wings unfurled, stopping her mid-flight and she attacked him again, her hands in front of her, reaching for his throat.

So far she'd barely inflicted discomfort on Amun. Killing him seemed impossible. Her only hope was to buy the girls enough time to escape.

Her magic waned quickly, and she hadn't the strength for even a small blast. Instead they grappled in the road, rolling over and over in the slush. Her wings grew wet and heavy and she realized she had no clue how to make them disappear. So much she didn't know about herself—would never know.

Amun dug his fingers into her arms and flipped her on her back. He pinned her shoulders with his knees while he dug in his coat pocket, producing a syringe.

"You've been more trouble than you're worth. If that little bastard in your belly doesn't kill you, I'll be happy to finish the job," he sneered. His long blond curls blew in the breeze as he uncapped the needle.

Gabriella trembled beneath him, knowing if he captured her now, she would never escape.

CHAPTER TWENTY TWO ✝

December 14ᵗʰ Paris

Lovely cat eyes blinked above Ian.

He came fully awake, sitting up with a start.

The tall blonde pinched his nose affectionately, kissed his forehead, and then stood away from the couch where he'd been lain out.

"Sasha? I thought you were dead. Did I die and go to hell?" He joked lamely.

"Hell should be so lucky." She laughed, sitting down in one of the wingback chairs.

Ian looked around, surprised to find himself in his own living room. A fired crackled in the hearth. Empty bags of blood littered the coffee table among outdated magazines.

Next to her, dressed in jeans and a sweatshirt, a boyish face grinned from beneath a mess of black curls.

"What the fuck is he doing here?" Ian glared at Anpu.

"He saved my life. Carried me in his arms for miles to his people's healer."

Ian's head ached, and he shook it, trying to make sense of her words.

"Gabriella," he muttered, as the world shifted back into focus. He shot to his feet, wobbled under a smashing wall of dizziness and sat down hard.

Sasha stared worriedly. "Erik and the Paris band are searching for her.

"Does he think she's still in France?"

"We raided the tunnels where Amun kept you and Gabriella. We captured one of the guards—killed the rest." She sneered, her eyes sparkling, remembering. "With a little persuasion, he told us Amun and Lilith are keeping the girls at a house in the country, west of the city. He wasn't sure where."

"He could have been lying."

A striped tail appeared over the arm of chair, twitching back and forth. "The guard did not lie. Not after I tore off his arms and threatened the same for his legs."

Ian snorted. Then it hit him. "Girls? What girls?"

Sasha bared her teeth. "They impregnate young women to bear their children. The girls die giving birth. The bitch and her lot raise the babes to fight in Amun's army. Your day walkers."

Ian remembered Amun's words about Alexander the great, the woman he'd impregnated. A new fear took seed. Would his child do the same to Gabriella? Tear her apart from the inside?

"He also told us where they meet—the Church of the Damned. At least the local faction. Erik's intelligence was correct. They are everywhere, in nearly every city around the world. Each city has a leader, and they all answer to Amun and his crazy bitch sister."

"His sister?"

"Yes, there are rumors that Lilith is actually his sister, Amunet."

Ian raked a hand through his hair. "I knew them once, more than a hundred years ago. They'd been Egyptian gods once, until so much time passed that they became something...more than gods."

Ian's mind returned to the tunnel, trying to recall her face. Could it really be her? So much damage, but now it all made sense.

He shook his head. "Yes, Amun and Amunet. Vlad attacked them while they slept, poured sacred water over them from the River Stxy.

"I thought they were dead. And then Amun showed up half a century ago, claiming to be one of the ancient ones. I always felt he was off, a little mad. His ideas were outlandish, even back then. He always hated free will, he felt it made his worshipers turn away from him to follow their own will. I should have recognized him."

Sasha raised a brow. "I thought the river water had healing powers, gave immortality."

"For mortals, yes. The water's toxic for immortals, which is why the entrance had been sealed and hidden."

"But Vlad found it?"

Ian nodded. "I don't know how, but he was very clever. He used the water to destroy all the ancient ones. The eldest of the vampires, the ones who were once God's."

"So the rumors are true," she said thoughtfully.

"What about Ramos and Catalina?"

Light glinted from Sasha's fangs. "Ah, the little spies. They ran away, but no worries. My people are hunting them, and the vamp governor of Spain has taken a team to search their home, see what other secrets the snakes let spill."

Ian shivered, suddenly aware that he was cold. Not an unusual sensation, only he hadn't experienced cold in more than a hundred years. Nor had his muscles ached, but hell, they ached now. Human sensations. He tugged a throw from the cushions and wrapped it around his bare shoulders. "How am I still alive?"

The silver should have killed him. No vampire had ever survived the poison.

Something stirred inside his head. Barely the echo of a thought. *I have saved you but at great cost to myself.*

He recognized the voice. Osiris, his demon-god struggled to reach his consciousness.

I returned your body to its original design. Changed your blood and removed the alterations made when we merged. In essence, I recreated you. I am weak now, and the Architects blood prevents me from rejoining you. Soon I will cease to exist on this plane. You are free of me. But know this, my host—though you have mortal sensations, you are not mortal. Her blood has changed you, made you stronger.

Ian felt a rush of excitement. This is what he'd wanted, more than anything. Freedom from the controlling demon in his body, his mind. Yet as a near mortal, he couldn't protect Gabriella, he realized, his mood plummeting.

Even with her blood, he already felt limitations. The cold, the soreness. Could he fight other immortals? Worse yet, he knew he was no longer strong enough to fight Amun. He would have to depend on Erik and the other vampires to keep them safe.

And Sasha. He glanced at the cat woman, who watched him curiously. Wouldn't she love that, babysitting a vampire?

He never imagined he would regret this moment, gaining his freedom, but the timing couldn't have been worse. And before he could protect Gabriella, he must find her.

"What can I do to repay you for saving me?" he whispered to Osiris.

There is only one thing that will restore me. You will have strength and powers beyond imagination, but I'm afraid it is too high a price to ask.

"Anything," Ian agreed. To save Gabriella and their unborn child, he would gladly forfeit his life.

Osiris laughed weakly. *Do not be so quick to trade away this new freedom, Ian. The only way to save me now is for you to allow me to become a part of you.*

Ian steeled against the words. *What does that mean?*

You would remain the same, but you would also absorb my memories...and my powers.

What?

You would become a true immortal—a demigod. You would live forever, and you would hold dominion over the dead.

Ian swallowed. *Does that mean I'd share my mind again?*

No. I would exist only in your memories, your powers. Every move, every decision you make would be your own.

What does it mean, holding dominion over the dead?

I am the lord of the Underworld. It is I who decides who passes on and whose souls are unworthy of continuing.

Ian's head throbbed. *And? I've no time for a history lesson. Just give me the bottom line.*

Another faint laugh. *It means you will have the power to destroy a soul. Forever. Vlad once had a mortal soul. Should he ever return to the earth, you could crush him. You could crush any soul while it is in its spirit form, save those of another god.*

You mean like Amun.

Yes.

How do I stop him?

There is only one way to kill a god.

How?

I am forbidden to tell you. No god may even speak the words. You must figure it out on your own.

But if you are really Osiris, then how could you be dying? Why must you come into me?

I am not dying in the human sense. I am fading to the underworld, beyond human ears. Unheard and alone in eternal darkness. What death could be worse than this damnation?

And the most important question. *Will I still be a blood drinker?*

Yes.

That was succinct.

Ian thought a long moment. The freedom he'd yearned

for, for so many years sat firmly in his palm. Yet freedom was no longer his greatest dream. All he yearned for, all he desired, was Gabriella. Gabriella and *his child*. What miracle of fate was this?

Fine. As long as you swear I keep control, go ahead and do whatever you need to do.

Even braced for it, nothing prepared him for the shredding pain. His eyes bulged as if they might burst from their sockets, his tongue swelled, blocking his throat until he couldn't breathe. Had this been a trick? Revenge for shutting Osiris out?

"Ian?" Sasha shouted, but she sounded on the far side of a raging waterfall.

Strange feelings and memories flooded his mind. Something foreign invaded his body, as if acid poured down his throat and raced through his veins. What a stupid shit I am, trusting the demon-god, he thought. Then the screams drown out everything.

CHAPTER TWENTY THREE ✝

December 14th The French Countryside

Oh no, not again. Gabriella spun beneath Amun, knocking him sideways. The needle plunged into her feathers, and she heard it snap. They were both on their feet in an instant. She couldn't fight him, he was too strong, and she had little strength left.

She kicked him center chest, sending him stumbling back a few steps. She used him as a springboard to propel herself upward, but the wings were soaked and heavy with mud. Exhausted and breathing hard, she rose slowly, laboriously into the sky.

"You'll pay for what you've done to my children!" A voice screeched behind her and she gasped. Lilith? She peeked beneath her wings. The wild woman stood in the misty road, her black cape flowing in the breeze, sunlight glinting off her pale face. Lilith was a day walker?

Lilith raised a rifle. Gabriella banked to the left, hoping to guard her exposed back while still gaining altitude. She braced herself for the assault of bullets. Instead of a roar, she heard a "pft" noise, and she felt a sharp thump in her left shoulder. A tranquilizer, she realized instantly as the drug spread quickly through her body.

No, no. She couldn't let them capture her. She flew higher, scanning the countryside below for somewhere to hide. Manor homes on large estates, forests here and there. Everything covered in snow.

She sucked the magic from the earth as fast as she expelled it, maintaining her ascent and fighting the drug. Up this high, she could see the tip of the Eiffel Tower straight ahead, but it was still very far. Too far.

Lilith's curses grew fainter until she heard them no more. Only the wind rushed past her ears. A bitter cold wind and silence. Directly beneath her, a white van raced along the curving road and she hoped she had bought them enough time.

Her vision blurred as her head swam.

At first she thought she was hallucinating. A black limo with dark tinted windows wound along the country road, heading toward the van. Her pulse quickened as hope fired through her. On the hood was the distinctive gold R.H. logo. Rogue Hunters. She slowed, rapidly blinking to keep her focus. Could it really be? Were they searching for her? If so, that meant Ian must still be alive. Relief and excitement bolstered her failing strength.

She flew lower, in a small circle until she was soaring straight down the road toward the car. Trees flashed by on either side. She glided so close to the ground that she could have dragged her toes in the gray slush.

The limo came too quickly around the corner, barreling right at her. She tried to fly over the roof, but she hadn't the strength. Glass shattered and brakes screeched. Pain was a deafening scream in her head as flesh ripped, bones splintered. She blinked blood from her eyes, and found a white faced driver staring at her. A speaker crackled and she heard a voice that made her weep.

"Gabriella, are you all right?" Erik asked.

"We escaped," she breathed. "The girls are coming...in a van. We've got to get out of here. He'll catch us and kill us all." She managed before slipping into the black abyss.

* * * *

Sasha and Anpu rose from their chairs, staring with huge eyes as Ian climbed up from the rug where he had fallen to his knees. He raised his left hand, then his right. Flexed his fingers. They looked the same, but they were not. A new strength steeled through him, as if liquid metal, not acid had flowed through him and encased his bones. His skin felt tough, like Kevlar. Yet every part of him looked the same. He touched his arms, his chest, his face. Just to be sure, he went to the mirror in the hall, relieved to see his own reflection staring back.

Osiris had been true to his word. Ian held the God's memories—his life, his loves, his murder, and his rage-filled decline into the demon form. Isis's desperate attempt to piece him back together. Only one part of the god remained missing. In a panic, Ian ripped open his jeans and pulled back his boxers, pleased to see his manhood still quite healthy and intact.

But the memories floated through his mind like wisps of dreams. Vivid, fleeting pictures and then gone.

"Are you okay?" Sasha peered into the hallway. Anpu remained just behind her, his eyes wide.

"I'm better than okay." He grinned, wondering from her wince if he looked a little maniacal. He would tell her everything, but not right this moment.

"I need to get to Gabriella. Do you have a cell phone I can use?"

Sasha found him a pack, stuffed in a revolver and a GPS. "Silver bullets in the gun. This is yours. Erik left it for you while you were unconscious." She tossed him a cell phone. "It's been programmed with everyone's numbers."

"You all had a lot of faith I'd come back."

"You're too damn stubborn to die."

"I could say the same about you." He glanced at Anpu. "I suppose I owe you an apology."

His own memories came swirling back, that beautiful elfin face, large green eyes. A sharp pain in his chest reminded him he must hurry. "How long have I been out?"

"Not long. An hour or so. Anpu and I arrived in Paris while you two were still missing, and Erik asked us to keep an eye on you while he searched for Gabriella."

"Do you have a car I can borrow?"

Sasha pulled her lip through sharp fangs. "We have a rented Fiat out front, but that won't do you any good."

Ian snarled a grin. "Where are the keys?"

"Ian you can't...the sun."

Ian saw a set of keys on the coffee table and snatched them up.

Sasha grabbed his arm, pulling him back as he rushed to the door.

"Don't do this."

He roughly shook her off, but smiled to soften the sting. "I'm not the same, Sasha. Don't waste your worry on me. It's Gabriella I'd be praying for."

"But Erik is out there already. And you've been sick. I don't think you know what you're doing."

Ian kissed her forehead. "I'll be fine, go back to your dog."

She snarled.

"He is right, Sasha. I know him," Anpu said, and he dropped down on one knee, bowing. "You have returned, master. I am here to serve."

Sasha rolled her eyes and yanked him up by the hair. "Embarrass me again, pup, and it's back to the kennel for you."

"But he is—"

"I do not care who he was. Right now he is Ian, the big stubborn pain in the ass."

"Forgive her, master."

"I am no one's master," Ian said. "I am eternally grateful for what you've done for Sasha and for keeping watch over me, but I command no one. I prize my freedom and so should you. Now, I've got to go." He threw open the front door.

For the first time in more than a hundred years, he stepped into the sun.

His breath caught, and he closed his eyes, waiting for the burn. In the frigid morning, he felt a blessed kiss of warmth on his cheeks. He raised his nose to the air. With a power beyond his comprehension, he caught a trace of her scent, like a thin string among thousands of threads. "I'm coming, my love."

"Ian!" Sasha shouted from the stoop. She disappeared inside, reappearing a moment later with a jacket, towing Anpu behind her. "We're coming with you."

CHAPTER TWENTY FOUR ✝

December 14ᵗʰ The French Countryside

"My God, it's Gabriella. John Pierre, get the first aid kit from the trunk."

Gabriella heard a voice through the fog. *Erik?*

"Yes, sir." Another male voice said.

The voices grew faint. Pain screamed through her body as arms were twisted and bandages applied, but she had no strength to speak.

A phone rang then, dragging her up through unconsciousness.

"Ian, thank God you're alive. We found Gabriella...or should I say, she found us," Erik said.

Ian. He was alive.

"She seemed very worried she was being followed. We're heading back to Paris now. If you could meet us and follow us back to my flat."

Yes, they're coming. Save the girls. The words shouted inside her head, but she knew her lips hadn't moved. And then a blanket of drugged blackness smothered her thoughts, and she knew nothing at all.

* * * *

Fury fired through Ian at the sight ahead of him. Amun stood in the road raising a white van above his head, readying to hurl it at a familiar black limo. Already the limo's roof was dented and the windshield smashed.

He slammed on the brakes and leapt from the vehicle before it stopped moving, leaving Sasha to scramble to the driver's seat.

"Summon the jackal warriors," Anpu called after him.

The jackal warriors? He shook his head as he raced down the road, reaching Amun in a blur. He tackled the demon-god, sending the van tumbling on its side, safety glass shattering over pavement. Ian grabbed Amun's neck,

193

momentum slid them until they smashed into a copse of trees. Wood splinters sprayed the air.

Amun shoved him off, sending him crashing into a stand of oaks. He leapt the distance, landing on Ian in a flash, his hands around this throat. Ian swung him around, scrambling on top of him, just as quickly getting knocked on his ass. Above him, like some harpy from Hell, Lilith leapt down from the treetops, her arms outstretched, and her black cape flowing around her. Her ruined face stretched in a hateful grimace as she approached him.

Down the road came the sound of running feet, dozens of them. Day walkers, Ian thought. Damn, he had to do something. He was barely holding his own with these two. He heard Sasha's roar. Ian flipped to his feet, Amun and Lilith circling, prepared to attack.

"Why does your brother use you like this?" he said to Lilith. "Do you remember Amun?"

Confusion flashed over her face. She sneered at him. "Shut up, liar."

"You're a goddess, Amunet, and he treats you worse than a pet dog."

She cast her gaze to the ground, her hand unconsciously stroking her ruined cheek.

"Don't listen to him!" Amun shouted, lunging at him, but Ian easily leapt away.

"Remember Vlad? He burned you with water from the river Styx, the one thing a god can't recover from. He damaged your mind, but you're still a goddess, Amunet." Ian glanced up the road. A dozen men in black commando suits raised weapons at Anpu and Sasha. He looked back toward the limo, knowing Erik was trapped by daylight. Where was Gabriella? In the van? Then he saw them, the hugely pregnant girls crawling from the wreckage.

"No, no, no," Lilith whimpered, blood tears sheeting down her cheeks. "He would never...he is my lord. He promised me..." She glanced at her brother, searching his face.

Ian said, "Amun is a liar, Amunet. He's using you."

"No!" she screeched, flinging herself at him, her nails raking Ian's face before he got his hands on her and flung her to the ground.

Sasha and Anpu stood at the edge of the road, braced for the approaching army.

Amun crouched for another attack, and just as quickly

Lilith flipped to her feet, snarling, ready to assail him again.

"Summon your guard," Anpu insisted.

"How?" Ian asked, desperate. Trouble came at them from all sides, and they were grievously outnumbered.

"Just say, 'I summon my guard.'" Anpu sounded exasperated.

Ian grinned and shouted, "I summon my guard."

Black steam curled like cobras from the snowy earth, each shaft a growing substance, until a dozen black haired men in black leather dusters stood around him in a wide arc. Closest, to his right, Anpu winked at him. Ian whipped to look out at the road. Sasha stood alone, holding a sword in front of her.

"Guards to my right, help Sasha," he ordered. The warriors at his right hand disappeared in a streak of black. "The rest of you, get Lilith!"

Six guards charged her. She screeched and took to the trees, leaping like a squirrel across their swaying tops.

Amun's face twisted in hatred. "This is not the end," he snarled, bent his knees, and launched into the trees behind his sister.

Ian raced after Amun, catapulting into the air. Pain ripped through his shoulders, startling him. Whoosh—he felt great wings unfurling, appendages as natural as his arms and legs. He flapped once, twice.

Was this a result of drinking Gabriella's blood?

Spreading at his sides, towering over him, he saw these wings were not like Gabriella's. Black as bats wings, the bones stretched with thick rubbery skin. Not angel's wings, these belonged on a devil! In a panic, he stroked the air. He twisted to see behind him, his mind a rush of fear at the sight of the flapping monstrosities. A gust caught him at an odd angle, sending him spiraling toward the earth, with foliage and fields growing larger at a frightening rate. He plummeted, slamming hard on the ground, and rolled to a stop beside a fat log. Growling, he flipped to his feet and searched the trees.

Amun and Lilith had disappeared.

Ian shook his fist at the sky. "This isn't the end. I'll send you to hell, demon."

Although he ached to pursue Amun, his body shook with a single minded drive. His vision seared red, bleeding rage that belonged just as strongly to Osiris as it did him.

He spread his wings, his knees crouched to take off, and

as he lifted, he swung around to watch the day walkers flee the leather clad guards. Sasha wildly helped the pregnant girls out of the van wreckage.

What the hell was happening? Because through all this, the single most important thought broke through his fury.

Gabriella.

"Ian! She needs you." Erik's voice pulled him back to himself. The rage receded, taking the wings with it, as if the two were mutually linked.

In a blink, he reached the limo, whipping the door open.

The sight of Gabriella's crumpled body nearly crushed his heart. He slid in beside her, pulling her into his lap. Air wheezed up from her crushed chest, her heart struggling, each beat excruciatingly weak.

He kissed her forehead, smoothing her hair.

Erik smiled at John Pierre, who stared with huge frightened eyes, but remained faithfully in place. "Please, friend, go help Sasha and the others."

John Pierre nearly sprang from the car.

"She's dying," Erik said softly from behind Ian. "You must make a choice."

"A choice?" Ian laughed bitterly. "I've got to end my child or save it—the child she thinks will somehow save the world. I've vowed to never pass this curse to another, and yet now it seems an even greater curse to bear."

Outside, metal scraped pavement. A loud thud sounded as if someone righted the van. He heard shouts, engines starting, cars driving off.

Then silence. Even the birds seemed to hold their breath waiting for the world to resolve itself.

"You're not the same. You walk in daylight now. Your blood may not affect her at all."

"Don't you think I know that?" he snapped. Then he turned to his friend, blowing out a long breath.

"You don't deserve my anger."

Erik shrugged. "Not the first time you've been an ass to me. I doubt it'll be the last."

Ian smiled. "'Tis true enough."

He slid the hair from her neck, answered instantly by the ripple of sharp teeth against his tongue. Her blood smelled mouthwatering, and he yearned to taste her sweetness on his tongue. That part of him hadn't changed. Yet his mind remained his own as he dipped his head to the weakly thrumming artery.

This was the ritual, as he remembered it from his own conversion on the Highlands. And though he'd tasted her blood in the catacombs, he dared not waver from it.

Fangs slashed through her delicate skin. Blood splashed down his throat. Sweet, sanguine nectar. He closed his eyes, warmth travelling through his arms, spreading inside his chest, and curling within his belly. Hardening his cock with such violence, he thought it might explode. He pulled back with a gasp. Furious that his body would betray his heart, mock his concern.

He raised his wrist, nicking the vein and held it to her lips. Her heart stuttered once, trembled and went silent.

"No," he cried out, squeezing her jaws open to drip his blood down her throat.

Still as stone, she did not swallow. He frantically massaged her throat, forcing down the liquid. He laid her out on the seat, sliding his hands to her chest, pumping the blood through her veins.

"Live, damn it!" he snarled, pushing again and again against her ribs. Tears burned his eyes, trailing down his cheeks. Crystal droplets spattered her filthy nightgown. Not blood tears.

"Ian, she's gone." Erik's hand came through the divider, resting on his shoulder.

"No!" he shouted, slapping it away. He pressed harder, faster. "Gabriella, I love you, damn it! Don't you dare leave me!" He collapsed against her, burying his head into her shoulder. Seeing that life he had imagined—the life where he and Gabriella played with their little one in front of the hearth—watching the hope slipping, slipping away. "Ah, Gabriella, I'm so sorry I failed you."

CHAPTER TWENTY FIVE ✝

December 14th The French Countryside

Downy softness brushed Ian's cheek.

He stiffened, terrified to hope. He lifted his head from where it rested on her shoulder and forced his eyes open. White feathers sprouted around him, stretching from spreading wings to embrace his shoulders.

His thumb stroked Gabriella's brow, tracing down her nose, to her cheekbone, and then to the line of her jaw. Her lids parted from those beautiful copper eyes, her hair white-blonde, her skin glowing pale silver.

Her bloodless lips trembled in a smile. "I've strength for one last goodbye, my love."

Arctic coldness blasted through him. "I thought.... Your wings...."

"Too much...damage on the inside. I'm so sorry." Blood burbled in her mouth, sliding down her chin.

"Then drink from me. You barely had a taste."

Her eyes widened, fear shining. "I don't know."

"I'll not beg for my sake." His hand slid to her belly, feeling his dying child struggling beneath his touch.

Her eyes fell away, and for one terrified moment he was sure she had left him, but then he felt her sigh. "Who am I to argue with fate? I'll do what I must."

He took her face between his hands, her humor tearing at his soul. "Are you sure?"

"Just shut up...and do it." Another trembling smile.

Ripped with emotions, he ran a nail over his wrist. He placed the seeping wound against her lips. Hesitant at first, he felt her mouth tighten, the first tentative suckling.

Without the demon, would this work?

Almost instantly, small points rippled over her teeth, anchoring onto his skin. Her eyes opened wide. He stared into them, horrified as crimson flooded the whites. Blood-red flowed from her roots, coloring the length of her pale hair. His breath caught as the feathers around him bled scarlet through the hollow shafts, fanning out in jagged stripes.

He fought to keep the revulsion from his face—not revulsion of her, but for himself, for what he'd done to her. She drank greedily until, once sure she was strong enough to survive, he pried himself free.

She grinned up with blood smeared teeth. Beneath his hand, still resting on her womb, he felt the strong steady thrumming of not one heart, but two. He gasped a breath. Twins.

Gabriella's gaze flitted from wing to wing, her smile fading. Her eyes turned to him, accusing.

"What have you done to me?"

"Just stay calm, love. You're fine."

She gasped, raising a hand tipped not with fingernails, but thin black claws.

Ian noticed then the black talons curling from his own hands like falcon claws.

That lying bastard, Osiris. What kind of trick was this?

"Get off me, get away," Gabriella hissed, flinging him backward out the car door.

The twelve guards who had remained nearby all tensed, but Ian raised a hand to still them. Anpu had remained with the others, but Sasha must have followed the girls in her rental car.

Weeping softly, Gabriella scrambled from the car, teetering to the road on unsteady legs. Turning in a circle, she twisted to see the macabre appendages, splashed crimson as if splattered by gore from the inside.

"I-I don't know what's happening." She stared with glistening eyes. "I need to speak to my grandfather. I don't even know what I am." The last words burst out in a sob.

Ian took a step closer, raised his hand to cup her face, feeling sickened when she stumbled away from him, hating the fear in her eyes.

"I'm sorry Ian, I can't."

She gazed up and raised her wings.

What had he done? Hot tears glazed Gabriella's cheeks as she stared into the winter sky. She just wanted to speak to her grandfather. Ask his advice. Beg his forgiveness. This creature she'd become—this couldn't be what the Architects had foreseen of her future.

She moved her hand to her belly, feeling the slightest flutter against her fingers. Had her bloodletting turned her baby into a monster? She listened to the tiny life inside her, and her breath caught. Two heartbeats played a quick staccato. Two babies?

Twelve muscled, russet-skinned men stood around the road, wearing black leather dusters over matching vests and pants. Semi-automatic rifles were strapped to their backs. Black curls tumbled over their faces. Anpu stood among them.

Her fists clenched. What was he doing here? Who were these men? At the moment, she didn't have time to worry about them. Power fired through her body in a volcanic rush. She searched the trees, the sky, wishing to catch a glimpse of Amun.

Try messing with me now, she thought, surprised by the growl in her throat.

She glanced at Ian through a crimson haze. Too confused to speak, she said nothing, afraid she might say something hateful. Yes, he'd saved her life, but was this a price she wanted to pay?

Hadn't she begged him to feed her his blood? But this was wrong. She needed to be away from him, to think. If only she could speak to her people.

If only she could trust her heart.

She thrust her wings and took to the sky, afraid she'd made a horrible mistake.

Terrified she'd doomed the earth with her decision.

* * * *

Ian's jaw clenched, watching her soar straight up.

"Give her some time," Erik said from the dark cave of the limo's back seat.

Jean Pierre climbed into the driver seat and started the engine.

"Come back to the city with us. I'll have a team clean out the house where they kept the girls."

Ian swung around, snarling. "How? You're all trapped in the darkness. All except Sasha, and even she can't fight every one of them."

"Sasha's cat people have arrived for the summit to plan the war. Maybe your new guard can help, too."

Ah yes, his guard. He turned to face them now. "Anpu, see if you can track Lilith and Amun. Don't engage if you find them."

Anpu bowed his head. Before Ian's eyes, the twelve

turned to black mist and disappeared.

"Eric, send the cat people to search the house. We need to find the scrolls and the Requiem."

"Come with me, friend." Erik leaned forward, and Ian noted his friend's frown, his worry-creased brow.

Ian shook his head, his tangled hair blowing across his face in the cool morning breeze. "No. I'll meet you in Paris."

He looked again to where his heart grew smaller in the sky and shook out his shoulders, spreading his wings. The air caught them instantly like two black sails and lifted him skyward.

Below, the limo sped off toward the city as he scanned the sky. Finding the red smudge against the blue haze, Ian went to claim her.

* * * *

Gabriella soared through the sky, barely conscious of the frigid air, her thoughts focused, consumed by one thought. *Ian.*

She wanted to hate him for turning her into this creature. But she didn't feel evil. She felt stronger than ever before. Her body hummed with magic, but her mind hadn't changed at all. And what Ian had described as vampirism had not come true for her. Only her personal demons swarmed in her mind. Yet still, the sight of her hands, the blood streaked wings, sickened her. Made her feel impure. But did her looks matter, if her heart felt the same?

She saw him then, rocketing up through thin clouds. Ian had wings? Had her blood changed him as well? For the briefest moment, she considered fleeing, but as fast as he moved, she thought is useless to try. No matter if her brain was furious for what he'd done to her, she knew by the pattering in her chest that her heart welcomed him, yearned for him.

The brain and heart still battled as Ian slammed into her. Not hard, but enough to send them into a spin, his thigh clamping around her bottom, his arms steel bands, pulling her tight against his rock hard body. Steely muscles smashed her breast, his hips grinding against her belly. Warmth fired through her body. Her nails dug into his back as her mouth sought his.

"I love you, Gabriella." His breath burned against her ear.

"I love you, too," she said, before his lips smashed against hers, his tongue sliding in a seductive dance with her own.

"I thought I'd lost you," he whispered between kisses. She knew his words held a double meaning.

"Never," she answered, sliding her hand between them, cupping him through his jeans.

He groaned into her open mouth, plunging his tongue between her teeth. He sought the hem of the nightgown, pushing it up her thigh, his fingers finding their way to that wonderful knot of nerves.

She shivered as he massaged her, scrambling to unfasten his jeans. No underwear. God, this man was sexy as hell. He nearly burst past the constraints, into her eager hand. She stroked him, loving how he shuddered at her touch. His fingers drove her mad. She wanted him inside her. Her body screamed for him, demanded him. Her stomach clenched with desire, fire burned through her core.

Then her eyes flashed open, remembering they soared a thousand feet above the earth.

She stiffened.

"What is it?" Ian asked.

"We're..."

He followed her gaze, seeing snow whitened squares of forests and fields, gray ribbons of slushy roads. Off to the east, the Eiffel tower glinted in the morning sunlight.

Their wings beat in an even rhythm as natural as breathing, spinning them in lazy circles. Sky, earth, sky, earth.

"Are you afraid?"

"No," she said quickly, and then she laughed. "Maybe, a little."

"You want me to stop?" His hand stilled.

"Yes," she said against his lips. "Enough teasing, I want this inside me." Her grip tightened on him.

His jaw clenched as he nearly exploded in her hand. "Up here?"

She glanced again at the earth far below, trembling and pressing herself tighter into his arms. "Yes."

He pulled her closer, kissing her hair, drinking in her lush scent, unchanged since the first time he held her. Thank the heavens for that.

"What about..." He hated to ask, hated to ruin the moment.

"The babies will be just fine. Come on, are you afraid of losing your pants?" she taunted, flashing her playful smile, the one that could rip his soul to shreds. Her body shifted, lifting her legs around his waist

A growl climbed up his throat as she lowered herself onto him. "You're killing me here. I've not that much control, love."

"Then don't."

How did the world cease to exist in his arms? Only her and Ian.

Electric nerve endings fired, blazing tremors through her entire body. She slammed herself down on him, gasping a sigh. Her legs wrapped his hips, and she drove herself onto him over and over.

Could a person die of sheer bliss? Her lips met his, the passion of his kisses, the power of their hungry, needful thrusts driving her to the edge of madness.

So many thoughts and fears tried to worm through her head. But her love, her lust for this man was a barrier, protecting her from everything but this perfection. Everything but him. He was ambrosia and poison all at once. He held her in his palm, a paper flower he could easily crush her. But he wouldn't.

They would raise their little ones and love each other so intensely their hearts would ache. They'd make love, hotly, passionately, driving each other, harder and harder.

She closed her eyes, her breaths quickened, growing more shallow as the fire built. Pleasure burned hotter and deeper until the skies exploded and stars rained down.

Gabriella screamed, her nails digging deep in his back. Startled, Ian nearly pulled away not wanting to finish too soon. With great restraint, he held back. But then he felt her pleasure, her internal waves of shuddering muscles sucking the seed from him and finally gave up in withering ecstasy.

He held her close, and they remained wrapped around each other while the orgasmic shudders slowly diminished. The leisurely motion of their spin added to the headiness of the moment. The entire encounter had taken just minutes, which was more time than they should have spent with the world coming apart beneath them.

Ian cupped her head for one final sweet kiss, hating to draw away from her. After all they had endured, it didn't seem too much to ask. One moment of peace, of pure happiness, stolen before throwing themselves back into the war. They had much to do.

Desire undiminished, Gabriella reluctantly loosened her grip on Ian. He slipped out of her, leaving her achingly empty. How had he become such a part of her? She knew with no doubt that Ian was the man foretold by her people. Perhaps not what they'd expected. Or was he? Between the dark and the light. Her hand went to her stomach. Her children—a perfect balance of both parents. Dark and light.

"At least you didn't lose your pants." She grinned, using humor to quell the lingering swirl of fear and awe. The awe at beholding his perfect, muscled body. Fear of those flapping black wings, the membrane so thin the veins glowed dark red in the sunlight. She drew a deep breath and held her hand out to him, ignoring the clicking as their clawed fingers met.

Ian smiled and they turned toward the city. She knew whatever hell rose to meet them, they would face it together.

CHAPTER TWENTY-SIX ✝

Three Months Later, Early March The French Countryside

Lightning streaked across the sky, thunder shook the windows. The skies split open, and rain sheeted against the glass.

Children cried. Many of them.

"I'll see to the kids." Ian sat up, stretching sore arms.

"Are you sure?" Gabriella murmured, her eyes never opening.

Ian smoothed back her lustrous dark hair, kissing her forehead before dragging himself up from the bed.

Four of the rescued girls had decided to keep their babies. They now lived at the complex, where Ian and Gabriella could help manage the children as they rapidly grew in strength and appetite. The other two, including Anya, had wanted nothing to do with the children. They'd left as soon as their sutures had healed.

Butter yellow squares shone from beneath a few doors. The girls were comforting their frightened children. He left the lights turned off as he made his way up the hall, opening the doors of the ones who had no mothers.

When Ian and Gabriella had taken over the mansion where the women had once been held as prisoners, they tore the bars out of bedroom windows and added homey furnishings.

Gabriella's grandfather had visited twice. The first time was for their small, private wedding. He'd brought a strange gift—four giant humanoid males to stand watch over their estate—but more specifically, to oversee the safety of his unborn grandchildren. Guardians, he called them. They were a head taller than Ian, and he was no small man. Still, with Paris under siege and the London vampires fighting to hold their city, Ian was happy for the extra protection.

Her grandfather visited again after their twins were born. The old man promised to speak with the other Architects to see if they might agree to take an active part in the coming war. So far, he hadn't made much progress. They would protect Gabriella's children and no more.

Ian went to the furthest room down the hall and lifted the crying little boy from his bed to comfort him. Perses, the child Gabriella had found beneath his dead mother's bed. He carried the boy to the next room where Anya's daughter, Sage, stood in her crib. A strong one, she was, clinging to his neck, her tears dampening his t-shirt as he carried the two to the last room where another boy with fiery red hair wailed and held out his arms.

Ian juggled two babes to one arm and snatched up Rufus. Sitting in a window seat, he sang songs and kissed their warm heads, smelling of baby sweat from sleep and shampoo from their baths. Finally, the storm settled, and all three children lay asleep in his arms.

"Let me help you get them back to bed."

He looked up to find Gabriella pushing away from the door frame, her dark hair parting like silk veiled around her breasts, and her succulent lips bent in a tired smile. She lifted Rufus and set him in his crib. The toddler stirred when she covered him, falling quickly sound asleep. She then took Sage and they shared a quick kiss before returning the others to their rooms.

Her sweet bouquet sent a shudder through him, like threads through his nerves, tugging him to her. He gently placed Perses in his bed and paused to check their own two before returning to his room. Their daughter, Aurora and their son, Dusk, had never awakened through the storm. Already fearless, he thought proudly.

Gabriella lay on her side in their bed, her silk gown in a heap on the floor, her head resting in her hand, breasts offered out in front of her. Ian nearly stumbled at the violent rush of blood to his groin, his boxers imitating a circus tent, raised and readied for the big show.

Ian never imagined a life of anything but pain. Now, he lived the dream he hadn't dared to wish for. He lay beside his beautiful wife, sharing passionate kisses as her hand traveled down his belly. Ah, yes, he was a lucky man, indeed.

* * * *

Morning paused at the edge of the eastern sky. Ian stood on the terrace clutching a mug of coffee, staring out across the snow covered fields to the forest surrounding their sanctuary. Normally this was his favorite time of day, those moments of peace before the children awoke, the time of day he could reflect and plan. But today an unwelcome tension invaded his serenity. He had no cause for it. The giant winged men stood on his roof, wicked swords at the ready. His own guards patrolled the perimeter walls—he could see them from here. He sniffed the air catching no trace of Amun or Lilith.

"Morning, love."

He jumped, spilling coffee over his hands.

"Didn't mean to startle you." Gabriella laughed, clutching her own mug.

"You didn't," he said crossly, which only made her laugh harder.

He smiled, shook his head. "Okay, maybe just a bit."

She stood close to him, and he put an arm around her, pulling her tight to his side. God, what a fool he'd been to pine for Angelica for so many years. He'd never had a clue what love really was, not until Gabriella. The swell of his heart, growing every day, so full he wondered how his chest could contain so much joy without bursting.

"Why so nervous?" she asked. She'd never let him off the hook.

He sighed, glanced again at the woods. "It's been too quiet. Where are they? Why hasn't he raised the Sorrows? It makes me nervous not knowing what his next move will be."

"We set them back by killing off his guard and stealing the young day walkers."

"Aye, but there are others. Many more than we dare to imagine, I fear. If you listen to Erik, the Church of the Damned has been spreadin' across Europe for decades. It's the violence that's recent."

He ran a finger over her forehead, smoothing the worried crease.

"I know. Maybe we should go on the offensive. Hunt them down."

Her words mirrored his own thoughts. "Love, you know the vamps everywhere are lookin' for him, fightin' his followers. We'll track them down soon."

"But it feels wrong, just waiting here while everyone else is out risking their lives."

"We're raising twelve kids, one who'll never grow up. I'd hardly call that doing nothing."

They had taken on the older children abandoned at the estate, along with Didier, who seemed truly happy here with the others close to his age.

"I know. Still, I hate sitting here."

"I do, too. But we have to keep these kids safe. Our wee ones, too. What's more important than that?"

She smiled thoughtfully. "Nothing. You're right, Ian. What greater way for Amun to hurt us, than to harm our children? This is where we belong, protecting them."

He took her mug and set it with his own on the porch railing before sweeping her into his arms. "Aye, and no one will get past us." He snarled, letting sharp tips ripple over his teeth.

She held him tightly, sighing, apparently reassured. But as he stared over her shoulder at the dark winter woods, the feeling of unrest grew stronger still. The wolf prowled at their door, cunning and watchful.

Ian buried his nose in the crook of Gabriella's neck, filling his lungs with her floral scent. He drew on her limitless strength, knowing as long as he had this amazing creature by his side, nothing or no one, would ever defeat them.

EPILOGUE ✝

Amun paced the halls of his crumbling palace. Ian probably thought he'd destroyed his guard. But thousands more awaited his orders, in every corner of the earth. He'd made his first day walker more than ten years earlier, and more were born every day.

Lilith had sunk deeper into madness since losing her pet, Didier. Her constant crying grated on his nerves. Perhaps he should kill her, put her out of her misery. Someday, certainly, but not quite yet. One never knew when they might need a mindless devoted minion to perform an unpleasant task.

He reached the main hall where the scrolls were stretched out on the long table. The vampire priest who'd stolen the copies now bent over the paper, studying the spells.

"Fascinating, aren't they?"

The dark haired man started, fear flashing over his face, barely masked by his smile.

Amun grinned, pleased that the priest respected his power.

"Yes, quite," he agreed. "Though aren't you worried these Sorrows could kill off your food source."

Amun shrugged. "I will stop them before they go too far."

The priest, dressed in street clothes, fingered the cross he still wore around his neck. He said it helped him control his demon. Another angle to explore, but at a later time. Right now he sensed the man had something to say.

"Come on, speak up. I'll not rip your head off."

"Well, don't you need the Requiem to stop the Sorrows?"

"Yes. We will not raise them until I have the spell I need."

The man pushed a hand through thick black waves. "Do you know where to find it?"

"Yes, that bitch Gabriella has it. My armies march now to retrieve it." He'd heard through his spies that she'd cleverly hidden the tome behind a panel in the jet on her way to Egypt.

"Very good, sir." The priest bowed his head and resumed studying the parchment.

Amun returned to his chamber, stepping out into the sea air above the Gulf of Lion. A thrill shivered through him, knowing his soldiers would soon attack. They'd been ordered to retrieve three things, and with their numbers, he had no doubt of their success.

Soon his soldiers would return with the Requiem and with Ian's beloved Gabriella. Revenge. More than anything, he wanted revenge. And he would have it.

Stolen from his cradle and raised by Amun himself, Ian's son, Dusk, would become his own. And someday the boy would rise up with armies to destroy his father's and send Ian McShane to his grave.

The End

A word about the author...

Sharron Riddle lives in west-central Florida with her husband and three cats. When she's not busy killing demons and fighting insane vampires, she enjoys cooking and long walks and dreaming up new ways to kill demons. But that's another story.

Thank you for purchasing
this Riddle Me A Story publication.
For other wonderful stories, more questions, or more
information contact us at
info@riddlemeastory.com

Riddle Me A Story Publishing, LLC.
www.RiddleMeAStoryPublishing.com

To visit with Riddle Me A Story Authors at
http://riddlemeastorypublishing.com/authors